For Alison

My soft, cool breeze on a hot, Texas day

My best friend

PRAISE FOR *SHADOWS BURNED IN*

What Other Writers Are Saying

This is that novel of childhood's end and adult's beginning. Of saying farewell to the things you love and that scare you and hello to things you're too scared to ever stop loving . . . written extremely well and with incredible heart. Complex. Bittersweet. It doesn't let you go. I highly recommend this haunted tale.
—Nick Cole, author of *The Wasteland Saga*

Chris Pourteau's *Shadows Burned In* turned out to be much more than I was expecting . . . I read a lot of books from debut authors and frankly, a lot of times it can be a chore. With SBI, Chris had me from the very beginning. This is a debut book that you really should catch . . . Very literary in its aspirations, an abuse story that is so much more.
—Michael Bunker, author of the *Pennsylvania Omnibus*

A great start for a new literary voice . . . the storytelling and uniqueness of Mr. Pourteau's voice kept me reading on. A wonderful first attempt, and a sign of great things to come.
—Roberto Calas, author of the *Scourge* series

What Readers Are Saying

The story smoothly follows several different vignettes involving unspeakable acts of the past, and their outcomes on the lives of the main characters. From old ghost stories to a teen's struggle for acceptance and love the stories haunt while maintaining a glimmer of hope for the future.
—Bridget Y. (Amazon reviewer)

This is one of those hard-to-put-down novels. The writing style is vivid and compelling.

—David B. (Amazon reviewer)

The author does a great job of developing the characters, and they stay true to themselves, which is refreshing. I would highly recommend this book to anyone who enjoys suspense, realistic family interactions, dogs (love the one in this book!), and/or just a good old well-written story.

—Supergenius (Amazon reviewer)

The characters are relatable in the sense that, even if you do not personally identify with any of them, you can see in them other people that you know. You may just see some of those people through a different lens after reading this book.

—LeaH1109 (Amazon reviewer)

You can interpret this book different ways, which is one of the good things about it, but I read it as a study of family dynamics and how a person can break the cycle of child abuse. The author handles the interactions deftly, without belaboring the point or becoming preachy.

—Aria (Amazon reviewer)

Upon starting this read, I was most reluctant to put it down . . . even to sleep. At times I was sure "The Tingler" had taken up residence in my spine. The author is quite a wordsmith.

—Beth M. (Amazon reviewer)

This book was not an easy read. Compelling, yes, but not easy. Simply put, this book affected me. I dreaded and hoped at the same time about the outcome of the story. I was angry and sad, but also, in the midst of uncertainty, I was surprised by hope found in the oddest places.

—Rachel V. (Amazon reviewer)

Shadows Burned In

BY

Chris Pourteau

First CreateSpace Edition: April 2014

ISBN 978-0-9899813-1-6

Shadows

Burned In

PART 1

(15 YEARS FROM NOW)

I'm not from here, I just live here,
Grew up somewhere far away.
Came here thinkin' I'd never stay long,
I'd be goin' back soon someday.
                    —James McMurtry
                    "I'm Not from Here"

CHAPTER 1

"Do you think it's haunted?"

The girl whispered the question, half hoping the boy beside her hadn't heard, half hoping he would answer yes. She stared open-mouthed at the old place, wondering if it stared back at her. Or if it could reach out this far, snatch her up, and carry her inside.

"Of course it's haunted," the boy answered. His tone said her question had been stupid in the first place. "It's Old Suzie's house. Everybody *knows* it's haunted."

The girl closed her mouth. The grass where she lay wasn't so cool anymore. The ditch they were in didn't feel so deep. She felt exposed, staring up through the Spanish moss hanging from the large oak trees surrounding the old house, guarding it from the sun. Wind breathed through the moss, making it sway.

"Haunted by what, do you think?"

The boy made a disgusted sound. "*Spirits*, dummy. What else?"

The girl fixed her eyes on the second-floor windows, ignoring his insult. Cracked by rocks thrown by brave children, they reminded her of jack-o'-lanterns on Halloween, hastily cut and cruel. She remembered something her mother told her more than once about how dangerous broken glass was, then heard herself saying to the boy, "Well, I thought maybe monsters or something."

The boy rolled his eyes. "Oh man, how old are you again? Everybody knows there's no such thing as *monsters*."

She didn't answer.

"Come on. Let's get closer."

Her heart skipped. His hand was on her elbow, urging her toward the broken glass and past the bushy beards in the trees.

"I don't know," she said. "Mom says to be home before sundown."

She could almost hear the boy rolling his eyes this time. "Mom says? Come on, you're in the seventh grade now. You still do everything your mom says?"

Embarrassed, she merely shook her head.

"Then come on. Don't be such a baby. You said you wanted me to show you around, didn't you?"

She nodded, giving in, still staring at the broken windows. The house seemed even more like a giant Halloween pumpkin now, its smile wrapped crookedly around razor-sharp teeth.

The boy moved up, hunched over and running like a commando. He reached the outermost oak tree and threw himself back first against it. The girl ran up next to him. She crouched down but felt even more exposed now. The tree wasn't quite wide enough to hide them both.

Screwing up her courage, she peered around the tree. The porch's railings were warped, and the slight smell of mold reached her as the wind blew through the old house. A limp screen hung, waving, and it seemed to carry a moan from inside the place. The girl thought she heard it inviting her in. But that was silly. *Just wind through the broken windows*, she told herself.

"Come on," the boy said and was off again. She followed because she was more scared what he might think of her if she didn't than she was of the house. She wiped her palms on her jeans as she caught up to him, and they hunkered down beside the porch.

"Damn, this place is old," the boy said. He hoped his cursing impressed her.

But her whole attention was focused on the house. Brown leaves and broken sticks littered the cracked wood of the porch, blown there by last night's storm. As the girl looked at the house, she thought she could see eaves that had once been painted baby blue and white. Now, after years of rain and wind and no upkeep, they'd faded to a pollen-pale green. Closer up, the empty windows seemed less like teeth now and more like sockets with their eyes plucked out. Somehow that made them scarier. A skull of a house, staring at her with empty eyes.

Scratches came from inside.

Fingernails. Bones scraping on rotting wood, she thought.

Inching closer.

"Come on," the boy whispered. He was on the porch now, and with a sudden *crack*, he fell over.

She started at the sound, almost screamed when she saw his leg was missing below the shin.

"Damned old wood," the boy said. With a grunt he pulled his leg out of the hole, careful to avoid the splintering edges. He needn't have worried. The planks were more rotten than dangerous. More careful this time, he approached the front room window.

The smell of old wood, wet blankets, and mildew flew up her nose. The girl almost gagged. *This is probably what Mom thinks my room smells like*, she thought.

"Well? Are you coming?"

She got onto the porch and looked at the hole his foot had made. She felt a bit of vertigo, as if she were looking over the edge of a cliff. The porch wood creaked under her steps, and she thought that whatever had made

(was making)

the scratching sounds inside would hear her feet, reach out with bony fingers through the window

(or up from beneath the broken wood)

and drag her inside.

The girl stepped over the gap in the porch. Her heart beat quickly, and only through a force of will was she able to look back at the hole. She saw only the broken wood and empty gloom beneath.

"*Boo!*"

She screamed, then lost her breath in the muteness of terror.

The boy laughed. "Come on, baby," he said. "Let's go in."

But the girl didn't like this game anymore. She could hear the house talking to her, like in a fairy tale.

(come into my parlor, dear)

Talking inside her head.

"Hey!" he yell-whispered. "Didn't you hear me?"

She stared at the shady doorway that held no door. She listened to the murmuring blackness inside but could only make out sounds, not words.

(I spy something)

"The scratches," she said, amazed her voice still worked at all.

"It's only rats," the boy said.

(with my missing eyes)

The girl shook her head.

"Hey, don't be a baby! C'mon! You said you wanted me to show you around."

(I spy something small)

He walked back across the porch, commando-hunched, snagging her by the arm. "What're you, scared?"

(I spy something new)

His grip on her arm brought her back. "Do you want to go in or not?"

She twisted to get away from him, her eyes still on the windows.

(nice to have a visitor, so lonely here)

"Hey!"

(won't you come in for tea)

She felt trapped by the clamp of his fist on her arm.

(I have sweets…and sweetmeats)

The girl wrenched herself free of his grip.

"*Hey!*"

Before she knew it, the girl was running back across the tall grass and vaulting over the ditch. She knew the boy would give her a hard time, knew the other kids would too, as if being new here wasn't bad enough already. But right now she didn't care. She only had to get away from that house, from the old voice and its moldy breath, from the mossy beards and shattered all-seeing eyes, from the smell of old women and their parlors.

Chapter 2

"Where's the fire?"

The girl walked quickly by, out of breath, not keen to stop and answer. Her mother looked after her, right index finger poised to begin cooking dinner.

"Elizabeth?"

She finally stopped but didn't turn around.

"What's so pressing that you can't even say hello to your mother?"

Forgetting for the moment her terror of Old Suzie's house, Elizabeth rolled her eyes. The habits of home kicked in quickly, and she made a deal with herself. She just had to say a few words to her mother, and then she could retreat to her room in peace. She turned around to begin.

"*Nothing*, Mom. I just want to go watch some—"

"Have you finished your homework?"

It's okay, Elizabeth thought. *We're almost finished with this for today*.

"It's not posted yet, Mom," she lied. She knew the assignments would've been available for download since noon for her morning classes and since four for the ones in the afternoon.

"Your monitor called today," her mother said. "He said your output is down. He said it happens often with new transfers, but still."

Oh no. This will make us talk longer. I'm going to have to talk to her longer. "Mom, I got the message from him already. I'll work faster, I promise."

Susan Jackson briefly contemplated her next comment. If pressed, her daughter would only shut down. "Elizabeth is at that awkward stage," she had told her sister on Skype the previous evening. "Somewhere between having tea parties and hosting them. And with the move and losing her friends, we've been pretty forgiving of her lately. It's just a stage."

Remembering that conversation, Susan pushed the button and dinner began cooking. "All right, but you've been online with this webschool for almost a month. You did so well on the other, and when we moved and changed providers, I'd hoped—"

"*Okay*, Mom, I get it." Elizabeth immediately regretted her comeback. If her mother had had a bad day, the tone might set her off.

Susan exhaled slowly. "Patience," her sister had said. "When she begins to fit in socially there, she'll be back to normal." She began to smell dinner cooking. "All right, then. Go on to your room."

Elizabeth nearly leapt from the kitchen.

Susan called after her, "But I want to review your work tonight before you submit it!"

"Yes, Mom," Elizabeth said behind her. A few more steps and she'd be home free, just get past the living room . . .

"E*liz*abeth."

A familiar mixture of dread, frustration, and subdued love seeped into her stomach. "Hi, Dad." She tried to sound upbeat. *If you're in a good mood, maybe he will be too*, she thought.

"How were classes today?" he asked. David Jackson glanced backward over the arm of the isometric recliner he called "my chair." His back didn't seem to be bothering him today, she noticed. That was always a good sign.

"Fine."

He half smiled. "Did you have any trouble getting online?"

She shook her head. "No."

"Hmmm?"

"No, sir."

"Mmmm. Your mother says your monitor called today." He sounded impatient, like he was making more conversation than he wanted to take the time for.

"I know. Mom told me."

"Mmmm. Did she also tell you that your output is slipping?"

God let me out of here before he—

"We've been here a month, Elizabeth. You should be adjusted by now."

She felt her hands beginning to sweat. The mixture in her stomach became thicker, colder.

"Come around here where I can see you," he said.

Elizabeth walked around the recliner, her knees feeling a little weak.

"You should be adjusted by now," he repeated.

"Yes, sir," she said.

"Mmmm," he said, nodding. "You've been hanging around with the Miller boy lately, haven't you? Michael?"

"Yes, sir," she said.

He drummed his fingers on the chair. Now he seemed anxious to get on with the conversation. *Never a good sign*, thought Elizabeth.

"Ken says Michael's pretty good in math and earth science. Maybe he could help you with the independent exercises."

She brightened at that. Elizabeth liked Michael despite his chiding, even after he'd called her a baby at Old Suzie's house. She felt giddy at the thought that he might like her too. He was the only real almost-friend she'd made in this little town of 3,000 people. It was hard enough making friends at school without being new on top of everything else.

"He's in my classes," she said. "I'll ask him if we can work the indies together if you want."

Her father nodded. "I think that would be a good idea."

"Okay," she said cheerily and turned to go.

He made a loud, exasperated sound, as if he were mustering all his goodwill to give her one last chance to earn a place in Heaven.

The feeling in her gut turned over like slow taffy, sweet and disgusting. But Elizabeth knew her father well enough to know the end of the conversation was coming soon. He wasn't in a bad mood tonight. She just had to wait it out. *One more minute and you'll be in your room*, she promised herself.

"You know, Elizabeth, if you don't apply yourself, you'll never—"

amount to anything, she supplied in her head

"and you'll end up—"

serving drinks somewhere

"in some cyberbar." He sounded concerned, contemptuous, and put out all at once.

"Even he's *getting bored with saying this over and over again,"* she said, smirking to herself. The voice in her head—her "3V voice," as she called it, because it always urged her to play 3V games and hated when the real world intruded—always had something smarmy to say.

Shhhh.

"Are you listening to me, girl?" His tone wasn't nonchalant anymore.

Elizabeth shut up her 3V voice and focused on his face. "Yes, sir," she breathed.

"You'd better be. Because if you're not careful, that's just exactly what will happen."

"Yes, sir."

"Mmmm." He seemed to relax as the conversation reached a familiar end. "Now I want you to go to your room and work on your homework. I'm going to call your monitor next week and see how you're progressing. If I don't hear from him you're improving, we're going to do more than talk about it."

Yes!

"Yes, sir."

"Do you understand, Elizabeth?"

"Yes, sir."

"Okay then." He turned away from her and focused on the 3V screen in front of him. She took that as her cue to leave and barely managed to walk without running to her room.

Shutting the door behind her, Elizabeth closed her eyes and unclenched her sweaty hands to dry them. She let out one long breath, and the 3V voice in her head said, *"He'll probably forget to call."*

But Elizabeth ignored it, saying, "Web on."

She crawled into bed and turned over on her back, spreading out and letting herself sink into the soft blankets, palms down. She lay there with her eyes closed, glad both her parents had been in a good mood tonight. She listened to the familiar and comforting hum of the system as it booted. In a few seconds it said, "Ready."

She took a breath. So many choices. What was tonight?

"Wednesday. Good interactive programs on Wednesdays," her 3V voice supplied.

Elizabeth shut her eyes tight, balling the blankets into her fists. What if her father didn't forget? What if he called and she was still doing badly in school? Then her 3V voice spoke again.

"Michael will help. Let's forget about it for now."

Better not.

"Select School," she said.

A few breaths, during which her other self tried again.

"You won't do any better, you know. Not without Michael's help. So why not—"

"Please identify yourself," the computer said.

Something clucked in her head, probably her 3V voice showing its disdain. Elizabeth sat up, swung her legs over the side of the bed and faced the screen. She recited her name and student number.

"Hello, Elizabeth. Are you ready to begin your homework for today?"

"No."

"Yes."

"You currently have three subjects in which homework is due before tomorrow: English, geometry, and geography. What class would you like to begin with?"

"English," she said. At least she liked that.

"I hate it."

Shut up!

She got to work. Thirty minutes into her reading and comprehension exercise, her mother brought her dinner. Elizabeth downed it without thinking. She even ate the stewed carrots without much complaint, trying to stay focused on the work at hand.

Susan waited for an hour after dinner. She'd let the food cool, put the dishes in the washer, and waited till she knew Elizabeth would be deep into her studies. Then she walked into the living room.

"David?"

"Mmmm?" He didn't move his eyes from the 3V screen.

She moved half a step to her left, edging into his peripheral vision. "David, I want to talk to you for a minute."

He wrinkled his forehead and mashed his lips together, disturbed and distracted. "I'm watching *Web Report*. President's talking tough to the Germans again. I may need to transfer our MerChrysler stocks out of the ECM and put them in U.S. accounts."

Susan nodded, feigning interest. "How *do* our finances look?" The topic was, at least, related to what she'd wanted to talk to him about.

He shrugged, barely listening, still staring at the screen. "If the Russo-German Consortium holds up, we'll be okay. But the Japanese are back as a buying power, and they've never been friends of the Russians."

"David—"

"What?" he said, disturbed again. "I'm watching *Web Report*."

She wanted to scream out loud, "Fuck the goddamned *Web Report*!" but she didn't. Instead she sat down in her chair next to his.

Taking a deep breath, she said, "I want to talk to you about Elizabeth."

He watched the numbers go by. German investors and Russian labor bosses were at it again. If this kept up, the Chinese, with American and Japanese investors behind them, might edge out their Russo-German competitors in the Eurasian markets, and *then* where would he be? *Down the tubes with MerChrysler, that's for damned sure. Whoever would've thought the Japanese and the Chinese would get together? Jesus.*

"David, are you listening to me?"

He looked away from the screen, his hands hanging off his knees. "All right, Susan, what *is* it? I've already talked to her about her schoolwork."

She smiled, grateful that the conversation hadn't started out more stressfully than it had. "Yes, I know. I did too."

"She'll whip into shape. I'll make sure of that."

Susan nodded, a little concerned by his choice of words. "I know. I think she'll shape up on her own." A little cheerleading from the Mom Section couldn't hurt. "But that's not really what I want to talk about."

He closed his eyes briefly. *Give in. Get it over with. Get back to* Web Report. "Volume, mute," he said to the screen. "What, then?"

"It's our moving here, David." Now that she'd reached the real purpose for the conversation, she was gaining determination. "Since we moved here, Elizabeth has been distant, reclusive. I'm worried about more than her grades."

"Oh, come on. Don't be a drama queen. She's in a new place. Kids adjust."

"I know," said Susan. "But it's been over a month now, and it seems to be getting worse, not better. She's not making friends like she had in Houston."

"This isn't Houston."

"That's my point."

15

He smirked, wincing one eye closed. "That makes a *lot* of sense."

Susan took a slow breath. "Why did we move back here, David?"

He smiled, a cat that's spied a mouse peering out of the hole. "Ah, there it is." He looked at his watch. "Nine o'clock. We're early tonight."

The hair on the back of her neck bristled. "Don't be an asshole."

"Stage Two: Name calling."

"You had a successful practice," she said. Her frustration was welling up in her throat like bile, burning and bitter. "We were doing well. I was thinking of going back to school—"

"To do what? What would you do?"

"I don't know!" What she did know was that she wanted to be more than she was, something she knew he would never understand. "It doesn't matter. The point is, we moved back here because you wanted to live here again."

"The crime in Houston is terrible," he said for the umpteenth time. "The traffic is worse—"

"And the pay? Did it beat this small-town practice?"

He looked at her, warning in his eyes. "We're doing okay. When was the last time you couldn't buy something you wanted, or something for Elizabeth?"

"But you sit in front of this damn 3V screen getting 'up-to-the-minute world market news,'" she said, quoting the *Web Report* slogan. "If we're so 'okay,' why are you so glued to the news?"

"It interests me," he said evenly.

"Mmmm," she said mockingly. "Does your daughter interest you? How about what your wife wants? Does *that* interest you?"

"What do you want from me—"

"*Why did we come back here*? All you've ever told me is how much you hate this place. How much you hated him and—"

"I never said I hated him," he said, his index finger in the air, on top of a fist. "I never said any such goddamned thing."

"No, that's true, you hardly ever say anything," she said. "But I'm telling you we're suffering for having come back here. This town is too small. I need a city. I need to go back to school. And Elizabeth needs her friends."

"Mmmm," he said. "Well, I tell you what . . . when you think you can make it out there, you go right ahead."

Susan's heart sank. She knew things were bad, but not this bad. What was he saying?

He saw he'd made an opening and pushed through it. "You go right ahead, Susan. I did us a favor by bringing us here. It's a small town, and that's a good thing these days. Living expenses, particularly top-rated webschools, are cheaper. I don't have to worry about presenting surveillance photos in divorce cases to prove infidelity here. I don't have to wonder if I break down on the wrong side of town that I'll get the crap beaten out of me. And I don't have to play the fucking *game* anymore."

"But what about *us*, David?" She was close to tears now but determined to hold them back.

"Why didn't you say something when I first proposed this?"

"I *did*! You brushed it aside because moving here was what *you* wanted to do. You've never given me *half* an ear of consideration over this whole issue."

"If you didn't want to come here, you always had a choice."

She drew back, totally thrown by his revision of history. She had all but begged him not to bring them here, once even with Elizabeth at her side, bawling because she didn't want to leave her friends. But they were here anyway. "*What* choice?"

"That one," he said, pointing to the front door. "Volume, normal." The commentators on the international stock and labor reports came to life again, speculating on speculation.

"David, you—"

"Volume, up." The voices got louder.

"You can't just shut out the—"

"Volume, up."

". . . without the necessary capital investment up front," the commentator was saying.

"Why don't you—"

"Volume, *up*."

"*. . . bringing better consumer prices from competition . . .*"

"God*damn* you!" she yelled, stalking out of the room, hands clamped over her ears.

When he heard her steps in the kitchen, David sighed heavily. "Volume, normal."

From behind her bedroom door, Elizabeth heard her dad mute the 3V. She knew what was coming, so she put on her headphones to work her lessons in solitude. It was almost ten P.M. when she finally finished her homework. Her mother would be coming in soon to tell her it was bedtime.

"Not enough time to play anything online," her 3V voice complained. *"Thanks a lot!"*

In answer, Elizabeth scrunched her face and curled up on her bed.

"Would you like to go offline?" queried the computer.

She blew out a breath as if the air tasted bad.

"What do *you* think?"

The system didn't even give her the satisfaction of being offended by her tone. "Please repeat."

"Go offline and video off."

"Thank you."

The low metallic hum faded and the room went black. It had gotten dark while she did her homework. Last year the lack of light might've bothered her, but now she found it strangely comforting. It was like a blanket of black air that kept her safe. She thought about earlier and how her dad kept telling her she'd never amount to anything if she didn't apply herself. She never really knew what he meant by that, but she knew she was tired of hearing that same old line. She thought she was trying. She was sure of it.

"Who cares? It's no fun," said her 3V voice.

"It's not supposed to be," she whispered back. "It's school."

"There, see? You're not so dumb."

"Gee, thanks."

"Michael will help you. He likes you, you know."

"No he doesn't!" she replied, secretly hoping she was wrong. Elizabeth felt funny about speaking out loud to herself. Her dad told her men in white coats would come and take her away if anyone heard her talking to herself. But she didn't believe that old saying, especially coming from *him*. Not *really*.

Would that be so bad if they did come and take you away? she wondered. "Michael doesn't like me," she said softly, though no one would hear her in her room, behind her closed door. "He tried to scare me today."

"Exactly. He likes *you."*

Now *that* made sense. Not. Well, kinda. Maybe.

Pondering Michael and his attempts to scare her made Elizabeth think about Old Suzie's house again. It was just up the street from her own home, a fact that both thrilled and frightened her. According to Michael, all the kids her age at least threw a rock through a window in the house when they moved into seventh grade, just to show they weren't babies anymore. In the seventh grade, closets were no longer gateways to other dimensions full of misshapen monsters. Beds no longer hid long-armed creatures with claws for hands just waiting for children to fall asleep before reaching up, slithering their hook-hands under the covers, and grabbing kids' ankles to pull them down into whatever torture pits the monsters called home. At least, that was the theory. And the way to prove the theory, to make sure it was true? Take a rock in your hand and break the eyes of the house, knock them clean out of their sockets. That'd prove that monsters weren't real once and for all.

"Then it can't see you when you pass by, and if it can't see you, it can't find you at night," teased her 3V voice.

But Elizabeth didn't think she believed that. She'd felt the empty eyes on her, seeing her from way back inside the lonely house. *Spirits don't need eyes to see*, she thought.

The more adventuresome, newly minted seventh graders actually went inside the house, into the monster's lair, braving the cockroaches, rats, and moldy furniture. Some ran, others crept on tiptoe past the gauntlet of gray shapes scraping and pungent smells floating on a sea of spores, challenging any who dared disturb Old Suzie's house.

Because Old Suzie was dead.

CHAPTER 3

As she laid her head on the pillow, Elizabeth recalled the stories Michael had told her about Old Suzie. The postman had found her sitting in her chair in the parlor, staring at an old television set. He'd knocked on the door first, then entered the house, calling "Miss Suzie?" Her mailbox had been full of ads for stores seventy miles away in Houston and clearinghouse $10 million giveaways and guaranteed credit card offers.

No one had seen Old Suzie for a while, which was how they preferred it if you'd asked them and they'd been honest. But the postman had smelled something. And it hadn't smelled good.

What he'd found was a two-week-old corpse still sitting in a dilapidated, greenish recliner, staring gape-mouthed and slack-eyed at "my shows," as Suzie had called them. No one really knew what she'd died of, but the story went around that it was something old people tend to die of a lot. Her position in the chair and the fact that dead bodies don't always know they're dead yet had forced her bowels and bladder to take their normal course. The hanging rot of flesh combined with the smell to impress an image on the postman he would not forget as long as he lived, which wasn't long. He soon retired from the postal service and from life shortly thereafter.

They brought in the fire department to move her. She was a big woman, muscle and fat mixed together as they often are in people who had once made their living with their backs but then reclined away everything hard work had built.

Suzie had been a spinster widow for nearly three decades before she was found in her chair. Her husband had run off right after he'd successfully settled with his company regarding injuries sustained during the blowout of a natural gas well. Suzie had never remarried and made her own living mostly from driving a tractor for local cotton farmers who couldn't afford to own their own equipment. When the larger, conglomerated farms took over production of the cotton fields, Suzie was out of business. She was close enough to retirement that she retreated to her home to live out the rest of her life watching reruns of *Wheel of Fortune* and *As the World Turns*.

The house around her began to crumble, but Suzie lost her will to care. "My give-a-shitter's broke," she'd say to anyone who'd listen. The house had been the center for a small but prosperous cotton plantation 200 years before, though the land itself had been sold off in parcels in the last few decades. Its banisters were less oak than spruce, and it had no tall columns out front the way you might expect from seeing *Gone with the Wind*. Still, the house had a quiet elegance that reminded people in the little town of Hampshire, Texas, of a proud Southern past. The county's historical preservation society had (around the turn of the 21st century, when Suzie still had interest in such things) gotten her permission to restore the house. But the effort had stopped partway due to lack of funding, and the sun had continued its assault on the old frame, bleaching and fracturing its naked wood. Still, as long as Suzie could get her mail and the local grocery store clerk could deliver the groceries without fear of falling through the porch, she was content to live inside the slow decay.

After she died, the place stood empty. No one would buy it. Most thought it was a money pit, and rumors of strange occurrences kept the weak-hearted away. Suzie had no family, and her will had given the house and the rest of her meager estate to the town of Hampshire on the condition that the old house be left standing until someone else bought it for market value. This was her last demand of the community that had promised to preserve the old structure and failed to deliver. These last wishes confounded those who desired to demolish the house—the same crowd who'd opposed the house's restoration in the first place—but the law was the law, and the court had upheld the will. Not even the great fire that had taken out much of the town years earlier had touched the weathering splendor of Old Suzie's house.

And so whenever people moved to Hampshire—which wasn't often if you trusted the census, and too often if you asked the townsfolk—or made a move within the little town, which was never, the local real estate agent (who was also the county clerk) made some attempt at selling the place. But since no great commission was attached to it and it was such an eyesore to begin with, he never made much of an attempt, and he never made a sale.

So there the house still stood behind its mimosa and oak trees and too-tall grass and weeds in the yard, a dare place for kids and a roach motel. Typical of the Victorian style of its heyday, the structure's great open doorways at the front and back encouraged what little hot and humid breeze could be coaxed through the house in August. Nowadays, the two doorways formed the start and finish lines for children-cum-teenagers as they dashed out their dares to prove they weren't scared anymore of closets and things under their beds and dead old ladies' houses.

Because no one really knew Suzie after she'd retreated to her television set, the local kids made up stories about her they passed down to one another, usually in the dark or around campfires on boy scout cookouts. Old Suzie, they said, was a tough old witch who wore a cowboy hat instead of a pointy one and who loved to play tricks on children come Halloween. The mailman had died so soon after finding her, they said, because he had disturbed her shows. She had finally gotten her wish and transferred her spirit into the TV through incantations and spells, and by finding her and having her corpse carted away, the mailman had made it impossible for her to ever reenter her body again. So she'd killed him, the stories said. And now her spirit moaned on the wind as it crept through the house, her broken eyes watching from jagged windows, waiting for someone to move in with a new television, her means to escape her own haunting.

This was more or less how Michael told the story to Elizabeth, and that same story, more or less, had been told to him by his older brother. Lying in bed and thinking of the house, Old Suzie, and Michael, Elizabeth had let her fear of the school monitor's report fade away. The sheets felt cool, the pillow soft beneath her head. She wondered if this is how it felt to lay in a coffin, on display for mourners. She'd been to several funerals for family members she barely knew and thought it funny, this ritual of painted people on display. Were they comfortable in their narrow beds, their heads resting on satin pillows, while the dearly undeparted wept over them? She wondered if anyone had come to Old Suzie's funeral. Slowly but surely her fatigue overtook her, and Elizabeth began to dream of what death must be like and Old Suzie's house.

"Come on," said Michael. He was looking back at her, a sneer on his face. "Baby baby, fraidy cat. It's just an old house."

Elizabeth stared up at the peeling wood as she had that afternoon. It looked to her like skin hanging in strips off an old face. She heard Michael but wasn't listening. Somewhere in the back of her head she wanted to scream at him that she wasn't a fraidy cat, that she could take this place at night all by herself, without a flashlight even. *Those* were the terms of the dare, after all. Walking through the house in the daytime wasn't enough. Even babies could do that.

It had to happen at night.

Without a flashlight.

Alone.

Unexpectedly, Michael's voice turned pleading. "Aw, come on," he said. "You made me bring you out here and now you won't even go in. I could be playing 3V games right now."

She swallowed and found, to her surprise, a little spit left in her mouth.

"All right," she said softly. "All right, let's go." She raised herself off the cool grass and began walking straight for the front doorway. No darting around behind trees, no hulking over and shuffle-running like this afternoon.

"Hey," he said, caught off guard by her bravery. Elizabeth was halfway across the high weeds in the front yard before he caught up to her.

The tall grass lay down beneath her tennis shoes with a satisfying crunch. She walked onto what was left of the shale front driveway, fists closing and opening. Elizabeth swallowed twice, sending less and less spit down her throat each time. She stopped at the front porch before stepping up.

Michael caught up to her. "This is it, huh?" His voice had lost its sneer. And did he sound just a little bit scared now too?

"You can't go in with me," said Elizabeth.

"Um . . . no, I can't. Else it doesn't count, right?"

She nodded, though she wasn't really paying much attention to him. Staring at the crusty porch, Elizabeth remembered its rotten wood and how easy it was to fall through.

"Um . . . night's almost here," said Michael behind her.

Cold electricity shot up her spine. As one sinking feeling of dread, all her old fears returned. *I was doing so well.* She sent the thought to her dream self, which she sometimes did when she knew she was dreaming but needed to reassure herself she was still in control, that it was her dream, after all. She stood there looking at the cracked gray wood of the porch, wondering where to step and only wanting to run home and play 3V games.

"But I'm *here* now," she said, more to herself than anyone. "I can't leave *now*." She expected a response from her 3V voice, from Michael, from someone. But there was nothing, and when she turned around, her friend had disappeared.

"Michael?" Elizabeth realized she was alone, standing before the house, fully clothed but feeling naked, as scared as she ever had been in her life and ashamed of her fear. "*Michael?*"

The light faded as the sun gave up for the day. She couldn't see the tall grass and weeds anymore, or the path her weight had made across the huge, overgrown front lawn. It was as if the grass and weeds had let her pass, then, when she wasn't looking, reset themselves, trapping her. She felt paralyzed, unable to move backward or forward, a plaything for the house's pleasure.

"Go on," she heard her father's voice say. "What are you, *lazy*? Want to end up serving drinks in a cyberbar somewhere?"

Dad, this isn't homework, she shot back. *This is an old house.* Her own dream-voice sounded like every exasperated child who's ever tried to explain something to an ignorant parent. But his voice was gone now, replaced by her other self, the self that wanted to play 3V games instead of doing homework.

"Come on," it said, mimicking Michael's voice. *"Let's go in and have some fun. We'll show 'em you can do it."*

With her 3V voice urging her on, Elizabeth found she had life in her limbs again; she could make them move. She glanced backward for the path her weight had made, then remembered it had already been erased.

"Baby!" charged her 3V voice, mimicking Michael.

"I'm not a baby," she answered angrily. "I'm *scared*. Adults get scared too, don't they?"

"Babybabybaby!"

"All right!" she screamed out loud in the dream.

She stepped onto the porch.

creak

She thought she could feel the paint cracking beneath her shoe, revealing the dead wood beneath. The sound it made reminded her of her father standing up from his living room chair, his knees and ankles popping. Elizabeth took a second step

creak

and the sound was like a memory waking up, as if the house itself were stirring from quiet years of solitary slumber. When she moved again

creak

she glanced back at her first step onto the porch, saw her footprint outlined by displaced dust, a record of her boldness.

(breadcrumbs like in the fairy tales to find your way back, little girl)

When Elizabeth turned around, she was facing the front doorway. She looked left on the porch, saw the old swing there, its seat more gaping hole than solid wood now, chains rusted a flaky, dull red. *The old woman must've sat here and watched kids playing in the neighborhood*, she thought. *Now that's creepy.* Shuddering, she wondered if Old Suzie's ghost had sat there and watched her and Michael playing earlier. She wondered if the house was putting these thoughts in her head, stoking her fear. Thoughts not of a nice old woman delighting in the play of children, but of a mean old witch sizing up kids to bake in a pie.

"Come on, babybaby," her 3V temptress said again. *"It's just an old house."*

"What would your monitor say?" her dream-father asked.

Elizabeth rolled her eyes. *He'd probably say I wasn't completing my homework assignments!* she mind-shouted. Yelling back at her father as she so often did, if only in her head, steadied her step. She looked back to the front door.

The sun had almost set now, so she could see only a little ways inside. Slanted rays captured the dust stirred up by the slight, dusky breeze. But beyond the snow of dust specks, she could see only dim shapes. Elizabeth looked back at her dusty footsteps again, and already they seemed to be disappearing beneath lightly stirring leaves. Screwing up her courage, she stepped through the door.

Her back felt warm as her eyes adjusted. Mold crept into her nose on itchy feet. She realized her hands were sweating when the cold, heavy air of the house began to tickle them. Somewhere in the back of her head, her father's voice lectured on airflow and wondered who paid the old woman to air-condition the neighborhood. Looking down the length of the breezeway, she saw the last rays of daylight streaming from the back of the house.

A light at the end of the tunnel, she thought hopefully. The light seemed to dim at just that moment.

Elizabeth took another step in, wiping her chilled hands on her T-shirt, coughing once as the mold settled in her lungs. Her eyes finally adjusted to the dusk light. To her left, the short, wide entryway led to a larger room off to one side, the parlor maybe, behind two large doors. She advanced slowly, staring at the dull, fuzzy knobs.

"Open the doors," said her 3V voice. *"Let's see what's inside."*

"No," she whispered.

"Babybaby, look at the baby!" Again the voice mimicked Michael.

"No."

I've done what I said, I've come inside, I've—

(not made it all the way to the back door yet)

Her thoughts paused. Was this the house speaking to her, then? Something. Not her 3V voice. Not her dream-voice. Not her at all, she didn't think.

"Fair enough," the 3V voice relented. *"The back door's that way."*

Elizabeth looked up the hallway. The sunlight was gone. She wondered what time it was. She thought she'd left her house around six, so she ought to have plenty of sunlight.

"Dreams don't have time," her 3V voice supplied smugly.

"Shut up."

She took timid, halting steps toward the double doors on her left. She held both hands out away from her, eyes still adjusting to the near-darkness. Elizabeth could taste the mold now, microscopic flakes of seaweed coating her tongue, acrid and slick. She worked her mouth as she walked farther into the house and spit once onto the dirty hardwood floor. At least she had enough spit to do that now.

Elizabeth pushed the doors open. Their hinges creaked. The latch snapped once.

Even as the doors parted, something in the main hall to the right caught her eye. It was hanging from the ceiling, swaying slightly. An old faux chandelier with broken bulbs and cobweb tendons drooping like cables on a suspension bridge. Her eyes moved to the vague outline of the cherry oak staircase that wound its way upward. It was a sharply steep, circular stair that seemed to reach the second floor too soon, a coiled spring meant to be stretched out more. The staircase looked ancient in its disrepair, its wooden elegance dusty and fragile. On the second floor, Elizabeth noticed, more closed doors invited her to explore. She turned back to the parlor, her eyes landing on what must have been Old Suzie's chair.

It rested in the center of the room, facing away from her toward a rickety cart that might have once held an old television set. The chair itself was a dirt-brown recliner, sitting straight upright with what looked like tendrils of gray hair hanging over the back of the headrest, drifting lightly on the breeze. She stopped and stared as the gray hair floated, thinking of the curly, gray beards drooping outside in the mimosa trees. Elizabeth felt goose bumps as the hair on her arms stood up. Was Old Suzie sitting there? Comfortable in the chair she died in, feet up, watching her shows?

"Don't interrupt my shows," said her 3V voice in a mocking imitation of an old woman who smokes. *"I don't like it when folks interrupt my shows."*

But the steely strands on the chair barely moved. Elizabeth thought then about turning around, heading back past the too-steep staircase and the two doors with dull knobs, retracing her fading footsteps across the splintered porch

(almost as gray as the hairy chair)

and running for home. But then she decided to go on, find out if what they said about Old Suzie was true, if she was fat and ugly and had actually become part of the chair itself. She inched her way into the parlor, waved forward by the gray creepers.

"That's right. Go on. Don't be a baby," her 3V voice said.

A shriek struck her dumb with fright, her limbs suddenly without energy, unable to move. Elizabeth saw it coming right at her across the floor, and her mouth opened to scream but nothing came out; she couldn't even breathe. She reached out to steady herself, but her arms were leaden, and she was in the parlor now, beyond the support of the entryway walls, and her arm that weighed a ton threatened to pull her over it was so heavy. She just stood and stared as the mouse came at her, then veered off and ran under Old Suzie's chair. Elizabeth couldn't inhale, and for the longest minute or ten, she felt like she might pass out. Finally, reluctantly, her lungs accepted the moldy air, leeching enough oxygen to keep her conscious. She instinctively wiped her hands on the front of her blouse and was surprised how soaked they were.

"God, that was scary, huh?" enthused her 3V voice.

"Shut *up*."

She was determined now to walk right up to the chair. Whatever the weather had forced into the house over the years now crunched under her tennis shoes, but she took a second step, not letting her 3V voice taunt her with thoughts of what she was grinding into the hardwood floor. A third and fourth step. Now Elizabeth could see the gray hair better, though the chair was tall backed, and she couldn't see over it.

"I'll bet Old Suzie's sitting right there and that's why all the kids run through the house, not creep through it like a baby mouse."

Old Suzie's dead, she thought back.

"Yes. Your point?"

Suddenly very angry for scaring herself so badly, Elizabeth took three gigantic steps forward and whirled on the chair, ready to face a skeleton with rotted flesh, its arms open, mouth shouting obscenities at the little girl who'd interrupted Old Suzie's shows. What she saw were cigarette burns in the arms of the chair, arms bloated with stuffing spilling out of the leather. Dust coated the old fabric. Elizabeth thought that if she patted the Naugahyde seat

(where they found Old Suzie, melted back into her chair, permanently joined, never to part)

a sandstorm might erupt and smother her. The gray hair, she saw now, was nothing more than airy cobwebs draped over the back of the chair, cousins to the hangers on the chandelier. Elizabeth thought she could see stains from years of Old Suzie's body sitting there

(or maybe just two weeks)

as if the old woman had left her shadow behind when she died.

"This is the chair where they found her," the 3V voice reminded her. *"This is where she started to go bad."*

Go bad?

"Like old milk left in the fridge too long. Lumpy and stinking."

Elizabeth wrinkled her nose, trying to block the picture out of her mind. But her 3V voice happily held it up with a big fat smile for Elizabeth to enjoy.

"Like old meat left out on the counter too long. Two weeks too long."

She turned away from the chair toward the old TV stand, her eyes shut, determined to make the voice shut up. *You're disgusting.*

"Yeah, yeah, and you love it too."

No I don't . . .

"Don't lie to me, you."

(Elizabeth)

She started, shaken by the voice. Who said that? It didn't sound like Michael. It wasn't her father.

"It wasn't me."

Who—

(Elizabeth, it's time)

She wanted to turn around, look at the chair again, make sure the shadow hadn't spoken.

"Shadows can't speak," the 3V voice reassured her. *"But corpses can. Bu-wa-ha-haaaa."*

"Shut up!"

(what)

"Shhhh . . ."

(what did you say to me)

Elizabeth opened her mouth to speak and gagged on her own breath. The spores closed up her throat, plugged her windpipe, and

31

then she wished she *had* climbed the too-steep stairs, done anything other than be standing here with her back to Old Suzie's chair.

"Should've run straight for the back door," she teased herself, *"like all the other kids."*

She felt the hand on her shoulder then, felt the force behind it
(Elizabeth)
and started to beat an airless scream against the dam of dust inside her throat. She sat up and opened her eyes wide and saw her mother sitting beside her, shaking her awake.

"If you don't wake up, you'll be late for login," said Susan. "And your monitor will report it to your father, and then you'll *really* be in for it . . . What's the matter?"

Elizabeth looked around. She was very cold. She shivered once as the ghost of her fear lifted from her, and then she looked at her mother. "Um . . ." she croaked from a throat full of cotton.

"Bad dream?"

"Umm hmmm," she managed.

"Well, you're awake now. Go and shower, get really awake. Fifteen minutes till you're online." Susan stood up and started to leave, then turned back to Elizabeth. "You're okay, honey. It was just a dream, okay?"

Elizabeth nodded, not really listening. "I'll be up in a second, Mom."

Her mother paused. *"Don't* go back to sleep," she said sternly.

"No ma'am," her daughter answered. Elizabeth had no intention of doing that.

After her mom had left the room and Elizabeth had taken a deep breath, she heard tiny giggling from the back of her head.

"Now what do you want?" she pleaded.

"When we get out of the shower . . ."

Yeah?

". . . let's boot up some 3V games."

I can't. If I don't get my grades up, my monitor—

"—will call your dad and then you'll really be in for it. Yeah, I know, I know."

I'm going to take a shower.

In a mocking imitation of an old woman who smokes, the 3V voice wheezed inside her head, saying, *"I don't like it when folks interrupt my shows either."*

CHAPTER 4

"Give me that other marker," said Wayne Alan Kitts. His cell mate, sitting across from him on the stone cold floor, handed him the black one.

"Dis de one?" Stu Metzger asked. "Dat wat you want?"

Kitts nodded, removing the cap. The water-based marker couldn't be sniffed, and that was its primary drawback as far as Kitts was concerned. Stu had his nephew bring them in. Kitts and Stu had a reputation around the cellblock as sweet on one another, something they encouraged along with the assumption that, since they were gay, they enjoyed making water-based art using magic markers. They weren't really lovers, but what other people thought didn't concern Kitts. Soon enough, they'd see what he was made of. Warden Ramirez in particular.

Warden fucking Ramirez.

It took a minute, but he worked the plug from the top of the marker, then poured the ink into a bucket of water he kept under his bunk. Kitts stirred it up a bit.

"You really tink dis gonna work?" asked Stu. His face held the simple, expectant wonder of a child's.

"Well, if it don't," said Kitts, "we ain't gonna be around to cry about it."

Stu grunted. "We be dead."

With the practice of thirty years of patience, Kitts resisted the urge to say, "No shit, you goddamned retard." Instead he said, "Yep. Dead, Stu." He pulled the marker out, shedding what black-stained water he could back into the cloudy bucket. "Okay, hand me the next one. And get to work on something, will ya? Do you want 'em to get wise?"

Stu quickly handed over the kelly-green marker, then moved the rest closer to Kitts so he wouldn't have to reach too far for them. "No, Kitts, no, 'course not. I just slow sometimes."

While Kitts began to pull the plug from the next marker, Stu took up the poster board and began to flesh out what he called his "painting." When Kitts had first cooked up the scheme to dye their clothes, they'd needed a cover story to explain all the markers Stu got in his packages from home. Kitts had demonstrated a serious ineptitude for making art. Stu, on the other hand, had taken pride in his vocation of forgery prior to incarceration. He'd taken on the role of prisoner-artiste with gusto. At times he actually seemed more excited about his current project than the notion he might just one day walk out of Huntsville's Goree Unit in a blue-black jumpsuit with a Mr. Goodwrench patch embroidered on the front.

Kitts, the plan's mastermind, thought he might just head back to Hampshire, that little shithole of a town that had produced him, maybe start over there. *Start over*? The thought made him laugh. *Start over at sixty-eight*? But he had distant relatives there that loved nothing more than to hear about the wilder exploits of his younger days. They'd feed and house him in exchange for the stories. He could live the rest of his life on the banks of the Brazos River in relative obscurity.

Stu, on the other hand, planned to head west to La Grange and the Texas Czechs he'd grown up with. He hadn't missed the family feeling of living there until it was gone, he told Kitts.

Yeah, whatever, thought Kitts. *Just keep drawing.*

Stu was pretty good, he had to admit. What God had cut out of Stu's head, He seemed to have stuffed into his eyes and hands. The pictures he turned out were something worth looking at.

It don't matter, thought Kitts. *None of it matters. We're gettin outta here.*

"That was real smart the way you thought up how to dye our clothes," Stu said. "*Real* smart."

Kitts shook the stained water off the green marker. "Next," he said. Stu handed him a red one. "It ain't the clothes I'm worried about," said Kitts. He pointed to his neck. "It's this." He tapped the skin below his ear.

The transponder felt like a hard rock deposit under his skin. A lithium-powered computer chip the size of a small wristwatch battery was inserted into each new prisoner's neck. It kept track of vital signs and fed the monitoring data back to the prison's central tracking system.

The company that made the devices had sold them to the legislature with the PR boost that the transponders made it possible for the prison doctor to more accurately diagnose inmates' medical problems, saving the state's health care system money. That might be the case, but Kitts knew their real purpose. All the prisoners did. They called them "tattlers." The transponders sent out a steady, unique locator signal, confirming every prisoner's whereabouts twenty-four hours a day. Guards could trigger the built-in electric stun at any time, minimizing the danger to prison personnel during an emergency and maximizing the deterrence to inmates who thought about creating one.

"Yeah, dees tangs is de devil all right," observed Stu.

"Shut up and draw."

Stu looked wounded for a moment, but Kitts didn't care. He was turning his brain on the last puzzle, the final obstacle to their escape. *How to get the goddamned thing out.* Tattlers had been in use for nearly a decade now, and prisons had come to rely heavily on them. Occasionally a guard would walk up and down the cellblock to check on the inmates in their bunks in the wee hours of the morning, but except for midnight rounds, prisoners were left to themselves overnight. And that's when Kitts and Stu made their dye.

Kitts knew the prison doctor implanted and extracted the tattlers. When necessary, the guards used a barcode device—called "the switcher" by inmates—that could turn them on and off. If the units were extracted without first being disarmed by the switcher, a prison-wide alarm would sound. The computer would know exactly which prisoner had set it off because each transponder was assigned a unique number. If an inmate attempted an escape, the transponder sent a charge of electricity like a mini-stun gun to the back of the skull as soon as the inmate crossed the prison's perimeter. Kitts had heard of other prisoners standing at the fence and putting their hands behind their neck in a mockery of standard police procedure. They weren't giving up; they were using a broken bottle to cut the tattler out before making a break. But the screws had thought of that too. If the tattler wasn't kept at standard body temperature, an alarm sounded. It usually took about ten seconds for an active, extracted tattler to cool enough and set off the facility-wide squawk box. An inmate wouldn't get fifty feet beyond the first fence, not even close to the second, before the whole prison was alerted. Kitts had thought about stealing a switcher from a guard, but try that and he might as well ask to be shot straight out. Besides, he'd have no idea how to use it once he had it. So that brought it down to one simple fact: The tattler had to come out . . . without setting off the alarm.

"Kitts," mouthed Stu quietly, breaking the other's concentration. Kitts made ready to snap at him, call him a moron—

"Guard, man," mouthed Stu, already putting the markers quietly back in the cigar box.

As Stu quietly scrambled to hide his latest masterpiece and the markers under his bunk, Kitts did the same with his bucket of dye, careful not to rush it and risk sloshing water everywhere. With practiced precision, both were in their bunks with only a squeak or two of sneakers on cement floor. Kitts slowed his breathing, the rise and fall of his blanket becoming restive. They heard the echo of the guard's boots on the floor, walking leisurely up the block. Occasionally, The Man spot-checked the prisoners, transponders or no, and tonight was one of those nights. The guard stopped outside their cell, shone the flashlight in.

It's a big fucking rat, you dickhead, Kitts thought at the guard. *That's the squeaking you heard.*

The guard mumbled something incoherent, flicked the light around once more, and moved on. Kitts lay there while he walked, worried Stu would freak out and give them away. But the retard had actually saved him, had to give him credit.

Figuring out how to get rid of the tattler while you've got a baton shoved up your ass ain't worth shit, dumbass, he thought. *Be more careful next time.*

He turned his mind on that problem again while the guard began his return patrol. The slow clock – clock – clock of his boots on the cement marked the time. To Kitts, it felt like watching molasses cure in a Mason jar. At some point he started counting the bootfalls of the guard as they fell on the block floor. Soon the sound spiraled him down into sleep.

"Dunk it," said Kitts.

He watched as Stu unfolded the overalls they'd pilfered from the laundry room that morning. Stu carefully laid them in the cloudy dye to soak them, then fed in the next portion of material, as if through a sewing machine. "Don't waste the water," hissed Kitts. Stu shook his head, mouthing, "No, no, no." He folded the treated cloth back over the bucket to catch whatever runoff there might be. Soon enough they were soaking wet in magic marker ink.

"Okay, we'll let them soak overnight," said Kitts. "Be sure and put them far under your bunk, away from the slightest ray of light, Stu. We're beyond innocent explanations now. They find that bucket, they know we're up to something, understand?"

Stu nodded as he wedged the overalls down in the bucket, then repeated the entire process for Kitts's suit while Kitts kept an ear cocked. Midnight rounds would begin soon. Kitts had made Stu dye his own suit first, in case something went wrong with the dying process. Kitts wore a size large because of his "stature and thickness," he liked to say. Stu wore a medium, and that seemed big on him. In both cases, it looked like the dye job was working. But they'd know for sure after the suits dried.

"Patches?"

"Right here," said Stu, smiling. As part of his homosexual façade, Stu had taken up cross-stitching, and he'd managed to conceal a single needle and enough black thread for stitching on two decently faked Mr. Goodwrench patches. Kitts had told him that once they were beyond the wall, with a little luck they'd get away with the charade long enough to boost a car and lie low until the manhunt was over.

"All right, then," Kitts said. "That's tomorrow night."

Stu had a goofy grin on his face, like that of a child seeing his parents wrap up the presents on Christmas Eve.

Kitts heard the slow clock – clock – clock of the guard's boots at the far end of the block. Butterflies invaded his bowels.

"Dey early," whispered Stu, but a little too loudly.

Kitts turned on him, raised a hand, then realized the guard might hear. He settled for whispering, "In your bunk, *now*."

It must've been a slow night. No sooner were they settled, had they breathed once, twice, than the boots passed their cell.

Kitts got no sleep. The pot was too close to boiling.

"*God it hurts*," Stu almost screamed. "*It feels like my guts is acid!*"

"What the hell'd he *eat*?" asked Thompson, the guard on duty the next night.

"Same thing's everybody else," Kitts answered, concern cracking his voice. "Come on, Wes, do somethin for him."

"*Ohhhhh.*"

"Do *what?*"

"I don't *know!*" Kitts tried his best to sound like a concerned wife. Though who was the husband and who was the wife, the guards often debated, was hard to tell.

"*Ahhhhhh, Jesus, let me die, please.*"

Wes The Guard looked down at the writhing prisoner, heard others begin to stir in their bunks. "All right, come on," he said reluctantly. He thought he probably ought to call for backup, but he was getting tired of the little one's wailing. "I'll take you down to the infirmary," he said to Stu.

"*Thank ye, Jesus,*" said Stu, sweat popping out on his forehead.

"I gotta go," said Kitts, as if it weren't open for debate.

"Can't do that, Kitts," said Thompson. "It's against regs. You ain't sick."

A look of utter defeat spread across Kitts's face. He kept thinking to himself, *Your wife is about to have a baby and they just told you you can't go with her to the hospital*, trying to create the right emotion. "Aw, come on, Wes, he's my . . . he's my *friend*, and this looks serious. I ain't never seen him like this before, not even with the arthritis. You got to let me go down with him!"

"Kitts, I—"

"*Oh*, please," cried Kitts, getting down on the floor and mewling as he grabbed Thompson's pant leg.

"*Ohhhhhh, sweet lord, let's gooooooo, I need a doctor bad!*"

Jesus, thought Thompson, *I hate to see a grown man cry. Even a fag.*

"All right, all right, let's just go!"

Other prisoners down the block were starting to make fun of faggy Stu's moaning and crying 'cause Kitty-cat must've gone in too deep this time.

"I don't know, Doc," said Kitts, concern written all over him. "He just doubled over and started screamin."

"That's right," confirmed Thompson. Even though he hadn't been there when the pain had started, he felt the need to show he was in charge of the situation. "Just doubled over."

"All right, we'll see what's going on," said the groggy doctor. "Unzip your uniform."

"Wahh?" Stu's agonized demeanor faltered a bit. "What'd you say?"

"I said take off your *uniform*," repeated the doctor wearily. It was obvious he begrudged wasting good sleeping time repeating the instruction.

"Umm." Stu looked over at Kitts, who gave him the slightest nod of his forehead. "Umm. Okay."

He reached up to unzip the prison uniform, while at the same time Kitts got Thompson's attention. "I really appreciate you lettin me come along, Wes. Nobody else woulda done it."

As Stu started to unzip, Thompson turned to look at Kitts. He didn't know whether to pity the old queen or lead a lynching party and be rid of him. "Kitts, you—"

"What the . . ." The doctor leaned over Stu to get a better look.

Thompson turned away from Kitts. "What's—"

But Thompson never finished his question. Kitts whacked him over the head with a bedpan. The doctor, who'd been focused on Stu, watched with disbelief as the guard crumpled. Stu came off the table and jumped on the doctor's back. The two pirouetted once, twice. While Stu and the doctor did their dance, Kitts took the baton off Thompson's belt and beat the back of the guard's skull till he heard it crack. Finally, the doctor collapsed as Stu vice-gripped his larynx.

Then all was perfectly quiet.

Kitts cocked an ear and listened. No one was coming. Stu had done a good job of choking the doctor into silence, and Thompson hadn't gotten off so much as a shout. "All right," he said, no time to waste. "Good-bye prisoner, hello Mr. Goodwrench."

He and Stu stripped off their prison whites to reveal the dyed bluish-black overalls beneath. From a distance, and even close-up to the unobservant, they were just two old mechanics who'd been more comfortable working on cars before all the electronic, satellite-linked gizmos were introduced into them.

Kitts fumbled around on the dead guard's belt, found the switcher, and passed it over the back of his neck. He didn't hear anything like a reassuring click, so he wasn't sure if the thing was off or not. Knowing he'd gone too far to stop now, he riffled through one of the drawers in the medical cabinet until he found a small scalpel.

"What you gonna do?" asked Stu.

Kitts ignored him, touching the tip of the blade gingerly on his finger. It was sharp, all right. Rubbing his thumb over the slightly raised area on the back of his neck, he guided the scalpel until it rested over the tattler.

"Kitts! What you—"

"Shaddup!"

Here it was. Everything on Red 36. Let it ride, Gambler Man.

He pressed down and began to scrape with the scalpel. He knew the tattler was only a little deeper than a splinter might've been. Kitts flinched as he cut. The blade finally scraped metal. He pulled aside one tiny flap of skin and knew the air was getting to the implant now.

(how fast does the temperature drop once the air hits the inside of the body)

He suddenly remembered he wasn't sure if he'd disarmed the tattler. Hurriedly, Kitts scraped aside a flap of skin on the other side and pushed the scalpel in deeper. The pain became intense, then he felt the tattler give as he pried it out. He looked at it for a moment, then the time clock in his head began to scream at him.

Only one way to make sure.

He plunged the scalpel into Thompson's throat and opened a thin slit of a hole, then forced the tattler in. Closing up the wound, he counted down the seconds until he was sure it wouldn't go off.

"Y'know, you coulda just put it in his mouth," said Stu.

Kitts turned to him. "Now you."

After removing Stu's tattler and forcing it down the unconscious doctor's throat, Kitts took a deep breath. As far as the main switchboard knew, both he and Stu were in the infirmary. And until the doctor woke up, that's all they'd know.

"Oh, that reminds me," said Kitts. "Excuse me," he said politely, pushing his way past Stu. Bending over the doctor, he put aside the scalpel and picked up Thompson's baton, then systematically bashed in the doctor's skull with repeated, measured, strained strokes.

"There now. That's better."

Stu looked on, his jaw dropping. "What'd you do that fer?" he asked. "Doc ain't never done us no wrong."

Kitts looked at him. "And now he never will, neither," he said. "It's too late to half-ass this, Stu. We're all in."

"Uhhh—"

"Be quiet and listen to me," said Kitts, brandishing the baton so Stu would pay attention. "We're goin out, and right now. One more thing . . ." Kitts unzipped his faux Mr. Goodwrench uniform and removed folded cardboard. Stu watched as Kitts opened up the little boxy one- and two-foot tubes held together with duct tape. Kitts slipped them on his extremities, then brought out one last untaped portion, which he wrapped around his torso like a girdle. "Stu, I need your help here," he said.

"What you doin?" asked Stu in wonder.

"Just do what I asked you and come over here and help me." Stu moved toward him, staring at the cardboard on Kitts's body. "Take this," said Kitts, handing him the role of duct tape, "and tape me up."

"Huh?"

"*Like a package, you . . .*" Kitts stopped, took a deep breath. "Like a *package*, Stu. Just like a package. Wrap the cardboard around my body with a few pieces of tape. Simple as that."

Stu still looked confused. "But what's it *for*?"

"It's for gettin over the razor wire in the fence. It'll help protect me from that."

Stu nodded, tearing a strip of tape off and wrapping it around Kitts. Then he stopped, his face dawning like it was the first time anyone had ever switched on its light bulb. "But I ain't got none!"

Kitts winked. "You won't need it, buddy. Trust me. Once I go over, the wire will be flattened underneath me. I'll lie on the fence, then you crawl over me. I could only steal enough cardboard for one set without gettin caught. I lie over the fence, let the razor dig into the cardboard, you just up-and-over me, and we're out!"

Stu thought about that a minute. "Oh, I see." Then Stu thought another step, and Kitts almost fell over at the look of gratitude coming over the smaller man's face. "You'd let me crawl over you, boss, while you hang on dat fence, wid dem lights and guns maybe poppin off an—"

"Don't worry about that. If we're careful, there won't be no guns poppin off. Trust me, Stu."

Stu thought about it another minute. "Yeah, okay. We friends, right? We been plannin this together for near-on thirty *years*."

Kitts smiled. "That's right, Stu. Now, tape me up afore they wonder why the infirmary light's on."

"Yeah, okay," said Stu, running the tape around a man he considered to be the greatest criminal mastermind since Al Capone. Meanwhile, Kitts applied shoe polish to his face and hands, then handed it to Stu to do the same.

"All right, buddy, this is it," Kitts said in his best pep-talk voice. "All those years of planning are about to pay off in spades."

Stu nodded. "I'm wit ya, boss."

"Let's go, then."

They inched out into the main yard from the infirmary. No one around except the tower guards that manned the spotlights and machine guns, and only two of them to worry about. The spotlights scanned the grounds regularly, like clockwork in fact, and Kitts caught their rhythm.

"*Now*," he said in a low voice, and they ran like Groucho Marx, bent over as far as their old backs would allow. The spotlights raked the concrete of the basketball courts. Stu nearly yelped as one touched his back leg, but he held his tongue. Kitts hunched down at the base of a basketball goal, pulling Stu, who was huffing and puffing already, down with him. They were in a blind spot from which they could reconnoiter the rest of the ground.

There was no alarm.

All was quiet.

"Okay, Stu. Fifty feet to the fence, up and over that and the razor wire, then over the outer fence, and we're home free."

Catching his breath, Stu said, "You want I should go first?"

Kitts rolled his eyes out of Stu's sight. *Jesus, you fucking retard* . . .

"No, Stu, I have to go first." He patted the cardboard armor. "The razor wire, remember?"

Stu rolled his own eyes at his own stupidity. "Oh yeah, boss. Sorreh."

"Don't sweat it. Ready? Here we go. Now remember . . . I have to lead the way. Understand? You don't go first. I have to lead the way."

"Yeah, boss, I don forget dis time."

Kitts nodded, feeling absolutely no confidence in that, and gauged the lights. One – two – three.

"*Now*."

Kitts led the way and Stu let him. Before they knew it, they were through the sweeping minefield of spotlights and at the fence. Kitts stared upward. It looked like the Empire State Building to him, it was so high. But he'd have to climb it.

"Okay, Stu, help me up. Help me get a foothold."

"Yeah, boss," said the other, cupping his hands and firming his back, worried that Kitts's weight might cut his own escape plans short. But Kitts quickly caught his arthritic fingers in the chain links of the fence. *Thank God they ain't electrified anymore*, he thought. The system had come to trust the tattlers and a series of crisscrossing electronic eyebeams between the first and second fences to hold the prisoners in.

Kitts reached the top and carefully lay across the slimmest, skinniest, dullest portion of the wire he could find. They had forty-five seconds to be down the other side before the lights passed this way again. "Now, Stu!" he yelled quietly down. "Hurry, buddy!"

Stu started up the fence. His own arthritis was more progressed than Kitts's and that made it hard as hell to keep a grip without screaming out loud. The bone-grating stiffness shot up his arms and into his heart, which beat faster than it had in years. But thoughts of failure, of failing *Kitts*, spurred him on, and then he was straddling Kitts's back, ready to go over.

"Go *on*," gasped Kitts under Stu's weight. "Twenty seconds to the lights!"

Stu did his best to hurry over his friend lying beneath him across the wire, cursing with Stu's every movement. Before he realized it, Stu was slung over the other side, his hands screeching their agony at him as he got his toeholds on the fence. Kitts was already struggling to release himself from the razor wire, which had dug its claws into the cardboard armor around his torso.

Shit!

Time ticked by as Kitts struggled to pull himself off the sharp talons. He figured he had less than ten seconds before the lights found him. Stu hit the ground on the other side. Kitts wondered if his brilliant plan was going to work, if Ramirez might not have the last laugh after all. *That old faggot died humped over, just like he lived*, he heard Ramirez cackling to the guards over a beer. *Fitting end, don't you think, boys? So to speak, that is, haw-haw-haw.*

Five seconds.

Kitts decided to hell with it, he had no choice, and tried to swing his legs up and over his head like a gymnast, hoping his weight and momentum would tumble him off the wire and down the other side. And if he was lucky, he'd catch himself on the fence, and if he weren't . . .

"Come on," said Stu, "I catch you!"

Kitts was lucky. The cardboard armor ripped on the razors' talons. He missed his grip on the fence, tumbling fifteen feet to land atop Stu. Overhead the lights raked the razor wire.

Catching his breath, Kitts asked, "You okay?" and Stu said, "Yeah." But lucky was the word for it all right, thought Kitts. *If I'd caught myself on that fence, I'd have broken fingers right now.* "Come on," he said. "We got one more fence to go."

But Stu held his arm. "But what about the electronic eyes? We gon trip ev'ry alarm dey got here."

"Too late for that now. We go now or we get shot. Your choice."

"But boss, de eyes, dey gon see us—"

"You comin?"

Stu looked Kitts in the eye, saw thirty years of planning, patience, and perseverance promising them that, one day, they'd be free. "Yeah, okay, boss," he said.

"All right, then. Now remember . . . me first."

They were up and loping across the no-man's-land as quickly as their old legs would carry them. Kitts imagined the invisible laser beams being broken, and sure enough barely five seconds had passed when a wailing alarm erupted inside the prison.

"Stay behind me, Stu, stay behind me!" yelled Kitts, trying to be heard over the screaming siren without giving away his location to the tower guards.

Searchlights scanned the area near both fences as the two prisoners pulled up short at the second one. Kitts pulled Stu down beside him, allowing the current sweep of the lights to pass overhead. The next pass would be at ground level. He said,

"Remember, Stu, me first, okay? Then you go over, just like last time, right?"

"Right, boss," puffed Stu.

The lights were gone for the moment, and up the fence Kitts went. He ignored the arthritis now. Too much adrenaline pumping. Guards were yelling at one another, trying to find the reason for the siren. About once a month, rabbits or possums would get under the fence and trip the alarm. There hadn't been an escape from Huntsville in almost thirty years. Since as far as Kitts knew the tattlers still hadn't set off the main board, he hoped the guards were looking for a possum instead of a prisoner.

He had crawled over the razor wire and begun descending the other side before Stu realized what was happening.

"Boss, what you doin? I need to crawl over you—de wire!"

Kitts looked him in the eyes. Thirty years of friendship was worth something, after all.

"Boss? What's goan on? You gon throw me de cardboard, so I can go over m'self? I don't haveta crawl over ya, that's okay."

"Stu, you dumb bastard." Kitts turned and ran as the searchlights traveled toward the second fence.

Stu stood for a moment watching Kitts run away. Then he began to panic. He couldn't make it without Kitts. Kitts did it all. He was Stu's friend. Kitts looked out for him. Had done so for thirty years.

"Boss?" The sound squeaked out, barely breathed. "*Boss*?" The scream brought the lights to him then as Stu tried to scramble up the hurricane fence.

"Hey, Charlie's in the wire!" whooped a guard, glad to find something besides a possum to shoot at. "Charlie's in the wire!"

Stu's fingers screamed at him and he screamed at Kitts as he went up the fence. The razors were slicing through his dyed jumpsuit as he desperately tried to get over the other side to freedom, and to Kitts. He hadn't been without Kitts for longer than he could remember.

"Hey, you!" The voice blared at him from a bullhorn. "This is the only warning you get! Come back down or you ain't never comin back anywhere!"

Stu was almost through the wire, struggling through it, ignoring it as it sliced flesh, tearing at the patch he'd so carefully sewn on like he'd once painted Ben Franklin's face on the hundred-dollar bill. He struggled through with blood leaking from him. Tears streaked the shoe polish on his face.

burrrrrp burrrrrrrrp burrp burrrp

The tracer bullets made a line from one tower, then another as they converged on the spotlight and the prisoner contorting in the wire at the top of the fence. At first Stu hardly noticed the bullets as they *thumped* into him, but then they ripped open his lungs and sliced through his muscles. The arthritis in his fingers didn't hurt anymore and he had a moment to wonder at that, to feel relief, before his heart shredded inside his chest. He had a thought of disbelief, then his hands betrayed him and he slipped, hanging loose on the wire.

Tough to breathe now, and hot fire inside him—inside his lungs, inside his chest—made the old arthritis feel like a pleasant memory. All he could think of was how glad he was that it was thanks to him that Kitts was free after thirty years, The Man hadn't got 'im, and that if he had to die, at least Kitts was free and The Man hadn't got 'im.

As the bright light overwhelmed his eyes, Stu Metzger's last thoughts were that he'd made it after all, and that he was freer than even Kitts now, and how happy that made him feel. How lucky he was to be rid of the pain now and how nothing else really mattered anymore.

CHAPTER 5

Last night was a real pisser, thought David Jackson as he got in the car to leave his new one-lawyer practice. *All Susan can do is complain about coming here because she lost her big-city life. What was that show in reruns when I was a kid?* Green Acres? *"You are my wife . . . good-bye, city life!"*

Well, that about sums it up, he thought. Sitting in his car, he stared at the outside of his new office. The brick exterior was only that, a cheap veneer meant to look like more than it was. *I think*, thought David, *if the big, bad wolf paid a visit to my office, he could blow it down, bricks and all.* The paint was peeling a bit along the trim, and the newest thing about the entire edifice—David Jackson, Attorney at Law, stenciled in gold on the glass door—looked oddly out of place. It was one story (*one boring story*, David japed to himself as he looked at the worn exterior), but it was cheap. And despite the fact it also looked cheap, he'd done some decent business for a local lawyer in a town this small. Will probates, mostly, with the occasional divorce or insurance settlement thrown in for good measure. It was late October, which meant heavy rains anytime now, and if he was lucky, a hailstorm might spark some enmity between the odd homeowner or two and their insurance companies. He could make a little off that. Not that he wished anyone ill fortune. At least he didn't chase ambulances.

The law practice in Houston had been profitable enough. He had to agree with Susan there. But the big-city life

(the cars)

had finally gotten to him

(the smog)

and he'd decided one day that it was a small-town practice he wanted after all, and the life there

(fresh air)

was bound to be safer for Elizabeth. So, he and Susan would lose their weekly dine-out at La Vie en Parmesan. So what? Susan had taken the news rather well, he thought, even enthusiastically; or at least that's how he remembered it. But now that they had been here for nearly six weeks, she was backbiting him about the move. She missed this and she missed that. She missed shopping with her girlfriends. She missed her nurse's job at the medical center. She missed her city. Despite the fact that the Web gave her daily (and sometimes expensive) access to her old girlfriends. They were less than an hour away should they want to get together. The local hospital, small as it was, had been delighted to get a nurse with Susan's experience on its staff. From all indications she would be head of nursing when the old biddy currently in charge retired.

And as for the shopping, hardly anyone shopped at malls anymore. About a decade ago, the Web had finally proven a viable alternative to department stores. Congress had passed the Internet Commerce Act of 2021, providing real incentives to virtual shopping. Brick-and-mortar stores were already following the dinosaur. Almost everything was Web based now—from virtual stores to virtual schools, where online monitors managed real-time discussions of five to ten students, each of whom accessed the teacher and subject from the comfort and safety of their own homes. The term *homeschooling* had taken on a whole new meaning. Street parties, neighborly barbecues, jaunts to the 3V monsterplex, and yes, even outings to what few specialty department stores remained were all things people did for entertainment now. The necessary day-to-day tasks of life were almost all done virtually.

Even preliminary diagnoses by the family doctor could be done by the patient's describing symptoms, the doctor's doing a cursory visual inspection over the Web, and the upload of the patient's vitals via data transfer from personal monitors. This made the insurance industry happy because it was so efficient. It made doctors happy because the pressure to spend no more than fifteen minutes with a patient was gone. And it made patients happy because they felt a lot more comfortable showing their symptoms in the privacy of their own home and over a secured Web line.

Why am I thinking about this stuff? David wondered as he stared at the old office with his name and title stenciled in gold. Maybe it was because he didn't really need this office. With technology such as it was, he could do all his client interactions from home, of course. *Well,* he thought, *maybe* that's *why I need it. To get out of the house for a while.* It was certainly cheap enough to maintain the space. Office real estate was inexpensive as hell nowadays, particularly in little towns like Hampshire.

So his office was a luxurious expression of the norm these days, eh? To get out of the house and enjoy himself a bit. Somehow, catching himself as such an obvious expression of the current culture put a bad taste in his mouth. He'd always considered himself so independent. But the simple fact was he had this office because he could afford to have it. *Because I want it,* he thought. That indulgence seemed to demand satisfaction a lot more often now that he was middle aged.

David put the car in reverse. Gravel and shale popped under the tires. *A mile and a half from now and I'll be in the comfort of my own home.* The thought came laced with sarcasm.

Stopped at a light on Main Street, he tapped his fingers on the steering wheel and thought about the evening to come. Maybe Susan would be in a good mood. Maybe he wouldn't come home to find another message from Elizabeth's monitor saying she was falling behind and holding up the rest of the class to boot. Maybe the stock report would be *up* for a change. Maybe this evening would actually be peaceful. What a pleasant thought that was . . .

Something off to the right caught his eye. An old man in a Columbo raincoat walking slowly along the side of the road. *It's the Walking Man,* thought David. He and Susan had named him that a few weeks ago, when they'd first seen him walking around town. The old man bent over the carcass of an animal, probably an armadillo, and used the flat shovel he had to pry it from the pavement. David winced his disgust. *Surely he won't eat that. I mean . . . come on. Surely not.* The Walking Man struggled to free the flattened animal from the glue its blood and bile had made with the road's surface. At last the animal was free. The Walking Man put it in the gunnysack he dragged around with him.

beep beeeeeeeeeeeeeeeeeeeeeeep

The impatient driver behind him pulled David's eyes off the grotesque scene, and he mechanically put the car into drive. With some effort he pushed away the picture of the old man roasting a flat armadillo over an open fire.

As muscle memory drove him the short distance to his home, David reviewed his decision-making process for moving back here. He'd thought getting out of Houston would reduce the whole family's stress level. Susan had been happier in Houston, that was true, but he'd been sorely worried about Elizabeth. Nowhere seemed safe to have a house anymore. Real crime, the kind where someone got hurt, had shot up in recent years. White collar crime had gone almost entirely cyber.

He hadn't counted on the new stresses caused by moving back here. Susan's disappointment. Elizabeth's distractions. *Maybe the big city wasn't so bad after all.* David grimaced at the thought, because it was giving in, giving up, admitting defeat. Couldn't do that. Certainly couldn't admit that Susan was right. Besides, Houston *wasn't* better. It was just *bigger.* And the bigger the town, the more opportunity for people to take advantage of you. Here, at least, life was quiet. Home life, such as it was, was at least secure.

He turned onto Elm Street, now only a few blocks from that security. And before he even knew what he was doing, he had pulled over near the high-grassed ditch where the street began.

What?

Had someone spoken? He surveyed the street around him but found no kids playing, no movement at all. He felt the sun on his neck as the day evolved into early evening. When he looked again, he barely noticed the house. And then it hit him exactly *what* he'd barely noticed.

The house.

A smile came across his face as he realized the sound he'd heard. The kids playing had been the whisper of memory. He put the car in park and stepped out and up on the driver's side doorframe to peer across the slightly stirring tall grass. *Needs mowing*, he thought. The Spanish moss around the cracking, gray porch danced on the breeze. He squinted, trying to look through the windows but saw only darkness.

Someone's probably boarded up the old place from the inside as a hazard to children, David mused.

That thought made the smile fade from his face. He remembered when he and Theron Taylor had come to the house on Halloween on a mutual dare to see if they could spook Old Suzie. She was a big woman then, and somewhere in the back of his mind David recalled she'd later died of something that makes other people just shrug and say, "Well, she was old," before going on with their day.

But not back then. Back when he was a kid, Suzie was in her mid-fifties, a big woman of . . . well, must've been 250 pounds. She wore her husband's old clothes after he'd run out on her. She'd literally stepped into his shoes, his pants, his shirt, and his cowboy hat and begun working the half-acre of vegetable gardens they had around back of the house.

She was a hard woman, David remembered, the fear echoing in his bones from that night long ago. Leaning on his car roof, he stared at the slouching house and remembered how much she'd scared two little boys. Suzie was a recluse who only came out to work or "get supplies," as he'd once overheard her say in the grocery store, or to rent old DVD movies from the 7-Eleven because she couldn't afford the satellite-based view-it-on-demand service that killed cable television. He remembered seeing her riding atop an old John Deere tractor in December, preparing the ground for seeding in January, bouncing up and down and manhandling the steering wheel.

When she wasn't working the land or buying supplies in town, the only other time he really saw her outside the house was when she mowed that big front yard of hers. On the odd cool evening between October and March, she'd sit out on her porch swing and watch the evening pass her by. Her thick legs pushed and pulled the swing lazily, its rusty chains creaking and twanging. And she'd just sit there looking out over the front yard, listening to the chirping of the crickets or the twittering of the birds and the distant

(always distant, if she was on the porch)

sounds of children playing down the street and cars passing on Elm Street as folks made their way home from work. When the Web made possible the work-at-home standard everyone enjoyed today, there was much less of that, and Old Suzie seemed to spend more time on the porch then. She'd rock and drink something out of a glass

("It's baby pee, it's baby pee!" Theron Taylor swore back then)

that was probably lemonade, now that David thought back on it. She'd listen and watch, and about the time the sun would go down, she'd call it a day and go inside.

All the children thought she was a witch. David wondered at that now, how children come up with those crazy ideas and torment other children (and adults) mercilessly to play them out, just to give themselves something to do and keep their own little lives from becoming too boring by making others miserable. Or was that the human condition in general? Maybe adults had learned how to be more subtle about it. Yes, they'd been convinced she was a witch all right, growing all those herbs and vegetables in her garden to brew concoctions in cauldrons that she used to poison little children

(and bake them in her oven)

and throw hexes on the townspeople. An entire mythology had built up around Old Suzie, so much so that the town's children refused to give her a choice on Halloween. No treats would they have. Only tricks for these kids, and those were the brave ones. For the first few days of November every year, Suzie would spend her time picking toilet paper out of trees and repairing at least one window after a rock had broken it. That was a festival ritual for the children, working off their year's worth of fears behind devil and skeleton masks. Even the parents, despite a public showing of admonition

("How're you doing today, Miss Suzie?"

"I'm fine. Just in gettin supplies."

"I heard what them kids did. I'm so sorry."

"That's okay," Suzie would always say, shrugging. "They's just kids.")

didn't really mind too much, because they didn't really like Suzie much either; they were just less obvious about it. She was a strange old bird who hadn't had sense enough to be ashamed when her husband ran away, and she didn't try to make friends, and isn't that old plantation house just running down more and more every year, and ain't it an eyesore, and what's she doin in there all alone every evenin, and why do you think she's watchin the children when she sits out there swingin on the porch?

So for the longest time, David and every other child in Hampshire had skirted her property rather than cross it. Occasionally someone would start a dare, and kids would walk up and knock on the door, only to run away again with sweat running down their backs. Now that he thought about it, David wondered how she ever kept from killing somebody if for no other reason than it might keep the rest of the little fuckers away from her front porch. Or at least kept from *maiming* someone. He thought about walking up to the house

(you're older now, there's nothing to be afraid of)

but looking first at the house and its broken windows

(how many rocks did you throw through them when Old Suzie was alive?)

and then at the sun as it was sinking farther west

(and how badly did you piss her off that night in her house?)

he decided it was too late. Susan and Elizabeth would be expecting him at home. So, with one last look at the old place, and a brief remembrance of that Halloween thirty years before

(wonder where Theron is these days, if he's even still alive)

David got back into his car and drove the remaining two blocks home.

As she heard the car pull into the garage, Susan tried to set herself in a positive frame of mind to receive her husband. When they'd first gotten married, she'd thought herself the luckiest woman in the world. She'd found a man she could honestly spend the rest of her life with. He was easygoing, didn't drink really, didn't smoke, didn't seem the cheating type, and had a bright future ahead of him as an attorney. They'd met in college in a literature class, arguing over whether or not the White Whale was truly evil.

They'd lived together for more than a year before getting married. In those days David had a sharp sense of humor, making others laugh at everything around them, and Susan loved him more than she ever thought it possible to love anyone who was not her own child. After graduating from law school, he'd thrown himself into his career, determined to make a mint before he was thirty, and they'd settled into the familiar patterns of a young married couple.

Then Elizabeth had come along and David had seemed to change slowly. His sense of humor, like abused vocal chords, had become scratchy and pained at first, then silent. His need to make more money quickly became an obsession. Still, he'd been a good father to the baby, changing diapers and taking his turn at early morning feedings. Then Elizabeth had begun to grow up and David had become even more distant, as if he no longer knew how to deal with her once she was no longer a helpless baby. Now, if they weren't talking about school or a 3V program, they hardly spoke at all. And Susan, for all her wish to do so, didn't seem able to bridge the gap between them.

"I hear *Web Report* was really positive today," she said as David came through the door. She hoped to strike up a conversation right away on something that would interest him, maybe erase last night's bout.

"Hmm?" he said, seeming distracted. "Oh, that's good." He walked on into the hallway, probably intent on changing out of his office clothes and relaxing in front of *Web Report* for a while. Susan let him go, glad for the fact that nothing more volatile had erupted from him. *Must've been a good day*, she thought.

David walked into the bedroom, changed into his sweat suit, then settled into his chair in the living room. "3V on," he said, then, "*Web Report*." Up came the screen with the commentators at their desk, their voices muted when David gave the command. "Portfolio activity," he said, and up came the dozen or so stocks he'd invested in.

Again today MerChrysler was doing poorly. *This is a bad sign*, David thought. *New models just came out, and the stock's going down?* Down by 2¼, which represented about a $10,000 loss to him for the day. He pursed his lips and quickly reviewed their other holdings. Microsoft-GlobalNet was up 1½. MGN would usually go up even when the rest of the market went down, even if only slightly. *At $1,150 per share, they ought to be dependable*, he thought. And Webmarket, the online matchmaker that brought consumers and vendors together, was up 3¼ on the news that, after years of debate regarding economic openness, China was finally drafting its own version of the Internet Commerce Act. *Some good news at last*, thought David. The good news ended when he looked at the oil stocks. BP was down again because oil was so damned plentiful. *Thanks a lot, peace in the Middle East.* World-Mart was up slightly, only ½, but at least it was *up*, and like MGN, you could always depend on World-Mart for that. Blue chips were expensive but still the least risky over time.

Still, in the balance he was down today, and though he was reasonably sure he'd make it back and more tomorrow, losing money never sat well with David Jackson. Nothing crawled under his skin and itched like the fear of financial failure. He'd tried to exorcise that demon for years, with no luck. When the market adjusted every few years, he would drink a little, rant a little, pull his hair out a little, and finally the line graph would start to ascend again and he'd pull the money he'd put in one market and invest in another. He wasn't a millionaire, but he hadn't lost his shirt either, and the promise of wealth tempted him every time.

But on days like today, the old fear of financial disaster reared its ugly head—a demon creeping up behind him, tapping him on the shoulder

(too greedy, David, if you'd just gotten out a few hours ago, just given up a little sooner)

and taunting him with his own failure. And no matter how many times the market came back or his holdings increased in overall value, the little demon with the sharp fingernail tapped him on the shoulder every time.

The portfolio auto-calculated his oil earnings, and he ran a heavy hand through his thinning hair at the apparent loss resulting from the oil glut. Where was a good jihad when you needed one?

"Daddy?"

David turned away from the bar graphs and his ruminations on ruin. "*What?*"

Elizabeth started at his tone, thought, *Oh great, I picked a great time.* "Um—"

"What *is* it Elizabeth? You see I'm reviewing the stocks, don't you? You know you're not supposed to disturb me when I'm doing that. Don't you?"

"Um . . . yes, Daddy," she said, her eyes focused on the floor.

"Well, now that you've done it, *what?*"

"Um . . . I, uh, I just wanted to tell you that the school monitor—"

"Did he call again? Am I going to find a message from him telling me that you're holding up the class again?"

Elizabeth closed her mouth as her heart sank. She had been so excited to tell him, so full of certainty that he'd call her over to him and give her a big hug and tell her how proud he was of her and how he'd known all along she could do it and that if she tried, she could do anything she set her mind to. That's how fathers talked to daughters in the 3V stories she'd experienced. But now she kicked herself inside for picking the wrong time, for not reading him better or talking to Mom first and finding out his mood. It was all wasted, all her effort for the day, and the words from the monitor that would never come again in a million years would fall on deaf, angry ears now. All because she was an idiot and had chosen the absolute *wrong* time to tell him.

Stupid, stupid, stupidstupidstupidstupid—

"Well?"

"I-I . . ."

"And now you're making it worse because you're paralyzed, you

big baby," said her 3V voice, imitating Michael. *"Now he's mad, and you're gonna get it!"*

Elizabeth's eyes began to well up.

"Spit it out, girl!"

"David!" Susan stood in the kitchen doorway. "Elizabeth, go to your room," she said evenly, trying not to sound too harsh to her daughter, but hoping her tone would short-circuit any more fury from her husband. "Go on. I'll bring you dinner in a little while."

Elizabeth turned around quickly and ran back down the hallway to her room, sobbing her defeat.

David sighed. "Jesus, Sue, am I going to find another message from the monitor? Am I going to have to take more drastic steps by cutting off her—"

"You know, David, if you'd listen instead of talking all the time, you might find life more pleasant," said Susan, her voice rising as she spoke. She didn't want it to happen, but her emotions took over, and she slipped into the rut that communication between them had become. "I know *we* would!"

"What the hell are you talking about?"

Susan walked into the living room as she spoke, her frustration spilling out of her, a snowball picking up speed as it rolled. "Her monitor called today all right, but not to tell us how *bad* she was doing. He called to tell us how much she had improved since yesterday. 'She must've spent all evening studying yesterday,' he said. But you didn't let her get that out, did you? You assumed she was having trouble again, and when she came to get a *little* encouragement from you, you squashed it! Jesus, David, you're such a self-centered bastard!"

She turned back and walked into the kitchen to finish dinner, leaving her husband to wonder why he was such an ogre for wanting his daughter to be successful in life.

And that made *him* angry.

"Now wait a minute, don't you walk away from me . . ."

The evening's match had begun.

CHAPTER 6

She'd thrown herself face down on her bed, burying her tears in the comforting softness. She clenched the pillows in her fists, hurt and defeated. Elizabeth had tried so hard to please the monitor, and when she'd achieved the unachievable, she'd just known her father would smile at her for a change, open his arms to her, tell her how proud he was of her, not yell at her. How hard was that? How much was that to expect?

Her frustration gave way to anger as she thought about how hard she'd worked, how long it had taken her to memorize the formulas and apply them in the monitor's exhausting makeup exam. He seemed to want her to fail, as if he and her father had an agreement that the monitor would do everything in his power to obstruct her. And what did her mother do to help? Occasionally she would try to explain to Elizabeth's father what Elizabeth was feeling and how hard the move had been for all of them, but then she'd knuckle under. Elizabeth knew the whole routine by heart now. It usually started with a conversation about how hard it had been on Elizabeth to leave Houston. That was Stage One. Stage Two began when her mother's railings became a lament on how hard it had been on Susan to move.

Her father's standard argument about the security of the smaller town and how much less stressful it was living here (*Ha!* Elizabeth always thought when she heard that) was Stage Three. Elizabeth would adjust, he'd say for the umpteenth time, and if her mom didn't like it, she could waddle right out the front door and don't let it bounce off her fat ass on the way out. This was when Mom would start crying, which Dad had learned to ignore by turning up *Web Report*.

The fourth and final stage usually began around nine o'clock when Susan would rap on Elizabeth's door with a sandwich or something, apologizing for not having made a better dinner. Elizabeth would say, "That's okay, Mom," or anything, really, to get her to leave her alone. Sometimes after an especially difficult argument, Susan felt the need to stay and comfort Elizabeth, which only added to her daughter's disgust at the whole situation. More and more Elizabeth was finding the less direct contact she had with her parents, the better she liked it. Occasionally Elizabeth feigned sleep so that her mother left the sandwich on her bureau and retreated from the room without waking her. Then Elizabeth would place a towel along the bottom of her bedroom door to hide any light escaping into the hallway and fire up the 3V network, losing herself in the games she loved to play alone.

She started giggling at the absurdity of it all and wiped her nose and eyes on the pillowcase. Cocking her ear at the closed door, she heard Stage Two beginning. Elizabeth thought the whole scripted thing even funnier now that she was already laughing—the predictability of it all, history repeating itself, over and over again. Now she was laughing and crying at the same time. How stupid her parents were! They read the same old lines from the same old scene over and over again, and neither's acting got any better! She buried her face in the pillow again, this time to keep her parents from hearing her laughter.

But her amusement quickly tapered off when she heard her father's raging voice. How she hated to hear their fighting! It ripped her apart inside to hear the only two people she really loved being so cruel to one another.

It twisted Elizabeth's stomach into knots. She felt certain she was the cause of it all and had that suspicion confirmed when the whole thing started over again as the result of something she'd done. Like today. *Maybe if they just got divorced*, she had thought a hundred-million times. But no, that idea filled her with a greater fear and loathing than any argument ever had, and she felt trapped between what she hated most and what she was most frightened of.

Now Elizabeth was crying again, and she wasn't sure if it was from giggling or frustration, because she couldn't tell the difference anymore. Her insides fluttered with the giddiness of it, the mixture of heavy pain and shaking laughter that made her want to throw up. She had found only one remedy, one thing that kept the heartache from bursting open her chest—to put on her interactive suit, climb in her 3V tank, and lose herself in another world. It was a race now as she jammed her arms and legs into the Lycra bodysuit and opened the top to the 3V tank. The suit soon covered her from head to toe, leaving only her face bare.

The sensory deprivation tank had become popular in the last decade as a way for the stressed-out to relieve their tense backs. Users climbed in and lost themselves in the coffin-womb, shutting out their troubles and floating on a sea of gravity-free endorphins. Before long the tanks merged with interactive gaming, and now they drew people into entirely new realities. Gamers could float away to Victorian Britain, Ancient Rome, or worlds that had never even existed. Feel the salty wind on the deck of a sailing ship. Smell the peaty odor of horses in a stable. Watch water trickle down the cold stone of an old English castle.

But at that sweetest of moments, as she anticipated leaving the real world, she could still hear her parents' voices. Elizabeth climbed into the tank and lay on her back in the thick but yielding liquid that had the power to transport her to her favorite fantasy.

(five)

"C-close and connect," she half whispered to the unit. Her insides were roiling, but her queasiness was soothed by the familiar feel of the tank's electrolytic solution. The doors to the outside world began to close.

(four)

"Where would you like to go today?" asked the too-placating voice of the Web.

(three)

"What did I ever do to deserve this?" came her mom's shrill voice from the living room.

(two)

"G-game Central," Elizabeth said, more loudly now, knowing she couldn't risk a misinterpretation by the Web. If she didn't get in-game, and soon, hearing her parents arguing might just cause her insides to explode all over her room.

(one)

". . . and don't let the goddamned door hit you on the way . . ."

snick

The quiet sound of the 3V tank's overhead doors latching gave her permission to breathe again. The screen above her flickered to life with a set of controls. She was now floating in an egg of electronica. Her entire body began to relax.

"Welcome to Game Central, Elizabeth Jackson. Begin game where previously ended?"

"God, yes," said Elizabeth as the soundtrack flooded her ears from the cocoon around her. Here, in the world of 3V, Elizabeth became another person, reveling in the freedom of a universe she'd created, forgetting everything outside it. She entered her fantasy world of simple choices she loved more dearly than real life.

The 3-D projectors inside the tank flickered to life, opening up a green landscape before her—hilly plains slowly rolling to meet the nearly cloudless blue sky of the horizon. A cool breeze touched her face and she smiled, smelling the scent of spring grass and the familiar, reassuring presence of nearby horses.

"Elsbyth!" shouted a man's voice. He emphasized the first syllable of the name so it came out *ELZ-bith*.

She turned toward him, noting the new weight of the heavy helm on her head. *The suit doesn't miss a trick*, she thought for the thousandth time. Whenever her character felt weight, like the helm, Elizabeth experienced it through the pressurized response of the sensors embedded in her Lycra suit. As the suit brought the game to life, she shed her old name like an old skin, becoming Elsbyth, Warrior-Queen of the Kingdom of Rheanna, who took up sword and shield in defense of her kingdom.

She reined around her horse, Caomos. Settling onto the saddle, she felt the firm leather and wood beneath her, the broad back of the stallion working between her thighs as he followed her lead. The shield. with the seal of Rheanna emblazoned upon it. rested heavily on her left arm. Her sword and scabbard bob-bobbed at her side as she faced the captain of the guard riding up the slight rise of a green hill.

Elsbyth looked past the approaching captain to the open plain beneath her. The hill swept down from her position into the open valley below, with nary a shrub to see till the gray trees of the Stone Forest to the northwest. But here the deep green valley of her home, the Kingdom of Rheanna, stretched from rolling hill to rolling hill. To the east flowed the River Adruwyn, the life's blood of the land running north and south. To the west lay the smaller River Faud, a tributary of the Adruwyn that split Rheanna in two. It was in the Y of the cradle formed by these rivers that she hoped to stop the overwhelming evil flooding from the dreaded kingdom to the south. If she could trap her enemy there, Rheanna's victory was certain.

"My Queen!" said the captain as he reined in his horse. "The enemy comes! The Dark Army is crossing in force over the Faud."

"Then our plan has worked perfectly," said Elsbyth, smiling.

For his part, Captain Moralir looked dubious. A force of 50,000 Orcs and Goblins, with their war machines and evil magicks, bore down upon them. They were clearing the way for the Dark King, the timeless Mallus, who had slain the mighty Ulaemeth, Elsbyth's husband. Driven by grief, she had snatched her beloved's sword from his funeral barge and pledged to cleave the Dark King's head from his shoulders. Now Elsbyth the Warrior-Queen and 10,000 Horse Companions of Rheanna stood, determined and grim, overlooking an open plain and awaiting their enemy.

"Elsbyth," said her captain more urgently now, "see their advanced scouts? They will be here in force within half a league!"

Elsbyth turned to the captain and drew Ulaemeth's sword. "Then that is where we shall meet them. Hah!" She kicked her heels and Caomos leapt forward. As she wheeled in and out of the ranks of her fellow horse lords, Elsbyth panted with the glory of the moment, all thoughts of parents and failure and fear gone. She reined up, and Caomos snorted and reared.

The wind carried the smell of the enemy to them—the rancid, flea-infested stench of sweat from days on the running march. The lead scouts of the enemy army crested over a low hill two slopes to the south. Running at a loping pace, the Orcs quickly spotted her and howled to alert their fellows.

"Captain, most of our Companions are, as yet, unseen by the enemy. Take half our forces and circle around the slope to the west. I will meet them here and charge down the hill to slow them down. You will, after our battle has begun, hit their right flank from the west." It was the plan she had mentioned earlier. If they could box them in against the Y the rivers made where they joined, Elsbyth's forces could limit the front upon which the enemy could fight, giving the mounted Companions the advantage. This was, at least, their hope.

"Yes, my Queen."

Moralir rode off. Elsbyth looked down the long, slow slope behind her and saw half her force turn and begin to gallop to the west.

"Horse Companions of Rheanna!" she called out. "For the glory of our fathers! And the hopes of your children! To me!"

A great cheer erupted from below, and 5,000 Horse Companions galloped up the hill to stand beside her. The Orc scouts topped the hill immediately to their front across the wide valley and halted. The number of the enemy swelled as they gathered for the charge, their howls increasingly murderous. The Companions consoled their horses, which snorted in fear at the stink and clamor of so foul an enemy so near. The afternoon sun provided the only brightness in the enemy's ranks as it bounced off axes, hammers, and maces. Covered in black armor, the Orcs and Goblins seemed to eat the sunlight, a mass of huge, black maggots covering the green grass of Rheanna. The war bosses, their whips cracking on the backs of their warriors, redoubled their efforts to drive forward and crush the thin line of horse before them.

When the enemy had mustered in force atop the opposite hill, Elsbyth raised her sword high again. Time seemed to slow as the enemy's main force began its steady advance downhill. Long moments of short breaths passed before the creatures reached the valley floor directly below the horse lords.

"For Rheanna!" screamed Elsbyth. Sweeping her blade around her head, she led her Companions in a galloping charge down the hill. The great tide of Orcs and Goblins slowed their advance, a low moan coming from the front ranks.

As the Companions brought the battle to them, the front-line Orcs turned back upon their fellows, as if the moon had shifted orbit and forced the ocean's tide back into an insistent sea. The great block that had moved as one now swarmed in confusion and in two different directions. Line sergeants cracked their whips and screamed, "Shield wall!" at their subordinates, but most ignored the order. Here the enemy's numbers worked against them, and they stumbled over one another.

The riders hit them with the full shock of thundering horse upon disordered foot soldiers. Charging downhill multiplied the impact. The Orcs swung their weapons wildly, hitting one another more often than a rider. The blades of the Companions, controlled and focused, found their marks much more often.

Spurred on by the whips of their war bosses, the Dark Army slowly began to assemble into more than a rabble with weapons. Having spent the shock of their attack, Elsbyth's troopers found themselves in the heart of every rider's fear—surrounded on all sides and, with the enemy aiming its blows at their horses, soon to be grounded and overwhelmed by hungry blades.

Now the screams of the horses drowned out the confusion of the enemy as the Orcs turned their axes to the task of grounding the riders. Companions raised their mounts from colts, breeding them not simply as warhorses but as beloved family members. The riders fought to keep their mounts safe, shielding them as best they could. But with the fighting so close, many began to fall. Holes in their line opened up, opportunities the invigorated enemy was quick to exploit.

Elsbyth's eyes filled with tears as she realized the price her Companions were paying.

(how could you have believed it possible to triumph)

"No!"

Elsbyth swung her sword, cleaving the head of an Orc in two.

(give up now, the odds are too great, you'll only lose in the end anyway)

"No!"

Caomos screamed as an iron axe bit into his shoulder, and Elsbyth felt him shudder beneath her.

"This isn't how it was supposed to be . . ."

(this is how it is, just give up now)

"No!" Elsbyth, the Warrior-Queen of Rheanna, struck down the Orc that had sliced Caomos with its axe, and its black blood spurted to the ground as another stepped up from the horde to take its place.

But in the face of the flood, as the Dark Army plugged the gap in its line with another of Mallus's minions, the doubt left Elsbyth's mind as she refocused on her certainty of victory. Elsbyth's faith that it could be done seemed to inspire her Companions, who fought on beside her with renewed vigor.

The great warhorn of Rheanna sounded and, almost as one, Companion and enemy alike turned their eyes toward the west. Two great foes stood intermingled, weapons raised to destroy one another, motionless for a single moment. And in the next, the hooves of 5,000 Horse Companions of Rheanna thundered from the west, riding stirrup to stirrup across the broad width of the valley.

A wail of yellow fear erupted from the Orcs, spreading eastward across the whole of the Dark Army as its soldiers realized they were boxed in by Companions to the front and right flank. Almost as one body they turned away from the battle and began pushing their fellows back, screaming about the tens of thousands of riders falling upon them. A grateful cheer went up from Elsbyth and her riders, who discovered new strength in the enemy's rout. Even Caomos, though bleeding heavily, snorted his enthusiasm.

The Dark Army disintegrated. If ever foot soldiers could outrace horses, it seemed today would be the day for it. As she rallied her Companions to pursue the fleeing enemy, Elsbyth knew this was the precise moment they could crush Mallus's forces against the rivers to the south.

"*Victory!*" Elsbyth shouted in elation, knowing in the space of a single second the Land of Rheanna was saved and that Mallus himself, the Dark King, the Enemy of the Ages, would be pushed from this world forever. She pulled Caomos up short and looked beyond the battlefield, now stained with blood, and watched as her Companions drove the evil from the field.

Elsbyth smiled her pride as she consoled Caomos against his wound. Her heart would have leapt from her chest had she given it leave to do so. Elizabeth, the young girl in the Lycra suit, rejoiced in her victory as Elsbyth, the Warrior-Queen of Rheanna.

Chapter 7

Still smiling, Elizabeth said, "Program, save" and stepped out of the tank. Removing the headset, she took a long, deep breath of satisfaction. She had written the story herself. Sometimes she played different characters, occasionally even on the Dark King's side, but most often as Elsbyth.

"Let's go back!" said her 3V self. *"Let's go back and finish 'em."*

Stripping off the interactive suit, she wrinkled her nose at the smell. She'd definitely sweated during the battle, no doubt about that. "No, that's enough for one night," she said, tired but delighted. *Well*, she thought, *at least the bodysuit is machine washable.*

That made her think of her mom, which brought up the prickly question from the back of her mind, forgotten in the Land of Rheanna. There was absolute silence in the other room. *They must've finished for the evening*, she thought sarcastically to herself. *I wonder how long they went on for this time.*

She looked at the clock.

Oh my God . . .

It was three o'clock in the morning. Her parents had been so wrapped up in their battle, they'd left her entirely to her own. She'd played for over eight hours, and that meant she'd be dead tired tomorrow.

Oh shit, oh shit, oh shit, oh shit.

Elizabeth quickly toweled off, shut down the 3V tank, and climbed under the covers. *I've got to get to sleep, I've got to get to sleep . . .*

She thought that mantra to herself for a full hour before finally drifting off.

"Monitor calling."

The feminine voice repeated its hail in an affectionate, may-I-be-of-service tone. There was nothing quite so perverse as that measured, not-quite-cheerful sound when you hadn't had enough rest.

"Attention, Elizabeth."

The prerecorded, helpful voice became a tad more insistent, as if saying, *No, really, for your own good . . .* "Monitor calling."

Elizabeth had been dreaming of her fictional husband, Ulaemeth, and how he'd wrapped his arms around her, kissed her, and told her how proud he was of her for defeating Mallus. He'd whirled her around in their joy and told her how she'd given meaning to his death through her victory. And then he'd stopped suddenly, looking around, as if hearing demons pricking at his ears with their pitchforks.

"What is it, dearest?" she'd asked. "What's the matter?"

Ulaemeth had looked her straight in the eye, his face falling, and suddenly he was her father, looking sternly at her. "There's an ale house in southern Rheanna that needs a barmaid," he said. "And that's where you'll end up. Queen of the Ale. That's what'll happen if you don't answer."

"Answer?"

(monitor calling)

"You think because you won the battle against the Dark King you *deserve* to wear that crown?" her father asked. Ulaemeth's armor had been replaced by his dress shirt and slacks, a loose tie dangling from his neck, his shirt sleeves rolled up. "If you don't answer, you'll amount to nada, zilcho. You'll be a huge disappointment to your mother and me."

"But—"

"*Wake up!*" he screamed, and she shot straight up in bed. Sweat plastered her hair to her forehead. She was panting, almost crying.

"Elizabeth Jackson. If you do not answer the monitor now, you will be counted as absent from today's lessons." The voice sounded downright prosecutorial now. But in a helpful way.

"Login Elizabeth Jackson!" she said desperately, knowing this delay would get back to her parents.

"Login complete," came the smug-sounding reply.

A video portrait of her monitor appeared in the upper-right corner of the screen, along with the four smaller portraits of her classmates lined up along the bottom. They all looked put out at having to wait on her. Monitor Skinner particularly. Debbie Maselic, class kiss-up and brain, seemed outraged at having to miss a minute of her education. Michael Miller looked relieved to see her at last, though he made a stern face and darted his eyes up and to the left to indicate that Mr. Skinner was not in a great mood. The others just looked bored to be there, but glad to see that Skinner's Evil Eye had settled on someone else for the moment.

"Good morning, Miss Jackson," said Skinner. "So glad you could join us this morning."

"Good morning, Mr. Skinner," she said, trying to put on a good face. "I'm sorry to be late, I just—"

"Overslept by the look of things," he finished for her. His eyes raked over her. As always, he could only see her from the shoulders up. But that was enough. He noted her disheveled hair, her rumpled clothes, her generally distracted, fatigued demeanor. "Were we up late playing 3V games again?"

Horrified at the question, Elizabeth stammered, "Uh, well, sir, I—"

"Mr. Skinner," broke in Michael, "didn't we finish up yesterday with the South firing on Fort Sumter?"

"Michael to the rescue!" her 3V self exulted.

"Quiet, Mr. Miller. When I require your newfound love of history to remind me of my lesson plan, you will be the first to know."

Michael's face deflated. Debbie Maselic smirked. The rest of the class continued looking bored as Elizabeth struggled with the decision to tell an obvious lie in hopes of keeping her 3V privileges. Or, at least, to try to keep the situation from getting any worse by telling the truth.

"We're waiting, Miss Jackson," breathed Skinner.

"Um, well, sir," she struggled, "I did play 3V games last night, but not past ten o'clock. But I had such a hard time sleeping. It was almost three o'clock this morning before I finally fell asleep." Well, a half-lie was, by definition, half of the truth. Wasn't it?

"Hmmm," said Skinner, giving the impression he almost believed her. "Then I must let the sysop for webgames know that his software is failing."

Elizabeth didn't understand. But she thought he was having a joke at her expense. "Sir?"

"Your game log here in front of me says you were on till nearly three A.M. *Actively*, I might add."

Michael rolled his eyes. Debbie smirked again.

I forgot the log! Now what do I do, what do I do?

Ever since the courts had ruled webschools legally liable for a child's educational achievements, certified monitors had full access to all recordable data regarding *anything* that might impact a student's ability to learn. Webgame logins were easy to keep track of, so they were loaded automatically as part of the monitor's morning checkup on his students before lessons began.

"Did you lie to me a moment ago, Miss Jackson?"

She thought desperately of a way out of it, of some way she could convince Skinner it had been a mistake, not a lie; an error, not a deception. Maybe she had fallen asleep online and, while dreaming in the bodysuit, had jerked enough to fool the program into thinking she was actively playing. Or maybe she could say someone else had taken over her game for her and played it late while she went to sleep, and it just *looked* like she'd still been playing all that time. But no, who could take the blame for that?

"Miss Jackson?"

"Blame Michael."

The thought appealed to her at first. She glanced at the lower left picture-in-picture on-screen. The look on his face melted her heart. He looked as if he only needed a horse and lance to ride to her rescue.

"Say it was a sleepover."

No.

"Miss Jackson, you are dis*missed* from class today."

Her brain cleared immediately. "Wh—?"

"You heard me," said Skinner. He raised an eyebrow. "Or, perhaps you didn't. Lack of sleep often leads to distracted behavior." Skinner's tone let her know his patience had run out. "So, I'll repeat it for you: You are dismissed from *class* today."

"But—"

"You will be required to make up the work before the end of the term."

Not another makeup exam. She'd gotten lucky yesterday, though she'd studied hard, it was true.

"Mr. Skinner, okay, I was playing last night . . ."

She darted her eyes to the others for help. Debbie looked smug, glad to be rid of the diversion from her lessons. Michael looked ready to cry out of sympathy. The others still just looked bored.

"Your parents will be notified that you have missed the day. Under the appropriate clause in the Parent-School Responsibility Sharing Act, it is *they*, not I, who will shoulder responsibility for your unexcused absence. The school will not be held accountable for your failure to learn today, and your parents will not be reimbursed for today's prorated tuition."

Her whole body felt numb with the certain fear of what was to come. "Mr. Skinner, *please*."

The monitor sighed. "It is unfortunate, Miss Jackson, particularly in light of your improvement yesterday. But discipline is not something that can be shirked. Perhaps some words from your parents will ensure your proper rest and prompt login in the future.

As it is, you have wasted ten minutes of the other students' class time already today."

Tears were streaming down her face now. "But you don't understand, if you call my father, he'll—"

"That is *all* for today, Miss Jackson. Good-bye." Skinner reached forward and tapped a button. His image disappeared.

Elizabeth sat on the bed, staring open-mouthed at the dead screen in front of her, listening to the prickly, fuzzy electrons dying on its surface. The final echo of Skinner's reprimand soaked into the walls, and her ears tried to catch and hold on to it, anything to keep what had just happened from being final.

But then, except for her sobbing, there was only silence. She wiped her nose with the bedcovers. She could see it all now, as if her own play were unfolding before her act by act, scene by scene. It would happen this way: After the day's lessons had ended, the monitor would call and her mother would get the message. And she might make a half-hearted attempt to deal with Elizabeth herself, but she was never very good at that sort of thing, so she would rely on Elizabeth's father to discipline their daughter. Then her father would get home and her mother would look for a good time to tell him what the monitor had said. But she would realize there *was* no good time and so, to get it off her chest, she would interrupt *Web Report*—the *worst* time to tell him. And he would be all the angrier because her mother's news would only confirm what he already suspected: that Elizabeth was a failure. Then he would lay into Elizabeth, ending his diatribe with a revocation of her 3V privileges for God knows how long

(depends on how bad *Web Report* is)

and then she would be in hell for that time, listening to them fight constantly with nowhere to hide from it.

Elizabeth sobbed harder at the paralyzing hopelessness she felt.

After a few moments, she gathered herself together and looked at the clock. Just after eight in the morning. Her father would have gone to his office already, but her mother would still be here cleaning up after breakfast and getting ready to go shopping online for the next couple of hours. Elizabeth knew she couldn't stay here all day, alone in her room, awaiting the inevitable. She began to plan how she might get past her mother on guard in the kitchen. Just thinking of her mother that way—*on guard*—made her wonder if Dad hadn't posted Mom there to ensure she attended webschool. It made her angry to think, despite today's evidence, that such diligence might actually be warranted. That was *beside* the point, after all. That her father might not trust her—that *really* made her mad!

"All right then," she said out loud to the empty 3V screen. "If that's what he thinks, then that's what he thinks. If we're going to be punished for last night, we might as well make it count!"

She wiped her eyes and nose one more time on her nightshirt and took it off to prepare for the day. She slipped on some jeans, tennis shoes, and a T-shirt with a 3-D imprint claiming that Elvis The King (whoever that was) was long dead but that Mick Forrest—his apparent replacement from Liverpool, birthplace of The Beatles (whoever they were)—should long live hereafter. She put a change of clothes in her backpack, which she'd bought for a family camping trip that had never happened, and put on a baseball cap, her hair hanging loosely beneath.

Elizabeth pushed the keypad next to her bedroom door, which slid open about two inches, swishing all too loudly as far as she was concerned. She could hear the morning news coming through the kitchen's 3V as her mother placed the morning's dishes into the washer for cleaning. She saw her mom's shadow dancing on the part of the kitchen floor she could see from her room.

About nine A.M. the webschool would break to let students go to the bathroom and grab a quick snack. They would be expected to be back in their places with bright shining faces by 9:30. So around nine, her mother would be looking for her to come out of her room. That meant Elizabeth would have to get out of the house as soon as possible, before her mother discovered she'd left.

She stared down the empty hall, opened the door wide, and dashed toward the safety of the bathroom. Elizabeth winced as the door hissed open. The dishwasher, just beginning to scour its contents, easily covered the sound.

She hid there for a moment, catching her breath and confirming the coast was still clear. A second door from the bathroom faced the kitchen, so she pushed its keypad and cracked it by a couple of inches.

Her mother was standing right there!

Susan Jackson stared at the 3V webnews in the glass of the microwave's door, which doubled as both a window on the cooking meal and a 3V screen. Elizabeth had one eye pressed to the crack, sure her mother would turn a fraction and see her squinting there. But Susan was listening intently to the report about a brewing crisis in Asia. A clanking from the dishwasher called her across the kitchen, out of Elizabeth's view.

Elizabeth opened the bathroom door and slid out. She was around the corner and out the front door almost before it opened all the way. She quietly keyed it closed behind her.

The sunshine felt like freedom. Her body lightened, like she'd just slipped off her interactive suit of virtual armor from Rheanna. Elizabeth actually stood a little straighter, a little taller, as her eyes adjusted to the natural light. She basked in its bright warmth.

She knew the feeling wouldn't last long. When Skinner called and her parents discovered she was missing, this glorious feeling would end. They would come and find her and drag her back here, chastise and punish her, and take the whole of Rheanna away from her.

"Don't think about that now," her 3V voice said, rebuking her for poisoning her few moments of liberation.

Yeah, Elizabeth thought. *Relax. Enjoy it while you can.*

"Don't think about them and their bitching at one another and Skinner and his holier-than-thou attitude and that brownnosing bitch Debbie Maselic," continued the 3V voice.

Skinner was Mallus, she thought to herself. But for now she'd beaten him.

"Don't even think about Michael right now. Try to enjoy the sunshine for a change."

And what a beautiful day it was! The early fall breeze was actually *cool*, a refreshing oasis after the muggy Texas summer. She rounded the corner of her house, well out of eyeshot of the front door. Elizabeth stood still for a moment, letting the ticklish warmth of the sunshine wash away the sterile cold of her bedroom. She looked around at the cul-de-sac of houses, then turned her eyes upward again to look through the branches of a pine tree and straight up at the most pleasant sky she had ever seen. It was the purest blue, and the most cottony of clouds floated above. They seemed to invite her to come and rest on their billowy softness, promising to take her away to a place without parents and webschools and worries.

She refocused her eyes on the houses around her. Though not the rolling hills and valleys of Rheanna, this sun was *really* warm. This sky was even *more pleasing* than Rheanna's. Most importantly, this adventure wasn't *programmed*. Elizabeth smiled at the clouds and promised to take a rain check on their offer to float her away. She set off down her street to see what she could see.

She wandered around most of the day, careful not to be too obvious about playing hooky. Elizabeth knew it was silly to even worry about that. Her parents would find out she wasn't in school anyway, and her mom had probably *already* discovered she wasn't in her room. Still, perhaps from some need to feel guilty, she kept to the neighborhood's side streets, avoiding the main streets in town.

Elizabeth walked toward Second Street, an older paved road that had almost crumbled to the gravel underneath. She walked past most of her own neighborhood before she realized she'd done so.

The houses she passed seemed old to her. But then everything in this town seemed old and worn down to her young eyes. The house they'd bought. The neighborhood. The tire-worn street they lived on. The smell of the air in Hampshire. Even *that* seemed old.

Her thoughts turned to Old Suzie's house and how it terrified her with its smell of ancient decay. Even though she'd only been inside in her dreams, she knew the air in there must smell like the breath of the dead, had they breathed—moist and foul. The paint of the house's exterior was cracked like her mother's hands in winter. In fact, the whole town seemed that way. Maybe not as old as that house, but old all the same, cracked and peeling and hunched over. Old and worn out and tired of living.

As she turned onto Second Street, she saw an old lady bending over rosebushes in her front yard. The old woman waved at her.

(come on in for dinner, honey, I ain't had a child for dinner in *ever* such a long while)

Elizabeth waved back and noticed how the old woman stooped when she returned to pruning her flowers.

snip – snip

Taking the dead blooms off.

The old woman resembled the mimosa tree drooping in the middle of her yard. Elizabeth looked at the two of them, the tree silhouetted behind the woman, and her 3V voice laughed, saying, *"The Hampshire Hunchback."*

That wasn't very nice, she chastised herself.

"Oh, puh-leeze."

She walked on down the street and past the old high school, which was mainly used as a community recreation center now. Local kids of all ages played sports there, and statewide football, baseball, and basketball teams competed against one another for bragging rights. But instead of school mascots, there were city and township teams now, still scaled into the A-system that once determined which teams played each other based on the size of the school's enrollment. The sports facilities for old Hampshire High were kept in pretty good shape by city taxes, but the rest of the school had largely fallen into disrepair. Though sometimes, for nostalgia's sake, the town would show old movies in the auditorium.

Elizabeth walked around town for most of the day, just looking around and glad to be away from her computer screen while it was still daylight. She stopped at a convenience store to grab a sandwich and a Coke. When she started walking the neighborhood again, she noticed a dog out of the corner of her eye.

She was startled by it at first. The dog was not quite collie and not quite shepherd, but a deep silky brown, almost-black furred beauty that stood straight on all four legs, ears perked up, its bushy brown tail wagging gently in the air. It stood looking at her intently, and that made Elizabeth stare back, standing stock-still.

"Don't ever try to pet a strange dog," she remembered her mother saying a long time ago. "Strange dogs bite you."

The collie-shepherd stood statue like, assessing Elizabeth, as if to say, *I see you too and I'm not sure I trust you either*. Elizabeth took another bite of her sandwich. The dog seemed more interested then, raising its head a little and sniffing at the air. She looked into its eyes, past the intelligence evident in them, and even from where she stood, Elizabeth could see large, brown pupils set deeply inside pumpkin irises. It was almost as if the dog had been carved from dark wood, so shining and perfect were the hues of its coat. All save for a patch of white that arced up from its belly and spread across its chest to disappear under its chin.

Don't ever try to pet a strange dog, her mother warned again.

The dog's brown-orange eyes entranced Elizabeth. So intense. So intelligent. So kind.

"Would you like a piece of my sandwich?"

The dog's ears perked up at the sound of her voice, and it turned its head, curious. She broke off a piece and held it out in her hand. The dog sniffed the air again and wagged its tail slowly, interested.

"Hungry?"

It looked away then, as if teasing her and saying, *I might be*.

"Come here."

The dog turned back to her and sniffed again. Then slowly it padded over, warily, eyes moving, as if looking for the trap beneath the food.

Elizabeth knelt down, and at first the dog stopped. *A-ha! I knew something was fishy about you*, its stance seemed to say. But then, as

Elizabeth held out the piece of sandwich, the dog's hunger trumped its caution. It padded closer.

"Go on," she said. "Go on, you can have it."

(strange dogs can bite you)

As it got closer, Elizabeth could see its fur was almost black, though really just a deep mahogany brown made up of many colors, but lighter around the eyes and muzzle. It was large for a collie but short for a shepherd. It came close enough to get a good sniff of Elizabeth's hand and the prize she held.

"Go on."

The dog put its nose right up to the piece, and Elizabeth readied herself to snatch her hand away at the first sign of her mother's being right.

But the dog opened its mouth and Elizabeth, without thinking twice, placed the sandwich on its tongue and pulled her hand away carefully, slowly. The dog chomped once, twice, and swallowed. It opened its mouth to pant and seemed to be smiling gratefully, at ease already with its newly discovered food source.

"Well," Elizabeth said. "Aren't you the friendly thing?"

The dog stared expectantly, panting.

"Want some more?"

Pant-pant. *What do you think?*

Elizabeth broke off another piece, and the dog took it more easily. She rubbed its head this time, and it accepted the praise gratefully.

"Whatever it takes to get another bite, huh, boy?"

Pant-pant.

"Hey, are you a boy?"

Elizabeth stood up and walked around the dog, which followed her with its head and eyes.

"It's hard to tell with all that fur!"

Pant-pant. *I won't freeze this winter, human.*

But the dog wagged its tail, and that gave Elizabeth the peek she needed.

"Why, you're a girl!" Elizabeth delighted herself with the revelation. "Here," she said, "I'll split the last bite with you." She broke the last part of the sandwich in two, took the first bite for herself while the dog licked her lips, then handed the second bite down to her new friend. "Pretty good, huh?" she mumbled around chews.

I've had better. Pant-pant. *But not today.*

Seeing no more food in the offing, the dog turned and walked away.

"Hey . . ." began Elizabeth dispiritedly.

The dog turned and looked back, wagging her tail slightly, panting her smile.

"Where are you going?"

But the dog looked away and walked on, stopping after a few steps and glancing back at her.

Elizabeth started after the dog slowly, so she wouldn't scare her. "Okay. Let's make a game of it," she said to herself.

"This isn't nearly as much fun as 3V."

Oh, shut up.

The dog glanced back once more without stopping this time, making sure that Elizabeth was ten or fifteen steps behind, then walked on down the sidewalk. As the wind picked up, cooling the late afternoon air, the collie-shepherd picked up her pace, her long fur flowing with the breeze. Elizabeth had to trot to keep up. Pretty soon the dog was playing a game with her, disappearing around corners. When Elizabeth made it around, the dog would be waiting there expectantly, looking up with her eyes shining. She'd get down on her front paws in front of Elizabeth, butt in the air, ready to pounce. As soon as Elizabeth started to giggle, the dog would jerk away and trot farther down the path. They played hide-and-seek around corners till it was almost dusk.

"Where are you, girl?"

Elizabeth followed the dog up a gravel driveway. She was ahead to be sure, but the failing daylight made it difficult for Elizabeth to spot her.

"Dog?"

She stopped and looked around, trying to find her new friend. Noticing the time, a part of Elizabeth delighted in the thought that her mother must be frantic looking for her right now.

"A-ha!"

She spotted the dog standing in a dilapidated doorway. The old mosquito netting of a screen door askew on its hinges waved in the soft breeze. The dog seemed tuckered out, but not quite ready yet to give up the game.

"Okay," said Elizabeth. "Here I come."

She walked past the brown rows that echoed an old garden long since abandoned, up the gravel driveway, and onto the back porch. The dog darted inside. Elizabeth stopped, not sure if she should go in or not. Looked innocent enough. No one lived here anymore. The partially opened screen door creaked on its one good hinge. Elizabeth cringed at the sound, but that and the quiet crickets of the early evening were all she could hear.

Pant-pant.

Almost all she could hear.

"There you are," she whispered. Elizabeth sidled inside the screen door. It struck her just how dense and thick an empty house can seem after the sun goes down. "Okay, girl, it's pretty dark in here. I can't see like you can."

Pant-pant.

Elizabeth's eyes adjusted. She was in an old kitchen. Cabinet doors dangled from their hinges. Roaches waking up for their evening patrols scurried one, then two across the floor, making reconnaissance between the old pantry and the sink. She curled her lip at the roaches, but the dog ignored them, passing through the doorway from the kitchen into the house. Elizabeth watched her go.

The dog woofed playfully from the other room.

Elizabeth turned toward the sound and walked a few steps in that direction. She deliberately averted her eyes from the roaches, some part of her thinking that if she ignored them, they really weren't there. She paused in the doorway that led to the heart of the house. *Must be the parlor*, she thought.

Elizabeth decided that if she sat down, maybe the dog would come to her instead. She looked around. No roaches.

They're more afraid of you than you are of them, she heard her mother's voice say.

Hope so, she thought back.

"Yeah, right," taunted her 3V voice.

Shut up!

She felt her way carefully down to the floor, sitting cross-legged. The wood felt old beneath her hands. She was careful of splinters. "Come here, girl," she said quietly. "Come here."

Pant-pant.

Then she smelled it. The same smell as when she and Michael had come here the other day at just about this time.

(Old Suzie's house)

But how could that be? She would've recognized it . . .

(from the front)

But the dog had led her around back. Had led her to the place she most feared in the whole damned, old, dead, decaying, smells-like-grandma town. The dog had been playing games, all right.

(we play games in the parlor)

Led her right here.

"Girl?"

Pant-pant.

(come into my parlor)

She felt something on her arm. Elizabeth tensed, sure the roaches had come for her.

"So stupid to sit down here," her 3V voice warned.

Elizabeth summoned Elsbyth's courage and looked down at her arm.

Nothing.

But there had been something. There had been the light down of hair rising on her arm.

And there was fear. A sense of being trapped, smothered in a blanket of *old*. As if her fate were in the hands of someone else. Someone who was not a good person. Someone she couldn't see.

She started to uncross her legs to ready herself to get out of there, roaches or no roaches, screen door in the way or no screen door in the way.

"D-dog?"

Pant-pant.

"Hello, little girl," croaked a tired male voice from the darkness.

PART 2

(15 YEARS AGO)

This place you say you're looking for,
That's a place I used to know.
Don't know the number of the road,
But I can tell you how to go.

Head on down 'til the pavement ends,
I used to go back there now and then.
I used to know it
Like the back of my hand,
When I was just a boy.
                    —James McMurtry
                    "Vague Directions"

CHAPTER 8

"On your knees."

The boy was crying. He focused on the entryway floor.

"*Now.*"

The boy knew—either he would get on his knees on his own, or his father would put him there. So he maneuvered carefully to the floor, sitting on his heels.

"You know better than *that.*"

Internally the boy rolled his eyes, though he knew he didn't dare show sass. That would only make it worse.

"And stop that goddamned blubbering," his father said. "Learn to be a man early on, boy, and you'll be better off for it later."

That was a laugh. How many times had he wished, *begged* God to make him a man so he could fight back? Somehow, he knew, this was supposed to make him tougher. But still he cried.

"Knees against the wall," said his old man. "I'm running out of patience."

The boy could already feel the cold tile of the floor digging into his knees. He wished he could burrow a hole through that floor, get away into some underworld refuge where his father would never find him.

"Now sit up straight. Ass off your heels."

He took a deep breath. Here's what he'd been avoiding—the full weight of his upper body on his knees. He would kneel here for an hour. Praying at the altar of forgiveness, sorry he'd made his father mad once again and wishing God would make him old enough to dole out some divine retribution of his own.

"I said *sit up*."

His father yanked the back of his shirt, the collar tightening around his throat until he pulled up straight. He wasn't a thin boy, nor was he fat, but forcing his center of gravity onto his kneecaps made him gasp.

Even in church, the kneelers have pads, he thought through the pain. He almost began to giggle, and a shock of fear coursed through him. It was bad enough to cry when punishment came. It would be worse if he laughed. *Much* worse.

"Keep that nose six inches from the wall, no farther," his father said. His voice was low. *These are your instructions for survival*, the voice said. *Screw it up and—well, figure it out.* "Keep that back straight. Understand?"

The boy nodded.

"What?"

"Yes, sir," he whispered.

"Mmmm," said his old man, nodding and turning to go. He looked at the grandfather clock behind his son. Noting the boy had started to slouch already, he turned back briefly.

"Up."

The boy immediately stiffened to attention despite the grinding in his knees.

"And the next time I tell you to have the grass mowed before I get home, maybe you'll have it done. You need to learn some discipline. You slouch your way through life, that's all you'll ever be. A slouch. Understand?"

The boy just wanted him to go, to get out, to leave him alone, to quit gloating over another round of humiliation and let him get the punishment over with. *Get out, get out, get out you motherfucking asshole! Leave me alone! Take your big arms and your discipline and your beer breath and your stupid weekend projects and your crappy job and your "Lazyass, get to work" and your "On your knees" and your "Mow the grass by the time I get back" and get the fuck out of here!*

"I'm talking to you, boy. You deaf now too?"

"N-no, sir," the boy said.

His father grunted, sounding like he might not agree. Then he heard footsteps trail off into the other room, probably headed for the kitchen.

Mix up another rum and something, he thought. *Good. Maybe he'll go to sleep soon. He'll be out for hours.*

He let himself relax a bit to take the pressure off his knees. He cocked his right ear toward the kitchen. Sure enough, he heard a chair at the breakfast table—*his* chair at the breakfast table—scrape slowly over the floor. The boy took some pleasure in knowing the chair was marking up the same floor that was killing his knees. The little television they kept in the kitchen flicked on, and a sports commentator came bubbling forth, the excited murmur of the crowd behind him. He sat back on his heels. His father would be back in to check on him soon enough, but for now he had a reprieve.

"Motherfucker," David whispered in defiance. "I hate him, I hate him, I *hate* him."

All because he hadn't had the grass mowed by the time the old man had gotten back from an emergency call from the company. Some power grid had gone offline somewhere. His father was on call, so off he'd gone in the truck. David had thought he'd be gone for hours, but the repair had been quick. Even if he'd fired up the mower as soon as his father had left, he doubted he'd have finished the yard in time. *I mean, don't I have better things to do on a Sunday afternoon?* David thought, defiant.

Too long.

(and look where it's gotten you)

A giddy rage boiled up inside him. He was helpless to do anything about the situation. David thought to himself, *You moron. If you hadn't pranced around making fun of him after he'd gone, you might've gotten it done instead of being here*

(on your knees)

and facing the wall.

93

He balled up his fists and relaxed them over and over again. He gritted his teeth until they slipped and made an awful screaming, grating noise that sent worms wiggling up his spine. He felt like such an idiot, when a simple thing like mowing the grass was all his father had asked

(you lazyass)

and now here he was

(on your knees)

for no better reason than because he was an idiot.

David felt his own frustration bearing down on him, pressing his knees into the floor. He closed his eyes, squeezing tears out of them like wringing water from a damp towel.

(don't cry, boy)

Then he lifted his head and opened his eyes. Opened them wide. Used the thumb and first finger of each hand to spread the lids open till he felt the cold air on his eyeballs. Till he felt like they might just roll right out of his head.

(men don't cry)

His nose was running, but he didn't spare a hand to wipe the mucous as it crept, warm and wet, onto his upper lip. He couldn't get his eyes to dry, no matter how wide he spread his lids. He dug at them with his knuckles, tried to squeeze them dry again, but that only made things worse. Now his eyes felt like they had something in them. All he wanted to do was rub them.

Making things worse seems to be the only thing you're good at, he thought.

He cursed at God for playing such a cruel joke on him, for making him such an idiot. He couldn't even kneel here and take his punishment like a man; instead, he sat back on his haunches

(like a slouch)

and cried about being punished.

"No one likes a whiner, David," he heard his old man's voice saying. "The world don't suffer complainers. Do what you have to do

94

and don't bitch and moan about it. Learn that and you'll save yourself a shitload of grief along the way."

He heard a chair leg screech from the kitchen. David sat bolt upright on his knees. The quick action pressed his kneecaps into the tile again, and pain shot up his thighs.

At least they're going to sleep, he thought mercifully.

He listened intently for his father to come, bare feet slapping on the cold, hard tile. But the slapping stopped in the kitchen with the creak of the refrigerator door. David cocked his ears to every sound, projecting the events on the screen in his mind. He heard containers scraping on the thick-wired shelves of the refrigerator, the muffled hollow hum of bottles as they were moved around. Obviously his father was searching for something. And by the cursing the boy heard, he wasn't finding it.

David cringed at the bellowing voice, then immediately realized his fear had bent him over, so he sat straight up again, his knees more numb now but still awake enough to feel pain.

"God*dammm*it!"

The boy closed his eyes and swallowed. The slapping started again. It was getting louder.

"David!"

He made sure he was sitting up straight. His knees were so numb now they barely hurt anymore. He smiled inwardly at his little secret. *I'll kneel here all damned day, you sonofa—*

"I'm out of beer," said his old man, his feet smacking to a stop behind the boy. "I'm going to the store. You stay in that position till I get back. Understand?"

"Y-yes, sir."

"Good," said his father, "but just to make sure . . ."

David heard some rustling—a paper bag, it sounded like—then felt little puffs of air wafting up from around his bent legs. He chanced a glance down once and saw the old man pouring flour around his kneeling position. *Why in the—*

"Eyes front!"

David jerked his head around.

"Move an inch and I'll be able to tell," said his father in a low voice. "This flour is spread for three feet around you, boy. You move an inch, you even breathe anywhere but right at the wall, and I'll see it. And then you'd wished you was only on your knees when I got through with you. Understand?"

All hope left David then. When he'd first heard his father announce he was off to buy beer, he'd seen a way out, at least a short parole from his sentence. But not now.

Why didn't you just mow the fucking yard! he screamed at himself. *Idiot!*

"I'm talking to you, boy."

"Y-yes, sir," he answered reflexively.

"Mmmm."

slap – slap, slap – slap

As his father's footfalls echoed away, David started crying and didn't care anymore that he shouldn't be. At least the old man was leaving. He closed his eyes and let the tears come, leaning his head against the wall and sagging back on his haunches, totally defeated. He heard his father's keys jingle, then the back door slam. David shuddered at the sound. Part of him was relieved to be alone in the house under any circumstances. Most of him hated his father for outsmarting him. Even gone, the old man had him trapped.

He looked around at the white powder prison walls. There was no way he could stand up and jump far enough without somehow disturbing the flour.

He was so angry he could hardly breathe!

So trapped.

The silence of the house pressed in on him then. The reality of living here with his father, alone. He swore he could feel his knees being crushed.

tick

Even if he wanted to get up, he couldn't move without flour going everywhere. His legs were asleep.

tock

Betrayed by his own legs now.

Idiot!

And beyond the echo in his head, he heard the grandfather clock behind him. Though he passed it every day, David hadn't really noticed it as anything but another piece of furniture. Never really listened to its pendulum count the seconds as they passed into the past. But now, with only his thoughts to scream at him, the clock's gears marked the time. With a maddening, measured

tick

the clock mocked him.

Pointed an hour hand at him and laughed.

tock

Made faces

(clock faces, with a mocking moon turning ever so slowly in its course to mark the seasons)

at him

(Mr. Moon, with one eye winking and a knowing grin)

as if to say

(I see you there, little boy, kneeling on the floor)

and cracking wisely

(each moment is worth remembering)

and saying helpfully

(let me count the moments for you)

and adding its own brand of timely humor

(by tick-tock-ticking them off for you)

because being a grandfather clock was so boring. Any little distraction, even a little boy kneeling, would surely help to pass the time, now wouldn't it?

David pictured Mr. Moon slowly revolving—so slow he couldn't even see him move. But Mr. Moon moved, oh yes he moved, and with every

tick

of the tick-tock clock he moved a little more, invisibly, through the course of the seasons.

David was suddenly very scared to have the grandfather clock behind him, where he could make his Mr. Moon clock faces at him, unseen. The boy could sense his mocking blue-cheese grin burning into the back of his skull. He turned his head to the left but couldn't see Mr. Moon very well. He was directly behind the boy. But David could hear the

(tsk-tsk)

of Mr. Moon the Tick-Tock Clock making fun of him for not doing as he was told

(should've mown the grass)

when he was told to do it.

He tried to shift around a little more to face his accuser, and his left leg went out from under him. His dead nerves couldn't pull it back in time. His foot shot out, cutting a wide swath through the flour. The white dust sprang into the air like the end of a magic trick.

Horror flooded his limbs. His heart beat hard. Blood raced adrenaline through him. His eyes, wide now at what he'd done, dried of their own accord. David glared at the clock, and Mr. Moon looked down at him with his blue-cheese, knowing smile

(tsk-tsk)

and marked the moments, one after the other.

(how many left till the Old Man returns)

The thought terrified the boy. He looked at the broad path his foot had made through the flour. The pumping blood began to revive his legs, and tiny pinpricks of pain pulsed through his knees and thighs. Knowing the mess was already made, he put his palms flat on the tile and tried to raise himself up. His legs were still slow to respond, but he willed them, *willed* them under him. As he drew his left leg up beneath him, he saw the flour clinging to his jeans. *How do you get flour out of clothes?* he wondered. David stood up now, leaning against the wall, and stared at the mess.

bong

David almost peed himself as the clock struck the hour.

(how long has he been gone, boy)

bong

(how long will he *be* gone, boy)

He stared desperately around. *Clean up the floor, idiot. See if you can do that right!*

bong

David forgot all about the punishment, all his thought bent on cleaning up the flour. He tiptoed through the mess and into the kitchen to get the broom and dustpan.

bong

As he walked back to the scene of the crime, David gasped. There was a short patch of carpet between the entryway and the kitchen, and he'd just tracked flour across it. The dirt-brown carpet was now bespeckled with white flecks. *Oh my God, oh my God—idiot!*

bong

"First the floor," he said to himself.

He went to the broken white semicircle and began sweeping it back into the pattern his father had made. The silence returned and he looked at the clock. It was five P.M. He had ten minutes, fifteen at most to clean all this up. The store wasn't that far away.

He brushed off his pant leg, then swept the flour into a little pile and scooped it into the dustpan with the broom. Then he resumed reconstructing the barrier his father had made. He was careful not to make it quite so wide, else he'd never be able to get back inside it. He hoped the old man wouldn't notice.

After cleaning the mess on the floor, he went to the coat closet, got the vacuum cleaner, and went to work on the carpet. David tried to work fast, because with the vacuum cleaner running, he wouldn't hear if his old man returned. *Maybe a little too spotless*, he thought, looking at the clean patch he'd just made. It seemed just the slightest bit cleaner than the surrounding carpet. *Maybe he won't notice*, David hoped again.

He put up the vacuum cleaner and returned the broom and dustpan to the kitchen after rinsing both off in the sink.

ding-ding-ding-dong . . .

The clock chimed the quarter hour.

(better hurry, boy)

David slipped it into overdrive, returning to the entryway and staring at the flour prison. He was free. He was out. *Escaped*. And here he was putting himself back in again, of his own free will.

Idiot.

He stared at the flour and thought his father, if he was lucky, would've started drinking the beer before he got back. If he'd had enough of it, David knew from experience, chances were he'd forget ever having punished the boy. On the other hand, there was all this flour here in a semicircle.

thrrrruuummmmmmmmmm

The distant, grinding mechanical sound startled the boy out of his options. The garage door was rising.

His father was home.

tick

He stood for a moment more, reveling in the rebellious thought of his father coming in and finding him outside the flour prison. He would take great pride in how upset, startled, and thrown for a loop his father would be to find the punishment abandoned. Right before David suffered retribution for his revolution.

tock

There was a pause from outside, then the thrumming started again as the garage door descended.

David carefully lifted his leg over the flour wall to climb back in again.

tick

His heart beat faster as the back door opened.

tock

He stood in the semicircle now, staring straight at the wall. Carefully he began to lower himself to the floor. His legs, as if they knew what was coming, tried to slow him down.

ticktock

His father was unloading the beer into the fridge. He didn't bother to take the cans out of their twelve-pack cartons. He just slid them onto the wire shelves.

David put one knee down, then the other, wincing. He heard the fridge door close and two shoes being kicked off two feet.

Knees still hurting from the last time, he sat straight up, facing the wall.

slap – slap – slap

So close to freedom. Tasted it. Walked it.

"David," said his father.

He closed his eyes. *I won't cry anymore, I won't, I* won't.

"You gonna mow the grass next time I tell you?"

David bit his lip and clenched his eyes shut, trying to squeeze the tears away.

"Y-yes, sir."

His father said, "Then you can get up." He heard the old man turn away.

David breathed deeply once and lifted himself up. He was determined not to disturb the flour when he did it. It was a test. To prove to himself that he could do it.

What, up again? his legs screamed at him. *Can't you make up your mind?*

But he stood up slowly, using the wall for balance, and not a bit of flour was moved. He smiled inwardly. A tiny victory.

His father poked his head back around the kitchen door. "Oh, and get the broom and dustpan and clean that shit up."

CHAPTER 9

While his father snored the evening away in his chair watching *60 Minutes*, David spent Sunday night stretching out his freedom. Sunday nights were always bittersweet for the boy. Even after he went to bed, he'd try to hold his eyes open as long as he could, savoring every moment before the school week began again.

Tonight he lay in bed, thinking about Halloween on Wednesday. He and Theron Taylor wanted to do something *really* special. No treats for this one. *Tricks only*, he thought. *That's all we want on Halloween.* A trick to end all tricks. But so far they hadn't decided what to do.

David stared up at the fan blades cutting blurry slices from the ceiling above him. It was nice and cool now. Fall blew into Texas like a sudden rain soaking a parched field. Chapped lips were soothed. Foreheads were dried. People came out of their houses again for the pure pleasure of standing outside and commenting on the cool.

Which makes it the perfect time for a Halloween trick, David thought as he fell asleep.

The boy was still thinking that the next morning in class when Mrs. McKinley repeated his name again.

"*Well*, Mr. Jackson?"

He came back to reality, looking around. The other kids sniggered. Even Theron. Freddie Martinez hadn't, though. He didn't want to attract Mrs. McKinley's attention. He didn't know the answer either.

"I said, how do we make a fraction into a whole number?" Her attitude made it seem like she half hoped he wouldn't get the answer right. *Come on*, it seemed to say. *Please mess up. Let me ridicule you in front of the* entire class.

David was a deer caught in the headlights. How did he get here? The last thing he remembered was lying in bed, planning Halloween . . . and then the monotony of the morning came back to him: waking up suddenly from some dream he didn't remember, looking at the clock, realizing he'd fallen asleep. *Back to jail again*, he'd thought, rising slowly to go to the bathroom. Monday morning, and time for school. New week, same old routine.

And here he was in first period. Math. They'd just finished learning how to find a common denominator in fractions, and Mrs. McKinley, the just-out-of-college teacher and advisor for the Hampshire Junior Varsity cheerleaders, was asking them the procedure for converting a fraction into a whole number.

Theron Taylor, David's best friend, watched Mrs.—or "Miss," as the students invariably called her—McKinley pace back and forth in front of the whiteboard. David, sitting next to him, was totally lost, but Theron had his mind on something else. Even as Mrs. McKinley repeated her question, he was planning his strategy.

There. Two more feet, thought Theron. *That's all. Just two more feet.*

"Mr. Jackson, will you kindly stay awake?" she asked, finally breaking the leaden silence. "I'll come back to you in a minute with another question." Mrs. McKinley sought another draftee, since no volunteer was forthcoming. Her eyes lit on Theron's face staring intently up at her. *Good as any, I guess*, she thought, smiling down at him.

Theron only partly heard her repeat the question to him. She was beautiful. *Young, blonde, and nice bazongas*, he thought. And almost right where he wanted her.

"How about you, Mr. Taylor? Any ideas how to make a fraction into the whole number one?"

Was she talking to him? Had she said something? He didn't know, but he *did* know that she was nearly positioned perfectly.

Mrs. McKinley cleared her throat. "Mr. Taylor? Has your hearing problem returned from yesterday?"

When he failed to answer her, she moved one step closer.

Off went the pencil from his desk, and no, she hadn't noticed he'd knocked it off on purpose. He smiled inwardly as he saw he'd damn near centered the No. 2 on top of the small, almost imperceptible "X" he and Freddie had made on the cheap carpet with the dry-erase marker. They had then rubbed it out, of course, leaving the slightest smudge to mark the spot.

"Oh . . ." he said. "I'm sorry, Miss McKinley."

She smirked slightly, sure that this had been one of those delaying tactics the boys in the class always pulled on her. They'd taught her all about such tactics in the education courses she'd taken at The University of Texas. "They all think they can fool you with their little games, Jill," her professor with benefits had warned her. "You need to take them by their freshly grown short hairs and show them who's boss." Yes, the boys in this class in particular were always ready and willing to test her, and she always met the test with the same resolve.

"Mr. Taylor, answer the question, please." Her unconscious smirk of triumph waited as the boy formed his answer. From the corner of her eye, she noticed David's right hand finally creep into the air, but Jill McKinley ignored it. *You're not going to pull one over on me, little mister. I've been trained by the* best.

"Uh—could you get my pencil for me, Miss McKinley?" asked Theron.

The smirk grew wider, more hungry, more satisfied. "After you answer the question, Mr. Taylor."

He shrugged. Whatever it took. "What was the question again?"

Now she was getting angry, and her eyes showed it. They reminded Theron of the way his mother looked when she was about to call his father to come and thwack him one. He wondered if Mrs. McKinley would also call him by all three of his names and grab him up by the ear the way his mother did.

Mrs. McKinley took a deep breath, still ignoring David's now fully extended arm. "The question was, Mr. Taylor, how do you make a fraction into a whole number?"

Theron actually looked pensive for a moment. Nothing like the promise of what was to come to spur his mathematical prowess, limited as it might be, into action.

"Um, you multiply it by its inverse, right?"

The class was silent. No one seemed to breathe. Jill McKinley paused and placed her right elbow in her left hand, regarding Theron with an amused stare and stroking her chin with thumb and forefinger. Theron noticed that her right breast was cupped quite nicely in the crook of her arm, squeezing it up to make the slightest raised hill peek out of her blouse. She stared at him for a moment, a smile creeping across her lips.

"Well, Mr. Taylor, as surprised as I am, you seem to have come up with the correct answer. Now, I'll be happy to pick up that pencil."

Mrs. McKinley bent over to pick it up, and in the short eternity she needed to grasp the pencil, Theron and every other boy in the class raised themselves six inches from their chairs. Theron, who had the best vantage point—as was only fair, since he'd taken the chance and dropped the pencil—could see right down the front of her blouse into her cleavage. *A white-lace bra today*, he thought, hoping beyond hope to catch a glimpse of that ever-elusive nipple. *Damn.* She rose and, as if choreographed with her movement, the boys all settled back into their seats. An audible breath—audible at least to the girls, who had all rolled their eyes in disgust—exhaled across the room.

"Here's your pencil, Mr. Taylor."

"Thank you, M-miss McKinley. Thank you *very* much."

He looked toward the whiteboard and the strategically placed eraser. She hadn't erased all morning, much to the boys' collective chagrin. Before class, Freddie had sneaked in and put one eraser on the floor in front of the board. About once a month they pulled this one, else she'd catch on and—yep!—she'd placed her hands on her hips.

Step one, thought David.

"Has anyone seen my erasers?" she asked, thinking, *I lose more erasers in this class than any other . . .*

Freddie said, "Um, there's one on the floor there, Miss McKinley."

"So I see," she said suspiciously. "Who keeps putting my erasers on the floor? And I know I have *two* of those things."

"I don't know, Miss McKinley," Freddie said innocently.

"Mm-hmm," she replied, walking toward the board.

The bell erupted with a loud clanging. Mrs. McKinley bent over to pick up the eraser.

Fourteen young boys raised themselves six inches in their chairs. Thirteen young girls rolled their eyes again. Theron's mouth opened slightly.

Mrs. McKinley stood back up and turned to face them, saying, "Tomorrow we start working on both sides of the equals sign, so read up on chapter five."

"Yes, Miss McKinley." More or less in unison, the class moaned at the prospect of homework. Some of the girls made disgusted clucking sounds.

"Theron?"

He hadn't moved from his desk.

"Yes, ma'am?" he asked, sounding shy, even embarrassed.

"You can go, honey. Class is over."

He was the one student left, and he hadn't moved from his chair. Hadn't stood up, even.

"Yes ma'am, I know," he said, cheeks a bit crimson. "But I just thought I'd sit here for a minute. I'm feelin a little . . . tired."

She regarded him for a minute, then nodded. "Okay. Take your time."

"Thank you, ma'am," he said sheepishly.

Taking a bite out of a sandwich, David motioned Theron over. "That was pretty good in class this morning," he said.

"Yeah," Theron nodded. "Getting a glance at Miss M's bazongas is always good. Getting her to bend over was just icing on the cake!"

David giggled a bit, almost choking on the bologna and bread. "Man, you're the best at it too," he said, trying to chew. It came out, "Manph, you de besht addit too." He finished up the mouthful and said, "She doesn't suspect nothing."

Theron smiled, impressed as usual with his own ability to get Mrs. McKinley to bend over in front of his desk. A stirring in his groin reminded him of the outcome, so he quickly started thinking about kickball, math, and helping his father with the car next weekend. That helped.

"I mean," continued David, "the way you got her to stand on *the spot*. Dude, you ought to be in the hall of—"

"Yeah-yeah," said Theron, trying to change the subject. "What's going on over there?"

Voices filtered toward them, like a group of kids singing a song or chanting a rhyme like "London Bridge Is Falling Down." Soon enough the words were clear, and one shrill, pleading voice broke the rhythm. Theron and David smiled. It was turning into a *very* good day.

"Regina, Regina, she's such a va-jeena," came the chant. "She's so poor she eats day-old farina!"

The chorus could be heard in rounds now, like "Row, Row, Row Your Boat," and it carried across the playground. The boys could see them now, a crowd of about six kids following one. The girl, pinch faced and red haired, stomped away from the crowd as fast as she could, occasionally turning back and hurling "Leave me alone! Just leave me *alone!*" at them, as she always did when they made fun of her. Her corduroy dress looked like it was made of sackcloth converted by her mother in an effort to dress her conservatively for school. Trying to be frugal, her mother made all her clothes, every stitch. But Regina hated her homemade dresses, since they only provided her classmates one more reason to tease her. The girl stomped away, fists tight, glasses smudged because she refused to wipe her eyes in front of her tormentors.

"Regina, Regina, she's such a va-jeena. She's so poor she eats day-old farina!"

"Shut *up!*" she screeched.

David and Theron watched her approach. Then they picked up the chant.

"Regina, Regina, she's such a va-jeena," they said again. "She's so poor she eats day-old farina!"

She walked into Theron and David accidentally, then suddenly found she was boxed in. She looked directly at the kids chanting at her, seemed to study their mouths as if trying to see the words coming out of them so she could catch them and throw them in the trashcan. Theron was laughing, and David asked, "Do you still sell magazine subscriptions, Regina? I'd like a copy, please," then laughed.

As she looked from one group of mockers to the other, the girl's eyes streamed. "My family ain't got the money y'all do! We all have to help out!"

"How about seeds, Regina the Va-jeena?" asked Theron. "Still selling seeds? I'll grow you something nice and big."

All the children laughed now, repeating the chant. But Regina had had enough. She turned to push her way through when a leg tripped her. The girl fell down with an "Ohhhhh!" The ring of children surrounding her looked down and laughed.

That's right, on your knees, was the thought that came to David's mind. He was about to take up the chant again with the rest of the crowd when he looked down at her and stopped. She was sitting on the rumpled skirt of her sackcloth dress, her right knee exposed and bleeding, and looking up at them with glasses so fogged and smudged from crying that she couldn't even see her persecutors anymore. The knee caught David's attention. He saw the blood and gravel from the lot ground into her flesh. The words of the chant refused to come out of his mouth again as he stared at her.

"Regina, Regina, she's such a va-jeena," the children said again. "She's so poor she eats day-old farina!"

Hey, thought David. *That's enough.*

"Look!" said one of the girls. "She's got her pretty dress dirty!"

Another kid said, "Ah, too bad her momma can't afford a washing machine!"

Regina had lost the will to fight back now. She just sat on the kickball lot and sobbed her defeat.

"Hey," said David. "That's enough."

But no one heard him as they mocked the girl. One of the boys drew back a leg.

"I said that's enough!"

The crowd hushed as the dust from the lot began to settle again. Within seconds there was only the sound of children playing across the playground. And Regina's sobbing.

"What's up, David?" asked Peter Lasco, the boy who'd almost kicked her. "It's just Regina."

"I know," said David, "but that's enough."

"What's your problem, man?"

David looked at Lasco. A bully if there ever was one. "I don't have a problem, Pete. But that's enough all the same."

Lasco walked up to him and thumped him on the chest. "Well, well, well. Looks like Regina's got a boyfriend."

The children standing around laughed. All except Regina, who still sat where she was, muttering something about how she'd be in trouble with her momma because her dress had been ripped.

"I'm not her boyfriend, Pete," said David. The thought filled him with revulsion, actually. Regina Va-jeena's boyfriend?

"Then you're just a pussy all by yourself," said Pete. "Maybe I oughta put *you* in the gravel, boy!"

The rage boiled up out of him before David even knew it was there. He advanced on the bigger boy quickly, reaching up and grabbing Lasco by the shirtfront as the other boy stepped back, startled.

"Try it, Lasco!" David was screaming. "See if you can get *me* on my knees. Go ahead and try it!"

Lasco backpedaled. One of the other boys started to grab David around the neck, but Theron intervened, saying, "Leave it alone."

"Get off me, you pussy!" Lasco was spouting. "Get off me 'fore I teach you a lesson!" He was trying to beat David's hands out of their locked grip, and the force of the blows brought David back to himself. The last thing he remembered was telling the other kids to quit. And now he had Peter Lasco ready to beat the crap out of him. He let go of the bigger boy's shirt. Lasco backed up.

"Goddamn, boy, I'm gonna kick your ass!"

"Well, we have *several* violations of school code here," said a calm voice behind Lasco. The bigger boy froze. "Language, number one, and fighting, number two."

Lasco turned around. Principal Sinclair, a balding former science teacher had his arms crossed, a cat in front of a mouse hole. And the mouse was outside the hole, and the hole was boarded up. The principal looked past the two of them and saw Regina still on the ground, crying.

"Regina!"

He brushed past David and Lasco, who gave David a look that said, *If you get me in trouble, so help me, I'll whip your ass.*

"What's happened here?" asked Sinclair. "Are you all right?"

Slowly the children began to slink away from the scene of the crime, but Sinclair had been a teacher for a very long time before becoming an administrator.

"That's far enough! All of you, in my office! Theron, help Regina here to the nurse's office. Let's go, *all* of you! My office. *Now*."

David and Theron walked home from school, and there was silence for a long time. Finally Theron asked, "Will you get in trouble with your dad?"

David shrugged. "Probably not. The principal was mad mostly at Pete. At least *I* didn't get suspended."

"No, but Sinclair *did* say he'd be talking to our parents."

David shrugged again dismissively. "He always says that. At least I ain't suspended."

Theron nodded and put his hands finger-deep in the front pockets of his jeans as they walked.

"Man, Miss McKinley was looking good today."

David smiled. "Oh yeah."

"I don't think I can wait another month to drop a pencil."

"Oh no," said David. "But the eraser thing is out for a while. I think she's starting to catch on."

"Yeah, I guess." Theron sounded forlorn. Another *month*.

"Hey, there it is!" said David.

They both stopped and looked up the street. Theron's eyes went to the old mansion that had stood at that corner for longer than even his father could remember, and Theron's father had lived in Hampshire all his life. Bob Taylor liked to say, "That house has stood strong since a time when Texas was one nation, under Sam." Whatever that meant.

The old mansion sat apart from the rest of the town despite its location in one of Hampshire's oldest neighborhoods. It stood on a lot a full acre wide, with the house proper nestled on the corner farthest from the sidewalk across a broad front yard of perfectly mowed grass. The white wood of the house, outlined with baby-blue eaves, still shined in places on early summer mornings. The oak trees dressed in Spanish moss shaded the old manse in the warm, sluggish afternoons of July and August. In winter, the drooping mimosas looked like old Christmas trees bent with age, mossy tinsel hanging from them. They surrounded the four corners of the house like gargoyles on an old cathedral, posted there as sentries, warning the evil summer sun to keep its distance.

Still, the trees could not protect their mistress from wind, rain, or time, and all three had had their way with her. The Old South exterior, though still intact in design, had lost much of its grandeur. The house was like the great-grandmother of the town. Bent with age and having a bit of memory trouble, she still lorded over her retirement-age children, who respected her enough not to point out her creaking faults. The look of the old place made David think there might be some home left in the house.

But then there was the caretaker of the place, Old Suzie herself. She too was something out of the past, a woman who dressed like a man and who had recently lost her husband to the "dipstick disease," as Theron's mother called it. She told Theron what she meant was that some husbands, being dipsticks, walked out on their wives when they got older and stupider, but that's not what Theron had once overheard his mom telling friends over margaritas. After he'd left, Suzie had taken over keeping the gardens in the back of the house and mowing the massive front lawn riding an old John Deere, bouncing up and down and singing old Hank Williams songs into the wind and out of tune.

David stared at the house and wondered: was it a grandmother house, or a grandfather house? Before he died, David's grandfather had always told him great stories, and he wondered if houses were fathers or mothers or both. He tried to peer past the windows, but they were too far away. That, plus the conspiring shade of the gargoyle-trees kept him from seeing anything more than his imagination wanted him to. Still, the house looked like it had great stories to tell. *It must be a grandfather house then*, David decided.

"Hey buddy, I just got an idea," said Theron. "I think I know what I want to do for our Halloween trick."

David looked over at him, then followed Theron's stare back to Old Suzie's house. Something in the pit of his stomach gurgled, though he wasn't really all that hungry. "What?" he asked, not sure he wanted to hear the answer.

But Theron was smiling.

"I want to make me a haunted house," he said.

Chapter 10

"You ain't a baby anymore."

"No, sir."

David lowered his tone, lowered his eyes, slumped his shoulders—everything but rolled over and showed his belly. Whatever it took to get his father to let him out of the house tonight.

It was Wednesday.

Halloween.

"Trick or treatin is for babies."

"Yes, sir."

His father stood in the doorway of David's room, leaning against the door facing

(preventing escape)

with his hands in his pockets and looking at the boy disgustedly, as if he'd just stepped in dog shit he should've seen plain as day on the sidewalk.

"Going out is a privilege, son," his old man was saying. "What have you done lately to earn the right to go out?"

David shrugged. The pity factor rarely, if ever, worked on his father. But he'd play that hand for all it was worth.

"I folded the clothes yesterday after school. And loaded the dishwasher."

His father snorted. "*After* I turned off the TV and reminded you of 'em, *sure*." The old man's voice was mocking. *Pull the other leg,* it challenged. "Have you fed the dog? And picked up the crap?"

David nodded. "I fed her. I poop-scoop on Saturdays."

His father cleared his throat. "I didn't *ask* you when you normally do it. I asked you if you *had* done it."

"No, sir."

"Then I suggest you get after it. Then ask me again if you can go out." Old Man Jackson straightened in the doorway. "Shoveling shit earns you a lot of things in this world, boy. Best to learn that now." He turned around and headed back for the kitchen.

David sat on the bed a moment longer. He saw the added chore for what it was. The toll. The offering. The tithe to the Father-God. If he did it *quickly*, before his father drank three beers. That seemed to be the foul line in their little game. After three beers, everything went foul, out of bounds.

He hopped off the bed and headed down the hall and through the kitchen to the backyard. *At least Mr. Sinclair hasn't called*, he thought. While Pete Lasco had been suspended for three days, David had been exonerated, largely because of Theron's testimony. Regina Va-jeena hadn't helped him any, but then he didn't figure she should have. Not after the way he'd treated her for so long.

As he walked out in the backyard, he made a quick survey around the fairly small fenced area. *Not too bad*, he thought. About half a dozen piles.

His dog, a dark-brown collie mix, looked warily from inside her doghouse till she saw and sniffed who it was, then came bounding out, a fluffy fireball of energy ready to race around and play with the boy. David smiled immediately when he saw her. She trotted up to him and sat down, looking up expectantly, as if to say, *What fine adventure can we have together today, my friend?*

He bent down and stroked her furry head, and she rolled her eyes up and circled her nose around to lick his hand. His father had named her Queenie for some reason he didn't know or much care about. She was sometimes the only friend he could talk to who would listen and not feel the need to talk back.

"How are you, old girl?"

Queenie stared up and licked and panted. Her cocoa-rusty fur was lined with silver now, her chin a prickly white. She was ten years old. David had known her almost all his life. But still she acted like a puppy, and except for a bladder problem whenever she got overly excited, he couldn't tell she was nearly seventy in dog years.

He knelt down and ruffled her ears, and she made a moaning sound.

"Have you been a good girl?" he asked. "Have you been making good poops?"

David always checked her stools to make sure she didn't have worms or something. She was never allowed in the house, so she was more likely to pick up something. David tried to do his best to keep up with her health. Only rarely—like when the bladder problems began last year—would his father spring for a vet visit.

"That's my good girl," he said. "I've got to scoop your poop, then I think I'll get to go out. The old man is in a good mood tonight. Better take advantage of it, huh?"

Queenie stood and wagged her tail at the hope in his voice. She licked his face. David patted her head again and went into the garage, where the lawn bag and shovel were.

As he scooped, he assessed the object of his cleanup. *Good*, he thought. *Good firm piles*. He smushed one a bit with the shovel. *Nope, no worms*. David picked up the rest of the piles and sealed up the bag, since it was full. His father would rather a partially filled bag stand open with the poop smelling and attracting flies than seal it up half empty. So wasteful as that was and all.

David washed off the shovel with the water hose, put it up, patted Queenie on the head again, and went back in the house. He washed his hands, looked himself over, and tried to think of any piece of the plot he might have missed.

Okay, if I've remembered everything, we should have about three or four questions, and then I'm free!

He walked into the living room. His father was propped up in his recliner, beer in his right hand, remote control in his left. The old man had taped the Dallas Cowboys game on Monday night and was finally getting around to watching it, though the boy never understood why he bothered. Usually the Cowboys sucked, and that just made his father angry.

David was pretty sure he knew the line the old man would use to greet him. He said it at least a jillion times during every Cowboys game.

"Dad—"

"Y'know," said his father, "they ain't played a goddamned decent game since Landry left. Not *one*."

"Yes, sir," came the automatic reply. "Dad, I finished the backyard. I scooped all the poop."

His father looked at him.

"You tied it up in the bag?"

"Yes, sir."

"Was the bag full?"

"Yes, sir."

"*Really* full?"

"Yes, sir."

"You washed the shovel?"

"Yes, sir."

"Dried it? To keep it from rusting?"

"Yes, sir," David lied without hesitation. He knew he'd forgotten *something*. He also knew his father would be too sloshed soon to check the shovel.

"All right then. You can go."

Exultation filled the boy. The governor had called at last!

"And see if you can't squeeze some of those bite-sized Snickers out of those stingy bitches over on Maple Street. I like those."

"Yes, sir."

He turned away and tried not to break into a sprint as he walked back to his room to grab his stuff for the evening's adventure.

"And would you look at *that*? He couldn't catch a ball if his hands were flypaper!"

But David was out of earshot and already planning the night's events in his head.

He met Theron over at the high school in front of the administration building. By 7:30, the mid-fall sun was mostly gone and a cool breeze had washed away the warmth baked into the pavement of the town's streets. Theron was dressed in a store-bought Spider-Man costume, and he and David had pooled their money to buy David a Batman costume.

Dad would come unhinged if he knew, David thought, *but he don't, so screw him.*

With their masks on top of their heads, they kneeled in front of the admin building, getting ready to take inventory. In the distance they could hear the shuffling feet of younger trick-or-treaters mingled with the calls of parents to stay to the side of the road as they walked. Theron dumped the contents of his trick-or-treat bag on the sidewalk.

"Okay," he said. "We've got firecrackers. Always good. Matches to light 'em. Rope. Toilet paper. What are we missing?"

David thought a minute. "I could've brought some dog poop."

Theron rolled his eyes. "You mean you *didn't*?"

David shook his head. "And I just cleaned up the backyard too."

"Aw, *man*. That would've been so fine. Right on the front porch. Knock – knock – knock, light her up, and . . . aw, that would've been *so* cool."

"Sorry, dude. But I ain't going back to the house." He thought his chances of recovering some of Queenie's droppings without his father noticing were pretty good, actually. The old man would be snoring in front of the television by now. But there was always the off chance he might get caught, so David decided against the whole idea right then and there.

Theron nodded. He'd seen firsthand how his friend's father could be. "That's okay. We've got enough. Come on."

They pulled their masks down over their faces and walked away from the high school, cutting across the parking lot and walking along Second Avenue. Goblins, ghosts, and other members of the Justice League passed them by. To all the world, Theron and David looked as intent as their fellows on amassing a ton of sweets. To be honest, neither of them knew *exactly* what was coming. But Theron knew he wanted to light a fire under Old Suzie's broomstick, and David was happy to be along for the ride.

Before long—perhaps, even, before they really *wanted* to be—the two boys were facing Old Suzie's house from the street. They stared across the expansive front lawn, which would look immaculate until the first freeze of the year turned it yellow-brown. Suzie must've mowed the lawn recently because the sweet, heavy smell of freshly cut grass hung in the air.

They tried to reconnoiter the house from the street as best they could. The long arms of the trees lifted and lowered with the wind. In the distance they could still hear trick-or-treaters and their parents going from house to house deeper in the neighborhood, but none ventured up Old Suzie's driveway. Still, there stood a pumpkin on her front porch—a massive one, with evil eyes and missing teeth, a heavy candle flickering inside. Lining the porch were several smaller pumpkins, each carved differently, with their own birthday-cake-sized candles inside. A queen and her court, all in a row. It must've taken a lot of effort to carve them. The front porch light was on and plagued by bugs, even this early in the evening. Only a light or two was on inside the house.

"She's probably in there watching her shows," Theron said. His voice seemed divided—part of him hoping he could guess her whereabouts and the other part wanting the local stories about her being a witch to really be true.

"Yeah," said David. "Probably busy mixing a cauldron of something in front of the TV."

Theron giggled. "Double, double, toil and trouble, cauldron boil and cauldron . . . Can I buy a vowel?"

David snickered.

"All right, Batman, let's go."

David's heart skipped a beat as he realized they were actually going forward with the plan. Tonight they'd have their way with Old Suzie and her house. "Right behind you," he said.

They ran across the front lawn and made their way to one of the oaks closest to the front porch. Panting and excited, they dropped down next to the tree and, remembering every war movie they'd ever seen, darted their eyes right and left to make sure no one had seen them. David's eyes focused on the trees around them, their limbs waving Spanish moss.

David had a creepy feeling, like he was in the Haunted Forest in *The Wizard of Oz*. He wondered if the trees would reach out for him, hold onto him until Old Suzie could come out and capture them. The trees looked taller all of a sudden. And was it the wind or something else that animated their limbs just a bit more than a moment before? But he took heart that he couldn't see any apples. Of course he couldn't, these *weren't* apple trees. Whew!

No ammunition, he thought, still thinking of the movie.

"Hey!" Theron yell-whispered.

David turned to him.

"What are you waiting on? I *said* let's get to the porch!"

David nodded and followed.

Their costumes made being stealthy a challenge. Theron almost tripped over something on the ground because of the limited vision through his mask's eye slits. But they made it and stepped carefully, almost reverently, up on the porch. Since the light was on, they had to be especially cautious. Theron stepped onto a board that creaked loudly, as if the house itself were announcing visitors to Old Suzie. A thought went through David's mind that it was like ringing the triangle for dinner, like the cowboys used to do out on the trail.

creak

(dinner's here)

creak

(special delivery)

The skin on their arms pimpled up. The hair on their necks rose. Theron thought he could actually feel his Spidey sense tingling.

What David could feel was exactly how full his bladder was. "Now what?" he asked.

"Now, we knock," said Theron. With his face behind the Spider-Man mask, his voice sounded hollow and muffled.

Theron inched his way up to the door.

creak

(spider and bat at the door)

creak

(just the ingredients I was looking for)

Theron looked back at David and counted off on his fingers—one, two, three.

knock – knock – knock

"Trick or treat!" they yelled in unison.

The boys jumped off the porch and darted around the railing to hide out of sight. They positioned themselves so they could still see the front door. A little out of breath—not so much from the running but because he was scared to death—David tried to calm himself down.

Maybe she could hear them breathing. Maybe she could smell their breath. Maybe she would know just where to look for them.

They heard the front door scrape against its facing. Into the light stepped Old Suzie. She wore a workman's shirt and heavy boots and overalls, but she was missing her trademark cowboy hat. It was hard to see her hair because the porch light cast weird shadows, but it looked like it didn't go below her collar. Short and iron gray. And she had a huge grin on her face. No, a huge *smile*.

David wondered what she was smiling at, then snapped to it immediately. What else? *Little boy pizza just arrived*, he thought. *And she looks hungry.*

"Hello?" she said, the porch creaking under her weight. Her voice sounded strange, like if it didn't get an answer, it might just never speak again. Then her smile started to fade back into the hard, tanned lines on her face. She looked left and right, strained her neck forward to get a better view of her own front yard. "Hello?" she said again. Suzie listened to the crickets chirping. In the distance, she could still hear trick-or-treating children down the street.

But none here.

She sighed once, stood up a bit straighter, and went back in. Normally when she closed the front door, she had to push it closed two or three times to get the warped wood past the facing. But this time Suzie closed it with one try.

David and Theron saw none of this. As soon as she'd opened the door and stepped out on the porch, Theron had grabbed his friend's arm and pulled him around toward the back of the house. This had been the diversion. Now they were putting the battle plan into action.

They made their way to the back door, keeping close to the house, just like in the movies. Theron peered through the screen. Low light shone from the windows in the kitchen.

"Come on!" said Theron. "This is it!"

David was less sure. "This is *what*?"

"We're going in, of course!"

"*What?*"

"We have to go now! While she's still around front!"

"But—"

"What are you, *scared*?"

"Yeah, no, I—"

"*I'm* going, then."

And with that, Spider-Man reached for the back door. David thought for a moment, wiped his cold palms on his polyester costume. *If I don't go, Theron will tell everyone at school. And then Pete Lasco won't be the only one wanting to kick my butt.* A shivering Batman followed after.

Theron opened the screen door and its loud spring made a sound

rrrrrrrrraaaaaaaaawwwww

that made them both pause. Then Theron screwed up his courage and placed his hand on the back door's handle. He slowly turned it to the right. It was unlocked. He carefully pushed it open.

The kitchen was smaller than David thought it would be. He could smell something cooking and wondered how witches preferred their children nowadays: fried, steamed, or baked in an oven?

(the old-fashioned way)

They inched into the kitchen. The front door slammed, and Theron nearly jumped out of his skin. Voices were coming from the other room. Anxious voices.

(children for the pot)

Plaintive.

David and Theron looked at one another. Their mouths hung open behind their masks. They could hear snippets of the conversation, and the words "afraid," "rescue," and "lovey" came to them.

Then there was laughter.

Theron crawled to the kitchen doorway. The door leading into Suzie's parlor was open. He saw her shadow approaching. Her big feet clunked on the hardwood floor as they came toward him. He could tell by her steps she was in a bad mood.

(want it quick and painless, kids)

Her feet pounded like they were trying to punch holes in the floor. The closer they got, the madder they sounded.

(don't think so)

Then they turned away and Theron heard her sit down heavily.

". . . rescued . . ."

David came up beside him and looked into the parlor. Suzie's chair sat at a thirty-degree angle to the kitchen, its back to the front door.

". . . impossible . . ."

If she turned her head left and bothered to look, she would've seen them kneeling in the doorway, trying to be inconspicuous superheroes.

". . . *Gilligan!* . . ."

Instead, she stared straight at the TV.

Theron pulled David back into the kitchen. "Okay," he whispered, "now we have some fun." He opened the bag he'd brought and took out firecrackers and matches.

"What are you gonna do with that?" David asked stupidly.

Theron's skin scraped the plastic as he smiled behind his mask. "Have some fun with the old witch." He lit a match. "Now here's what we're gonna do. We'll set off a few firecrackers, then run straight for the front door and out of here, okay?"

In the other room the boom of commercials began with bright music, loud voices, and hyperactive announcers. David suddenly felt very sick—that queasy feeling you get inside when you realize the milk you just drank must've started to curdle. "Why not go back out the back door?" he asked.

Spider-Man cocked his head to one side. "Because, dummy, then there wouldn't be any *fun* in it."

David swallowed. "Oh."

"Here we go . . ."

Theron touched off a string of five firecrackers and was preparing to toss it into the parlor when Old Suzie stepped into the kitchen for a beer.

"What the . . . ?"

Batman peed himself.

Spider-Man stood in the center of the kitchen like a plastic army man, legs spread apart, left arm forward for balance, right arm cocked back, poised to throw the firecrackers.

"What are you kids doin in my house?"

The fuse sizzled.

David couldn't speak. His lips just scraped against his mask. Theron tried to move and felt as if his joints had frozen. One look at the much-talked-about Medusa had turned him to stone.

"You gonna answer me, or—"

CRACK . . . CRACKCRACKCRACK . . . CRACK

The firecrackers exploded in rapid succession, and only after the first one went off did Theron remember to drop them. The tiny explosion set his hand to stinging and he cried out. Suzie screamed at the noise and David just sat there on the floor, working his mouth and not breathing, feeling his lower half getting warmer.

"Great God Almighty!" Suzie yelled. David managed to get his feet under him. She was going for Theron. *Good*, one part of David's mind thought, *more time for me to get out*.

But Theron had found his feet too. David scampered toward the parlor as fast as he could, Theron on his heels.

"*Wait!*" came the heavy, been-doing-her-husband's-work-for-years voice. "You boys come back here, damn it!"

"Ahhhhhhhhhhhhhhhh!" screamed David, imagining what she'd do to them if they got caught.

Her work boots came clomp-clomp-clomping after them. The boys split up, running around the parlor like chickens in a farmyard, trying to keep Suzie's furniture between them and her.

"You boys have some explaining to do!"

Theron led the charge for the front door.

"Oh, *no* you don't!"

clomp – clomp – clomp

But the boys beat her to the hallway and that's when David saw it, he *saw* it! The cauldron she mixed her children up in with

(spiders and bats)

eye of toad and tongue of snake to make them *mmm mmm good*.

Suzie grabbed him by the cape.

"Ahhhhhhhhhhhhhhhh!" screamed David again.

"Great God Almighty!"

"Let him go!" Theron yelled bravely as he opened the door to make his own escape.

"I don't think so," said Suzie as David struggled to get free. She tugged, trying to get a better grip while he squirmed, and suddenly there was a loud

rrrrrrriiiiiiiiiip

and Batman was de-caped. David fell forward, knocking the huge cauldron-bowl onto the floor, where it shattered. He could hear Suzie audibly gasp at the sight as dozens of crystal pieces and hundreds of tiny candies went everywhere. David made the obscure observation that Suzie had been planning on giving out those tiny bite-sized Snickers his father liked so much, and thinking about the old man filled him with dread. But the boy pushed all that aside and ran through the front door onto the porch, where he and Theron made good their escape.

Behind them Old Suzie stood in the doorway, looking back and forth from their forms growing smaller by the second to the broken mess on her floor but unable to coax any words from her throat. She stood there, rubbing her eyes from time to time, just stood there and stared into the night, long after the boys had vanished. Then she slowly closed the door and went to the kitchen to get the broom and dustpan and trashcan. And that beer.

knock – knock – knock
"Trick or treat."

The girl stood there for a moment, giving the homeowner time to come to the door. She imagined their picking up a bowl of candy and gripping the knob to turn it. Maybe the person inside would expect several kids to be trick-or-treating together, so they'd bring a lot of candy to the door. Since she was alone, that would mean more for her, right?

No one answered. She could hear scraping noises inside. She knew she was at Old Suzie's house and the other kids said she was a witch. But the girl didn't believe that. She decided to try one more time.

knock – knock – knock
"Trick or *treat*."

The front porch light was suddenly flicked off.

That's weird, she thought. *Maybe they ran out of candy*. She blew out a disappointed breath. *Momma always says when the porch light is out, it means they're out of candy*. She turned to leave and scraped one of her rays on the front door. She had come as the sun. A simple enough costume her mother could make for her. But the cardboard bent easily. Now she had a ray that flapped when she walked. Tonight just wasn't her night.

"Light's off," called the girl's mother from the street. "They ain't got no more candy. Come on, Regina."

Chapter 11

Wayne Alan Kitts walked the length of the wall again, judged the distance again. He looked at the guards looking at him, then glanced away and counted the seconds when they weren't watching him watching them. He flexed his hands once, twice, used the action to count the seconds. Then he turned away as he saw the guard on the south tower turn back toward him. He had five minutes to go before out-time was over. Leaning against the wall, Kitts tried to be cool, like Steve McQueen in that old World War II movie where he tries to jump the motorcycle over the barbed wire and gets tangled up. He even styled himself "Cooler King" inside, the nickname for McQueen's character in the movie. *A motorcycle would help right about now*, he thought, looking again at the razor wire that lined the prison fences, thinking how hard it would be to climb those things without getting sliced up.

Or shot, bendejo, Kitts thought.

Yeah, or shot.

He looked around the compound, trying to seem nonchalant, when he saw her walking in. He preferred blondes, but without much of a choice these days, he wouldn't have kicked this one out of bed. Her jeans were painted on, her boots cracking on the hard cement as she walked across the basketball court. She passed close enough that, had Kitts stretched his arm out, he could've touched her. And he was mightily tempted.

With the wind blowing, he thought, and with the right angle, he could see just inside the armhole of her sleeveless shirt. He imagined more than saw the curve of her right breast, just a glimpse. He could almost feel its weight in his hand. And the sunglasses. *Jesus, women look so much better in three dimensions*, he thought. He heard someone call what must have been her name, Caroline, and he stood and stared. Kitts put aside all thoughts of escape, replaced them with a downright desire to *stay*, boy. He almost fell over when she leaned up to kiss her boyfriend. As they walked across the yard together, the boyfriend looked in his direction.

"Hey!"

Kitts was startled back to reality. *Never let 'em see you sweat, boy. That's how you stay alive in here.* But it was a bit late for that now.

"Yeah, Sarge?"

"Keep your eyes to yourself," said the sergeant of the watch, placing his arm protectively around the woman.

She was *his* woman. *Ramirez's* woman. And God, how he hated Ramirez. But Cooler King Kitts played it cool. "Aw, c'mon, Sarge, I'm just window-shoppin. I ain't buyin."

Then Ramirez did the one thing Kitts hadn't expected. He smiled. It was a sunny day, a hot day for this time of year, and he had those damned mirrored sunglasses on. Kitts hated not being able to see the sergeant's eyes. *The eyes are the windows to the soul*, his grandmother had taught him. And on more than one occasion Kitts had found it to be true. It had saved his life and cost other people theirs. He always knew how to handle someone after he looked hard into their eyes.

But that damned smile. *Wipe it off, lawman*, thought the Cooler King. *Or I'll fucking cut it off your face and shove it up your ass.*

With one thumb hooked in a belt loop of Caroline's bodypaint jeans, his hand resting on her ass, the sergeant ambled in his direction. Kitts's breathing got shallow. *He's bringing her over here.* Fantasies blossomed in his head.

Ramirez took a drag on his cigarette, standing at ease. "You still planning your breakout?" he asked. "'Cause me and the boys got a bet. Y'know, kinda like a baby pool. We figure you'll be over the wall before the first real warm day. Course, to be fair, that's to say the first *real* warm day. None of those iced-tea-on-the-porch winter days we have around here. The month of June is right popular with the pool, in fact."

Kitts heard Caroline giggle a bit as she mock-swatted her beau's badged chest.

Goddamn him. Goddamn the fucking bastard. First thing I'll do when I get out . . .

The guards on the towers, which couldn't have been more than two-hundred feet apart, were laughing at him. They couldn't've heard Ramirez. Could they? Or was Kitts such a joke to them that they must've known what Ramirez was chiding him about?

Goddamn bastard.

Kitts just shrugged, which was a bit difficult because he was also trying to lean further into the wall behind him to present the most unconcerned portrait possible. Indifferent nonchalance. A look that said, *Sticks and stones, motherfucker.* "I figure I might go as early as December," he said, smiling back. "Cooler then. Who wants to break out in the heat?"

Ramirez nodded. "Cooler then, for the 'Cooler King,'" he said, laughing. Turning to Caroline, he flicked his eyes Kitts's direction. "Ever seen *The Great Escape*, doll? This guy thinks he's Steve fucking McQueen. Digging tunnels and riding bikes across Germany like some goddamned movie star war hero."

First thing I'll do, motherfucker. First thing.

"December, eh? Good idea," Ramirez mused. "Let me know when it's gonna be, and I'll split the kitty with you. Fifty-fifty."

Kitts forced himself to laugh for the audience. "Yeah, man. And I've been looking for some swampland to buy for a homestead—know of any?"

"Yeah," said the sergeant, grabbing his crotch. "You can take up residence right here anytime you want. A little grassy, and one great big hard rock to climb, sweetcheeks."

Despite their distance, the tower guards laughed out loud. And some of the prisoners were looking on and smiling, currying favor with the deck warden, their title for Ramirez. Then Caroline laughed too, though she swiped playfully at Ramirez's chest again as if to say he shouldn't make such jokes when she was around. She did laugh, though, a lilting giggle that put the lie to her false modesty. Her sunglasses flashed on Kitts, taking in the funny little man.

Goddamn bastard. Fucking humiliate me. Cooler King Kitts said, "Really? That's not what I heard. I heard Franklin damn near went blind looking for it and you beat him to death because he couldn't find it. Lethal injection, my ass."

(too far)

The warning came from way back inside Kitts's head. This was a game they were playing, always fixed in its outcome. Guards and prisoners traded insults, mostly one-on-one, sometimes with an audience, but never with the prisoner getting the better line. This was a game, and he'd just jumped out of bounds. And now, the penalty phase.

"You fucking red-haired bastard," said Ramirez, advancing. The yard went quiet, and the tower guards took the safeties off their weapons smoothly, with the flip of a thumb hidden beneath a covering arm. "You best learn to keep that mouth to yourself."

The Cooler King went cold. His heart skipped fear into his veins. In another place, the street, anywhere but here, he'd meet Ramirez head-on, damn the weapons and everything else. But here he was helpless, a chained dog about to be whipped with nothing to do but stand there and take it and hope the beating didn't break anything vital. He stood up from the wall so he wouldn't be off-balance. But it was the wrong thing to do because, off-balance or not, he just came off as more threatening to Ramirez.

"Ramirez, I—"

"What? I can't quite hear you."

"I was about to say that—"

The billy club went up so fast and across Kitts's mouth that he was still trying to finish his sentence as he hit the ground, wondering why his mouth wouldn't move. He realized, finally, through the numbness, that he'd been hit, hit hard, as the warm, coppery blood flooded his mouth. Pain began to radiate like a thousand tiny pinpricks in his jaw.

"Still can't hear you," Ramirez said.

Kitts tentatively touched a loose tooth with his tongue. The club came down three times quickly on the back of his knees, and he forgot all about his mouth. The rest of the prisoners looked on, some in impotent rage at the abuse of a fellow inmate, some in happy appreciation for the entertainment before them. Most were just glad it wasn't their day in the barrel. Kitts cried out, and he thought he saw at least one prisoner begin walking toward them.

Nonono, don't make it worse, goddammit—

But then the tower guards chambered rounds in stereo, and the blurry figure coming in his direction stopped.

"Don't ever open your mouth to me like that again, Cooler King," said Ramirez. "Get up."

"Mmmmph." Kitts struggled with his rage, his pain. He tried to put on a properly cowed manner for Ramirez, anything to end the beating sooner rather than later. Then the baton came down three more times on him, and his lower back went numb. He dropped to the concrete again.

"I'm not fucking with you, you little prick," said the sergeant. "Next time I'll take more than teeth out of you." He turned around to the audience, picked the one prisoner who'd walked forward as if to help Kitts, looked him right in the eye and said, "Break it up! Everybody to your cells. Lock down." The inmate eyed him a moment longer, then cast his eyes down to show the proper respect and headed slowly toward the door to the cellblock.

"Get up, Kitts," said Ramirez. "Get up or you won't be able to get up again."

Gasping for breath, Kitts put his palms flat on the concrete and pushed. Pain shot through his lower back and legs. Blood drooled out with spittle onto the ground. He lifted himself up onto his knees.

"You haven't been here that long, Kitts," said Ramirez. "That's why I went easy on you. Fuck with me again and they'll have to dredge the Trinity to find you. Understand me?"

Kitts nodded, whatever it took to get past Ramirez now. This didn't make any difference. It wasn't important. *Live to fight another day*, said his head, then added, *Cooler King* in Ramirez's snide voice, just to mock himself.

"Walk to the infirmary," said Ramirez.

Kitts stood up warily, his head spinning, his lower body in agony. He saw the baton coming at his head then and shied away, staggering, arm up. Ramirez stopped the swing before it hit. He bent down and whispered in the prisoner's ear.

"That's right. Know your betters, Kitts. Keep it that way and your fucking mouth shut when we have an audience, and you and me'll do fine." The sunglasses reflected Kitts's scared, bloody expression back to him along with his knowledge that Ramirez had beaten him, was in total charge of his life, no quarter.

"Now get to the fucking infirmary," said Ramirez. "And when the doc asks you how you got your injuries for his files, you just tell 'im you were playing basketball and fell on the court . . . *hard*. Understand?"

Kitts nodded as he staggered away toward the main building. All the other prisoners had been herded back into the cellblock by now. All he could see was a blurry, kelly-green surface he knew was the basketball court and a great stone building in front of him he knew housed the infirmary. His hearing was acutely attuned, however. Maybe that was his body making up for the blurred vision. Or maybe it wasn't his body at all; maybe it was God or the devil having a joke on him. The only sounds he heard were the wet squeaks of his bloody-bottomed sneakers, a light slap as Ramirez bounced the baton in his open palm, and the mocking laughter of the tower guards as they watched him stagger away. He stopped for a moment as his palm found the doorjamb to the main building, where he caught his breath.

I'll bring that motherfucker to his knees, Kitts promised himself. *I'll stick that baton so far up his ass he'll choke on it.*

He walked into the building rubbing his eyes, and his vision began to clear a little.

"Fall down, Kitts?" asked the door guard sitting behind the first gate desk.

"Uhmm," he mumbled, trying to nod.

"Yeah, I saw it. Damned shame, but accidents happen."

The guard began to laugh, and Kitts's spine froze with hatred for Ramirez, for all of them. And especially for the woman who'd just stood there. *Caroline.* He waited till he heard the chamber turn in the cell door and advanced as the guard swung it open. Kitts tried to ignore the laughter behind him and turned left down the first hallway. He still couldn't read the sign, but he knew where the infirmary was and let memory guide him. One final chuckling bellow from the guard rankled him as the door closed, shutting everything but the memory out.

The doctor looked up from his paperwork, frowned at him, and took off his glasses. "Well, what happened to you?" he asked, getting up from the desk.

If it's the last thing I fucking do . . .

"I fell," Kitts mumbled. "Playing basketball."

The doctor took a bottle of alcohol and a handful of cotton balls off his shelf. "Uh-humm," he said, shaking his head. "Sit down."

Kitts lay in his bunk, his mouth screaming at him. The doctor had had to pull two more teeth, one in the front up top and one on the upper-left side. They'd be able to make him a bridge, the doctor said, but not till the dentist made his monthly rounds. For now, it would be painkillers and a mouthful of gauze to soak up the bloody seepage that was still coming now and then. The bruises on his back and the backs of his knees were purpling up, but the drugs for his mouth were keeping the pain at bay for now. He'd floated away for an unknown amount of time on a lake of painkillers. They'd brought him dinner in his cell, had slipped it through the slot, and the shit on a shingle still sat there, cold on the concrete floor. He looked at it. Chicken-fried steak, mashed potatoes, green beans, a half-ear of corn, and a hard roll. *Cold comfort for the Cooler King*, he joked in his head. All of it but the beans and potatoes would be impossible for him to eat.

Ramirez probably knows that too, Kitts thought. *Probably had it specially prepared for me so I could lie here and look at it and know I can't eat it. God, I hate that sonofabitch.*

"Kitts!" came the urgent whisper. It was after midnight, after lockdown, and the man in the cell next to him knew the penalty for talking after hours. "Kitts, you 'wake?" the voice came again. "You der?"

Kitts pulled the cotton out of his mouth, wiping away the rope of spittle it dragged out of him. "I'm here," he whispered back. It was hard to talk at all. And he was tempted to be silent for fear of another round with a guard. But he and his fellows had so little privacy that any stolen moment to speak without worrying a guard would hear was usually worth the risk. "Whatayou want, Stu?" he slobber-mumbled. "Been beat once 'day."

"Yeah," said Stu Metzger, more quietly this time. "We saw. What happened, man? Refuse to give old Ramirez a blowjob?"

Kitts semi-smiled at that and winced at the pain it caused. *Yeah*, he thought. *That's what happened. And it's how I lost my teeth too. I finally got fed up with blowing the bastard and chomped down hard. Then he beat me off. Get it? He* beat *me* off. *Funny, huh?*

"I one-upped him," he said simply. "Never one-up a guard, Stu. Number One Rule." He thought on that a minute, then amended, "Make that Rule Number Two. Number One Rule is, find the daddy of the family you want to join, then spread your cheeks wide the first week. Less painful that way in the long run."

"Yeah," said Stu again in that long, drawn-out whine of acquiescence of his. "You know a lot, just bein here a few months."

Then Stu's tone changed, as if he'd just scratched off the final winning lottery number. "I can't believe nobody knows de udder reason you here, man—"

"*Shut up*," Kitts hissed. It came out less menacing because of his missing teeth, something like *Shuth uph*. "I told you I had your number with Daddy Wallace. Best keep your mouth *shut*, Stu." Kitts raised himself up off the cot, though it was painful to do so and Stu couldn't see him anyway. "Got it?"

"Yeah, yeah, I got it. Sorreh, man, I don't wanna git you in no trouble. I just—"

"You just shut up is all. It's enough they know I killed somebody. The other don't matter anyhow," he lied. Stu knew he was lying and Kitts knew he knew, but he had Stu cowed enough that it didn't matter. Ramirez hadn't told anyone either, which Kitts couldn't quite believe. Maybe that would change after today. But for now he was graced with the space most will give a confessed murderer. Maybe Ramirez hadn't told anyone because he knew, like everyone else in here, that one word about it and Kitts would be butt-fucked with a broom handle and his head stove in with crowbars. And Ramirez wanted Kitts to enjoy his time in here, oh yeah. No easy outs for Kitts. *That must be it*, he thought. *Nothing else makes any sense.*

"Now drop it, y'hear? Never bring it up again. Y'hear?"

"Yeah, yeah, okay. Sorreh, man."

There was a long silence in which Kitts closed his eyes and wondered at his luck for having to place confidence in a mole like Stu. First free BJ or pack of cigarettes, and he'd spill his guts. *Honor among thieves, my ass.* He breathed through the holes in his teeth. The warm air soothed the sockets. He made sure to inhale through his nose. *But at least somebody has to ask the right question. At least Stu don't have the presence of mind to volunteer it unasked. At least—*

"So you embarrassed Ramirez, ay?" Stu asked. Kitts could tell he was forcing his tone to be light, hoping Kitts wasn't still mad at him. *Good*, Kitts thought. *As long as he stays worried, I'm okay.*

"Yeah," whispered Kitts. *Follow the scolding with a little soothing*, he thought.

"What'd you say, hey?"

Kitts smiled as he remembered, then let it drop since stretching his face even that much caused him pain. "I said he had a small dick," he said. "In front of his woman."

"*Ooooo*," started Stu, and Kitts shushed him down. Stu went on laughing, but Kitts could tell he had his face shoved in a pillow.

Jesus, if he don't get us both beat for talking . . .

Kitts cocked his ear toward the cell bars, listening for any echo of footsteps on the stone floor outside. After a minute Stu caught his breath and said, "Oh man, you good. You got balls wi'dat one, Kitts. Oh man, balls wi'dat one."

Kitts half smiled again, ignoring the pain this time. The beating was almost worth it. Even if halfpennies like Stu were the only ones impressed, it was *almost* worth it.

He lay on his bunk, staring up at the gray stone. He imagined the wheels of Stu's brain cranking to come up with more conversation. He could hear the little gerbil churning away in there, wheel spinning, axle squeaking from lack of maintenance.

"Well, don't worry 'bout de beatin," said Stu. "It wurd it to get ole Sarge in public like dat." Kitts could hear the self-satisfied smile. He cleared his throat, though not too loudly, so Stu could hear for effect.

"You ever been beat, Stu?"

Stu had been in the joint forever. He'd been beat when beating didn't make the news exposés. He'd been beat when beating was the way you woke inmates up in the morning.

"Yeah," he muttered. "I seen my share."

"Then shut the fuck up," said Kitts. "Next time *you* take on Ramirez. Tag, you're it."

"I sorreh, Kitts, I didn't mean nuthin . . ."

Kitts blew out a warm, soothing breath. *Best not be too hard on him*, he thought. *Else they find out about those kids and you'll get more than a baton from Ramirez. The fucking bastard. All of 'em. Every last goddamned one. Including this shit-for-brains here.*

"Go to sleep, Stu," he said. "It don't mean nothin. Go on to sleep."

"Yeah, okay," whispered Stu, as quietly as he'd spoken in their whole conversation. "G'night, Kitts. But you got balls, man, you got—"

"Yeah, yeah, g'night, Stu."

He heard Stu turn over in his bunk and sigh out the day, long and loud. Kitts stared up at the blackness above him, tried to make out the cracks in the ceiling he knew were there. Just for something to do to pass the time because now, thanks to Numbnuts Metzger, he wasn't sleepy. Stu's mention of Kitts's other reason for being in the joint had riled him, got the juices flowing again. The throbbing ache had finally beaten back the painkillers. His mouth pounded.

I'm getting out of here, he thought. *Come hell or high water, I'm getting out of here. A little patience, a little planning, that's all it'll take. I'm getting the fuck out of here.*

He thought about turning over to relieve the pressure on his back, decided against it, and closed his eyes.

And I'm gonna kill that motherfucker Ramirez. And that cunt he's with. If it's the last *fucking thing I ever do.*

CHAPTER 12

Theron walked—bounded, really—ahead of David. Every few steps he would turn around, throw his hands up and say, "Oh man, that rocked!"

For his part, David was still shivering. He thought about the hairlipped maw of Old Suzie standing over him, her great bulk blocking his escape, her iron grip clutching his cape, reeling him in

(you're pretty small, boy)

like a fish on a line, closer and closer

(but I won't throw you back, no sir)

until finally the material had ripped and he'd pulled free and run for his life onto the porch

creakcreakcreak

and into the night.

"Did that rock or what?" Theron's voice seemed to plead for a little support. A little recognition. *Hey, buddy, help me out here. Did that rock or what?*

"Yeah," said David. "I guess so."

"You *guess* so?" Theron stopped dead in his tracks and David walked into him.

David rolled his eyes. *I should've just played along. Like with the Old Man.*

Turning around, Theron said, "Man, that was the most fun I've had in this shithole of a town in a long time!"

David nodded, looking down at his shoes. They had mud on them. Old Suzie's mud. "Yeah, I g—I mean, yeah, it was a *blast*!" He tried to animate the word to make it sound like what it said.

"So, what's up with you?" asked Theron. His voice had a sarcastic quality to it, like he was pissed David had dared to spoil the most fun he'd had in this shithole of a town in a long time.

"Dude, I don't know," said David, dropping the pretense. "But that old woman scares the living shit outta me. Always has. And when she had hold of me and was pulling me toward her—dude, I could *smell* her *breath*. It smelled like cigarettes and beer, pouring out on me like she was trying to gas me or something. I can't explain it better'n'that. But I don't ever want to go back and do it again. Scared the shit outta me. I'm telling you, I came *this* close to being Batman stew. I just know it."

Theron looked at him for a moment. He wore his Spider-Man mask on top of his head again, like a hat. He cocked his head to one side, and it reminded David of Queenie. Then Theron burst out laughing. It wasn't slow in coming. It didn't bubble up. It gushed out of him like a dam bursting.

David stood there and let it flow over him, his head lowering, his eyes looking out from under his brows at his friend. "It's not funny," he said softly.

Theron draped one hand onto David's shoulder for support, as if he might fall over otherwise. David sloughed off the hand. "Aw . . . come on, man . . . you're not serious?" Theron managed to ask between quick breaths.

"You know I'm serious, you fucker." David's voice was barely audible. Like it was challenging Theron's ears to hear it.

The other boy's laughter tapered off after a few more jerky breaths. His Joker's grin faded into a stern wall. "Hey, don't call me a fucker. Just because you're a *coward*."

David stared at him. *Coward? Did he just call me a coward?* "Why not? That's what you are." David's voice was heavier, somehow, though still low and slow. A lion stretching a rope taut. "Fucker."

Theron pushed him once in the chest.

"Don't push me," said David. "Fucker."

Theron swung a roundhouse. David ducked, wondering somewhat seriously, *How would Batman handle this?* Theron's weight carried him through. David caught his friend's swinging arm and used the other boy's momentum to turn him around, wrapping Theron's arm behind his back. With Theron off-balance and facing him side-on, David planted the sole of his right foot in the back of Theron's right knee, forcing the hinge to buckle just like he'd done more than once to ornery folding table legs at school picnics. Before he knew it, Theron was on the ground, screaming "Heeeyyyyyyy," and trying in vain to get up. But David's weight was on him now, so whatever the other boy did only brought pain to his knee or his right shoulder. "Heeyyyy, get off me, you shithead! That *hurts!*"

"I'll get off you when you say you're sorry," said David matter of factly. It was only now dawning on him what he'd done. He hadn't even realized he'd put Theron on the ground till he'd demanded the apology. Then, suddenly being quite aware of what he'd done, he had no idea what to do next.

"Screw you!" said Theron in a burst of prideful testosterone.

Now it had sunk in. He had Theron down. And Theron was pissed. And David was scared again.

"You weren't caught, Theron," he said trying to explain himself. "You didn't smell her *breath*. You didn't see inside her *mouth*."

The pain was getting to Theron now. "All right, all right! I'm sorry, dude. Let me up, goddammit!"

David released him and backed up, ready for the fight to continue. He really hadn't meant to hurt Theron. But he couldn't stand that goddamned laughing at him. Couldn't *stand* it.

Theron pushed himself up off the ground, massaging his shoulder. "Damn, David! You really hurt me, man!"

David put out his hands in front of him to ward off the coming fight. "I'm sorry, dude. You shouldn't have laughed at me."

Theron stared at him a moment. David waited for the *real* fight to start. And he wasn't sure if he'd fight back, either. He wasn't sure he deserved the *right* to fight back. He really hadn't meant to hurt his friend.

"All right, man, I'm sorry. *Geez*. Remind me to stay on your *good* side."

David exhaled.

"I'm going home," Theron announced, turning toward his house.

David looked after him, tempted to apologize again, then grew mad at himself for being such a pussy. Theron *had* laughed at him.

He walked the rest of the way home. David hated feeling like he was two people all the time. One, the boy he wanted to be, tough and strong and nice and thoughtful, all at the same time. The other: angry, just angry, everything about him red with rage and ready to fight over anything. Maybe he should've gone as The Hulk, he thought. Bruce Banner never remembered what he did when he got angry and went crazy either. He thought again about attacking Theron and how he didn't even remember how it happened, just remembered standing there, uncertain what to do next. The Hulk had gone back into hiding, and David in his Batman costume had come back, scared and unsure. And that just made him angry again, this time at himself and not even knowing why.

He stalked quietly up to his house, making his way through the garage. Tiny padding sounds came at him, and he hurried the large garage door down, trying to be as quiet as he could. Behind him a growl sounded.

"It's *me*, girl," he said. "Shhhh." Queenie wagged her tail. Her mouth dropped open in a welcoming pant as she looked up at him with those big eyes. He bent down to pet her on the head and scratched behind her ears. She took it in with a moan of contentment. Petting her always made him feel better, Hulk or no Hulk.

"You still got food?" he asked, and she perked up her ears and turned her head slightly at the question. It was like she'd trained herself to respond in certain ways when the humans made certain sounds and used certain tones. This sound was one she recognized. She wagged her tail faster.

David walked through the door leading from the garage to the small breezeway that connected it to the house. He found her empty bowl just outside the back door and dipped it in the bin of Ken-L Ration dry food. She waved her tail more excitedly at the sound. As he set the bowl down, it made a satisfying, heavy landing on the cement.

"Water?"

But she was too busy snuffling the contents of the bowl. She looked up at him, seemingly disappointed.

"No scraps tonight, girl," he said. "You're stuck with what you've got."

She huffed loudly, then thrust her snout into the bowl again.

David walked over to the hose and began to fill the large water bowl. He chastised himself for not remembering to fill the bowl up before running off to light firecrackers under Old Suzie's broomstick.

Dumbass, his brain said in his father's voice. *First things first and second things second, and that's if you have time for them.* This was another of his father's life lessons that plagued him from time to time. He knew Queenie was his first priority compared to Halloween shenanigans, as his father would've called them. But sometimes he forgot.

Dumbass.

He finished filling the tub and turned the water off. Fed. Watered. Ears ruffled. And it was late. "Time to brave the Old Man, girl," he said as he walked to the back door. Being busy with more important things, she didn't raise her head.

As he walked into the kitchen, he heard the television going in the living room. He glanced at the oven clock, which read 9:38. By now his father would be on his second six-pack, which meant he didn't leave his chair except to urinate and go to bed, right after the sports on the ten o'clock news. David walked past the oven, turned left immediately, and went down the short hallway to his room. He wanted to get out of his costume before his father heard him and came looking for him on one of his bathroom jaunts. If his father found the costume ripped, he'd take David to task for not being more careful, for being wasteful. Then he'd take him to task for buying the thing in the first place. His father's parents had grown up in the Depression, and like all Depression-era children, thought it better to eat a rotten apple than let it go to waste because you just never knew if you'd have food tomorrow.

David made it to his room unmolested. *Base!* he always thought at this point in the game of hide-and-seek he often played with his old man. When he made it to his room he felt safe, though he'd learned more than once that the feeling was just an illusion. But at least in this house, his room felt the safest. The most *his*.

He walked in, shut the door, and turned on the light. He hoped his father wouldn't need to pee before he got his costume off and his bedclothes on. Otherwise, he might notice the closed door and light underneath, and then he'd just come barreling through it without knocking and lecture David on airflow and how the electric bill was too high because David had to have his goddamned *privacy*. Old Man Jackson would say it in a tone strikingly similar to how the kids at school, including David, taunted Regina Va-jeena. But for now, he could hear a rerun of an old show his father loved called *Hunter* mumbling through the door from the living room. As usual, his old man seemed to prefer the volume up louder when he drank.

David shed the Batman costume quickly, not much caring if he ripped it any more in the process. His father had opened all the windows in the house, so the airflow thing might be a *real* problem if he had to pee anytime soon. The cool air of October's final evening kissed David's cheek as he stood there only in his underwear. It tickled the sweat he'd worked up in Old Suzie's house and the fight with Theron. He opened his closet and sifted through the huge box of comic books (*Batman*, of course, but also *Superman*, the entire *Justice League*, and his personal favorite, the reprints of the late 1960s' *Sgt. Fury and His Howling Commandos*). He lifted a stack of those, went one level deeper and pulled back the one issue each of *Playboy*, *Penthouse*, and *Hustler* Theron had given him last year as a birthday present—which he guarded dearer than just about anything else he had—and stored the costume underneath. He would dispose of it in the morning. His father never went through his closet, so it should be safe till he could get rid of it.

Smirking at himself, he pulled out an Incredible Hulk T-shirt and put it on. He decided he'd better change his soggy underwear, which he peeled off and tossed on a pile of dirty clothes. Something in the back of his mind suggested he might've showered before putting on a fresh pair of underwear but, oh well, too late now.

David looked around. All the evidence seemed to be taken care of. And wonder of wonders, his room actually looked in good order. *Let the old man bitch about* that, he thought. He turned on the black-and-white television in his room and found the tail end of an *A-Team* rerun. With that providing light to see by, David went back to his door and turned off his room light, then cracked the door slowly. Hunter's husky voice filled the house, then two gunshots. He cocked his ear for his father's tread, which sometimes he could hear even on the carpet. David particularly appreciated the air conditioner's intake vent in the hallway. He could tell from the change in the airflow when his father walked past. That was his two-second warning. Tonight, of course, the A/C was off and the windows were open. "Let mother nature do what she's supposed to do," his father said when it was cool like this. "Save me a buck or two for a goddamned change."

But the old man was nowhere to be heard. David retreated to his bed to lie down, staring intently at the screen. His cover was secure. If his father walked in now, there was nothing out of place. *On base!* he thought to himself again.

He watched the jeeps fly through the air and the A-Team shoot about 10,000 rounds of machine-gun fire at the bad guys without ever hitting anyone. He always wondered how trained, elite soldiers could be such bad shots. After the show ended, he got up to go to the bathroom and used that as an excuse for reconnaissance on the old man. The television in the living room was still blaring, slivers of light dancing on the ceiling and carpet. He closed the door to the bathroom and took a leak. When he was finished, he opened the door again slowly and cocked an ear. The ten o'clock overture had begun with a man's deep voice introducing the newscasters. His father must've fallen asleep. Usually he grabbed a last beer from the fridge to finish off the evening. Yep, he was asleep. David could hear his rumbling snores as the music faded out and a woman started talking about the president and Congress.

So it was a "B"-night. *Good*, David thought. *Could've been worse.*

Recognizing patterns, David had learned to categorize his father's behavior. An "A"-night would've seen that final beer lasting through the sports; then the old man would've raised himself up out of his chair, paused to fart or burp or both—it varied—and stumbled to bed. A "B"-night meant he was already asleep by the time the news was on and might very well sleep till morning in the chair, or at least until his bladder woke him up. A "C"-night meant he'd gotten bored with the television fare and decided to amuse himself in other ways. David didn't like C-nights. On C-nights, David thought of his father as the devil incarnate, sent down by God to punish the boy for his sins. So by comparison, B-nights were fine, although sleeping in his chair often hurt his old man's back, and that made him irritable the next day. A-nights were great . . . David didn't have to talk to him at all— also a bonus of B-nights—and his father was usually able to sleep off the beer, until he woke up early the next morning and started drinking again before heading to work.

David made his way back to his bedroom, making sure to leave the door cocked open with a shoe. At least he got some privacy with the door partly closed, but the air could still move through the house. He tumbled into bed and turned over on his back, watching the moonlight dance on the ceiling through his fan's rotating blades. He had school tomorrow, the first day of a new month. A Thursday. "Thor's Day," whispered David as he thought of *The Mighty Thor* and the gods of Asgaard from the comic book. He never could quite understand why a hero as mighty as Thor looked like a cross-dressing clown with big muscles and wings on his head. And speaking of Marvel superheroes . . .

He thought again over the whole escapade at Old Suzie's house. He wondered why he'd let Theron talk him into it. He'd known that going into anyone's house without permission—particularly *her* house—was wrong. Tricks were one thing. But they'd invaded her house, her *home*. He'd been terrified, maybe more of doing what he knew he shouldn't than of her. And *that* was saying something. And when he'd seen her standing there in the kitchen door and felt his bladder empty, the flowing warmth had felt reassuring and terrifying at the same time. He knew he'd remember her face as long as he lived, that grunting grimace as she grabbed him to keep him from escaping. How dare Theron laugh at him! How *dare* he! He was never in any danger.

He went right for the front door! And he called me *a coward . . . Theron's such a fucker.*

Theron didn't know what real bravery was. Didn't have a fucking *clue*. He didn't see her mouth. He didn't see the hair growing on her top lip. And maybe her husband hadn't run off like everybody said. Maybe she'd taken a hatchet to him and chopped him up

(all the better to eat him)

and put him in her cauldron

(with candy for flavoring)

and boiled him up for supper one evening. And her mouth—exuding the smell of an old woman who's got no reason to smell good anymore, who decides not to bother because she's accustomed to her own smells and the grainy touch and dead-rodent taste in her own mouth. And Suzie was so big! She only had to sit on you to snuff out your life, push the air out of your lungs like they used to do to witches with stones. *Sweet revenge that, no doubt*, thought David. And it was only by the grace of God and poor Made-in-China tailoring that he was alive to remember it all now. No, they'd had no business going in there at all. He had Theron to thank for that too.

Fucker.

He turned over on his side and stared at the shoe-wide crack of light cast by his door. He could hear the soft swooping of his ceiling fan as it breezed his face with the cool, outside air.

Sometimes on nights like this, when he felt relatively safe from his father's intrusions, when the world seemed ready to sigh itself to sleep, his mother would come and sit on the bed beside him. She wasn't warm, but then, on nights like this, cool was nice. Her mere presence reassured him in a way that nothing—no other time of day, no other place, certainly no other person—ever could. The first time she'd visited him, he'd been afraid. She hadn't spoken that time, just sat beside him stroking his hair as he slept. It was like he'd watched the whole scene play out while hovering over his own bed.

Soon he came to long for her visits and how protected he felt when she was with him. David would have quiet conversations with her and tell her about his day and what had happened to him, how things had gone; and she would smile and listen and look like she might be enjoying the sound of his voice for its own sake. But she didn't come now, and he blamed the noisy television in the other room for disrupting the peace that seemed to draw her to him on soft nights.

From the living room he could hear the echoes of the news announcers as they promised the first half of the weather after the next commercial break. Again his mind wandered back to his confrontation with Theron. He thought he'd felt sorry about picking a fight with Theron, then realized he didn't feel sorry at all, not one damned bit. And he hadn't picked a fight either. He'd just picked up the gauntlet Theron had thrown down. *I'll never back down from anyone else, ever*, he fumed to himself. *Never ever ever!* He closed his eyes, and thoughts of Old Suzie played against the sparkly orange backdrop of his eyelids.

"In this corner," began the booming announcer, "in the workman's boots and grass-stained overalls, weighing two hundred fifty pounds, Old Suzie the Witch!" An invisible crowd broke out in wild applause. The kids in the audience threw Halloween candy into the ring like rice after a wedding.

"In *this* corner, in underwear and with beer in hand, weighing pretty much damned near the same, the Old Man!"

The crowd went cricket silent as the image of his father raised his arms in the ring. It sounded like someone might've farted approval from the back row.

Now that *would be a matchup*, David thought, staring at the picture of the two of them in a ring together, pounding the tar out of each other, fighting over a beer or maybe whose show they'd watch. He was a long time getting to sleep.

On this night, his mother never came.

CHAPTER 13

David went to school sleepy on Thursday. All in all, it was a very boring day. Theron wasn't speaking to him, and he wasn't speaking back. Theron had evidently said something to the other kids, because they were giving David a wide berth as well. That left focusing on schoolwork to pass the time. But in math class, at least, he never got bored looking at Mrs. McKinley. So Thursday became a mix of doodling, answering questions when he absolutely had to, and sitting on the low brick wall that fronted the playground. He watched the other kids play kickball while he ate a peanut butter and jelly sandwich. All in all, a *very* boring day.

He walked home by himself. Theron took an alternate route, cutting across the track and football field of Hampshire High. Along the way, David reassured himself again he hadn't been too hard on Theron, not after the other boy had started making fun of him. There were some lines you just didn't cross, and that was one of them. The thought was cold comfort as David walked with his hands in his pockets, staring at the sidewalk

(step on a crack, break your mother's back)

and the fractured lines between the breaks in the concrete. He wondered if they broke in some mystical pattern, some Ancient Alien Code that, if read just right, would reveal the secrets of life to a young boy.

He walked around town for a long time, studiously avoiding Old Suzie's street. As evening began to fall, he finally headed up his own driveway. Going home didn't seem like such a bad thing for a change, not after school today.

It looked like his dad was home early. There was his work truck, with the telephone equipment, extra line, splicers, circuit jumpers, and all the rest of his tools. It would be time to wash it again soon, now that November had arrived.

Oh boy, what fun, thought David with fake enthusiasm.

He walked through the garage, stopped to pet Queenie and give her water and food, then entered the house to get the evening's check-in over with. His father was in the living room watching the evening news and drinking a beer.

"Hi Dad," he said, poking his head around the corner. A commentator's deep and halting baritone spoke about the next election and how the president and Congress were squaring off over tax issues. His father liked to flip between news programs, trying to maximize his absorption of current events, saying the commercials were a waste of his time and by God, *his* time was worth more than whatever a damned commercial had to say. Whenever the Big Three networks had commercials simultaneously, he'd settle on one, usually NBC, and curse the screen for wasting his time, then crack himself up by making fun of the people in the commercials. Sometimes David thought he actually enjoyed the commercials more than the news, despite his grousing. "I'm home," David said.

"Hi son," came the gravelly voice. *Two beers down*, David guestimated. "How was school?"

"Fine," lied the boy.

"Good. Grades okay? Test tomorrow?"

"Yes, sir. I mean no, sir. Grades are good, I mean. No test tomorrow."

"That's good," his father said, muting the commercial as it came on. "Shouldn't have tests on Friday. You ask me, the Bible's all wrong. God rested on *Friday*. To get ready for the weekend."

"Yes, sir."

"What are you up to tonight?"

"Homework," the boy said immediately. "Math. We've started fractions."

His father made a noise. "I always hated math. Adding, subtracting, and multiplying. Long division. Fractions, huh?"

"Yes, sir."

"Well, you best get to it then."

"Yes, sir," he said with relief, glad the interrogation was over. With luck, after a little dinner, he might not have to talk to his old man at all again before tomorrow.

"By the way," his father said, "don't answer the phone tonight without checking the caller ID."

David blinked. "Okay," he said.

"I'm thinking of taking a sick day tomorrow. If the company calls, I'm not here. I don't want you to tell 'em that or nuthin, just don't answer it if you don't recognize the number. It's safer just not to answer at all. Got it?"

"Yes, sir."

"I'm feeling downright croopy, I am," his father said with a smile. He made a practice of taking the odd Friday off, though not too often, lest they get wise to him. "Maybe a little fishin'll make me feel better," he mused. He unmuted the TV. "Those tits ain't real," he said, gesturing at the screen, "but you gotta squeeze to know for sure." He laughed as David turned away, heading to his room.

He flipped on the fan as he walked in, tossing his book bag on the floor next to the bed. The boy felt relieved to get it off his shoulder. He had a test in history on Monday—not tomorrow, so technically he hadn't lied—and he'd brought some library books home today so he wouldn't have so much to lug home tomorrow.

He jumped belly first onto the bed and reveled in the secret knowledge that, had his father seen him do it, he would've gotten in trouble for it because "Beds cost money" and "When you get older and have to pay for it yourself, you'll appreciate it more." He reached over and flipped on the TV. Since it was coming up on six o'clock, nothing was on, save some lame sitcom reruns and the local news, which was even more lame. He flipped around from channel to channel, scanning Hitler's secrets, the life of a three-legged dog, why the Edsel had flopped, his local forecast, how to weave baskets from old grocery bags, some lousy cartoon with characters with angular faces and an irritating soundtrack, and about thirty other boring programs. *That's the word for the day all right,* David decided. He finally settled on one of the lame sitcom reruns and turned his brain off while the lame laugh track patronized the lame jokes.

Unchallenged, his mind wandered again to his falling out with Theron. David hated this about himself. He always wanted to make peace with people. He always wanted to smooth things over, even if it was *they,* not he, who needed to make amends. And so he started thinking about Theron and how someone had to make the first move and how it wouldn't be Theron, because he didn't think he'd done anything wrong

(did you tell him)

and that it was all David's fault

(or did you just goad him into swinging first)

for spoiling their fun.

But truth be told, David hadn't told him *why* he was angry. And when Theron swung, David had gotten his excuse to Hulk up. So who was at fault here? Theron had been a dick, sure, but David had known what he was doing. Even through his anger, through the raw hatred he'd felt for his friend at that moment, he'd *known.* And today in school, neither had spoken to the other because they both knew that Theron had been a dick and that David had gone out of his way to provoke him, and that Theron had let himself be provoked. Almost as if they both had been forced to perform the roles they had to play out, each with his part, to usher in the finale of a fistfight. He wondered who should call whom until the lame laugh track from the lame sitcom was in his head, laughing at him. David thought about taking a swing at the air that laughed at him, which only made it laugh harder.

He lay there staring at the TV and thinking about Theron, with his eyes getting heavy, until a ringing woke him up. The show on TV was different now, but the canned laugh track was the same. A new episode of something was on, and it wasn't the show he'd been watching, but the telephone had rung and a character was answering it—

No, wait.

riiiiiiiiiiiiiing

It was his phone that was ringing with that old Ma Bell ringer his father preferred.

Maybe it's Theron.

The thought came to him, cutting through the laughter in the room. Maybe Theron had bitten the bullet and decided to call. If so, David would tell him how sorry he was—after Theron apologized first, of course—and ask him what he wanted to do this weekend.

The bed creaked as he rolled over and swung his legs around and reached for the phone.

"Hello?"

"Hi!" The exuberant voice seemed to reach out of the phone, then withdraw, like something revving up and then easing off, an engine of enthusiasm. "Can I speak to Mr. Jackson?" The question was chocked full of goodness, downright friendly.

"Um . . ." David hesitated. He'd been sure it was Theron. He'd almost answered the phone with "Hey, turdhead," but decided not to at the last moment. Now there was a man's voice on the other end of the line. Men only called here for four reasons—to invite his father out for a beer; to call his father into work because a pole was down and somebody was pissed; to try to sell his father something; or to try to get his father to pay for something he'd already bought. David was desperately afraid it was Door Number Two this time. He hadn't checked caller ID first. "He's not feeling very well," he finally eked out. "He feels real bad tonight."

"Oh, son, I'm sorry to hear that!" The voice sounded genuinely depressed at the news. "But I tell ya, I promise not to take up too much of his time."

He felt his father behind him before he heard him. David must've missed the warning of the A/C intake. Too sleepy, maybe, to notice it. He turned around slowly, with the phone pressed to his ear. The old man stood in the doorway. David flitted a glance at him first out of the corner of his eye. His father was just standing there, staring at him. *Willing* David to put down the phone, turn back time, not answer it at all.

"Hello? Son, you there?"

"Um—"

"Who is it, boy?" his father hoarse-whispered. He stretched out the last word, as if emphasizing David's place in the food chain.

"Yeah, I'm here."

Out of the corner of his eye he could see his father move. It was like he was spreading out to fill up the doorway. "I *said* who is it?"

"Are you from Dad's company?" David asked. He was scared now. Between a rock and a hard place.

"No, son," said the voice, laughing on the other end of the phone. It felt to David like the man knew the punch line to a joke but was unwilling to share it with him. At his age David felt that a lot when he talked to adults. *You'll understand when you're older.* "No, son, I'm not with your dad's company."

"Okay, so you're not with his company," David repeated for his father's benefit. The mass in the doorway seemed to shrink a little. "Who are you, then? Why do you need to talk to my dad?"

"Well, son, no need to—"

"And stop calling me that. I ain't *your* son."

"All right, Mr. Jackson's boy—"

"And don't call me *that*, neither. My name's David."

"All right, *David*," said the man. His happy-happy voice seemed to be losing some of its phone-smile. "I'm not from your father's company. But I *do* need to speak with him."

"Like I told you, he—"

"Gimme that."

The receiver was ripped out of his hand.

"Hello?" came the gruff you've-invaded-my-territory voice. "Who is this?"

"Mr. Jackson?"

"*Yes.*"

"This is Ford Motor Company, Finance Division. We're calling about your car note."

He rounded on David, who had retreated to his bed and sat down. The boy saw the furor rising in the old man's eyes. He looked from his father to the door and wondered what kind of chance he had of making it out of the room before the old man caught him. But his father was hunched like a spring. David thought the receiver might break in two, he was holding it so tightly.

"Yes, sir, I'm so glad you called," his father said, glaring at David. He had put on the fake phone voice people get when they're in the middle of something unpleasant and yet feel the perverse obligation to stop being shitty and answer the phone. "I was planning on ringing you up myself tomorrow," he lied.

"Oh, great," said the man. David could hear the tinny, faked brightness from where he sat on the bed. His old man continued staring at him with volcanic eyes. The room was a pitch blackness of silence but for the phone conversation. David heard as much as felt the throbbing in his ears. "Then I've saved you the trouble!"

"Ah," said David's father, and his guard went down a bit, his voice betraying a bit of the anger he truly felt, "so you have."

"Well, it's about your truck payment, Mr. Jackson," said the man, his voice sounding concerned again, like when David first told him that his father wasn't feeling well. "It's three months overdue, you see."

"Ah," Jackson said again. "Yes, that *was* what I wanted to call you guys about."

"Well, again, I've saved you the trouble then. Mr. Jackson, I'll be frank with you . . . your credit history isn't what we'd call first rate. And the fact that you've missed payments before—"

"I always made those up," Jackson said, defensive now. He hated no-nuts salesmen. He fucking hated them. Either they tried to screw him out of money or they bitched because he hadn't given them enough of it soon enough. He fucking *hated* no-nuts salesmen.

"Yes, so you did," acknowledged the man, a prosecutor allowing a small point in favor of the defense because he knew it wouldn't matter to the case. "But it's in your file here that you agreed that the last time *would be* the last time. And here we are again, Mr. Jackson." Now the district attorney had shown up. He had the evidence. The violation was clear. There was no way out for Mr. Jackson, no sir.

"Yes, I realize that." Jackson's tone was infuriatingly passive all of a sudden. But his eyes weren't. They were staring hard, flat as black stones, at David.

Idiot! David thought. *Why did you have to answer the phone?*

"And I realize I'm three months behind schedule with the payment." The words panted out of him, the labored breath of a man running for his life. Through his creeping fear, David noted the change in his father's voice. The old man had gone from tyrant to bootlicking slave in seconds. It made the boy feel queasy. But his father's eyes hadn't changed. "Well, it's November now, and I get paid tomorrow. I can guarantee you one thousand dollars in the mail by Friday afternoon."

"Mr. Jackson—"

"What, isn't that enough?" Some of the defensiveness crept back. "I mean"—with a toned-down voice—"what's it gonna take so I can keep my truck?"

There was a sigh on the other end. It sounded as if the salesman were battling his own conscience—please his manager or do this pitiful fool a favor. Blood burned crimson in Jackson's cheeks. If he could have, he would have reached through the phone and grabbed the no-nuts prick by the shirt and punched him in the fucking face.

"Mr. Jackson, I'm really tempted to believe you, but your record isn't conducive to that."

You calling me a liar, *you fucking little—*

"Look," said Jackson, "I can appreciate where you're coming from. You're right. I've fallen down on the job here." David's stomach got queasier. "But I can guarantee a check in the mail tomorrow afternoon. If it's not, you guys come out and take the truck on Monday. No questions asked, huh?"

Another sigh. "Mr. Jackson, I'm making a record of this conversation in my database. I will expect a check overnighted to our office here in Houston tomorrow. If there's not a FedEx letter delivered to me by lunch on Monday, we're going to do just that."

"Overnighted? But that costs . . . I mean the mail will get there in two days—"

"Take it or leave it." All pretense of cordiality was gone. The plea bargain was set. The judge-salesman was smiling over the phone.

"All right, all right," the old man grumbled. "It'll be there."

"Good. I look forward to receiving it. Good-bye."

Jackson pulled the phone away from his ear and looked at it. "I've got something you can receive," he said quietly, then brought the receiver ringing down onto the cradle. "You fucking little *prick*!" He screamed the last word and it echoed in the otherwise silent room for a moment. David wanted to hold on to the sound, keep it going, capture the moment to hold it in place for a thousand years. Because as soon as it was over, the next phase would begin.

His father turned to him. "Stand up," he said.

"Daddy, I . . ."

Jackson slumped his shoulders as if to say, *Why string this out, boy? You know where we're headed, so let's just get there and get it over with.*

"I said," he said, "stand up."

The boy stood up off the bed. He was within arm's reach, and his father made good use of that fact. David was on the floor before he realized it. The left side of his face was numb. It started to burn, slowly, a little sun of pain spreading to his brain.

"What did I tell you about answering the phone?"

David was dazed, shocked by the blow, despite knowing it would come. His hand went to his face and felt the heat there. He was careful not to touch it. A bruise would settle in by morning.

His father was moving on him. The boy inched away, and immediately he knew it was a mistake.

"Don't draw away from me, boy," his father raged, the lava finally boiling out of him. All his impotent anger at the salesman, all his frustration at his financial situation, the crap job, all of it, coursing through his veins, balled in his fists. He grabbed the boy and held him in both hands, arms pinned to his sides. "I asked you a *question!*"

"I-I…" David was starting to cry. *Another mistake, idiot!* his brain shouted at him.

"Stop blubbering like a baby and answer my question!"

"It wasn't the company!" David cried. "I didn't *know* who it was!"

His father set him down on the ground, then slapped him again. David cried out this time. His face was burning and now his brain was working overtime to tell every inch of his body that his left cheek was in a bad way.

"If you hadn't answered it, like I *told* you, it wouldn't have mattered!"

The boy lay on the floor and looked up at him. All of a sudden it was very important to win this argument.

Idiot!

"You told me to check the caller ID first, not to not answer the phone!" Some part of him knew that wasn't entirely true, but that detail wasn't important. Making his stand was all that mattered.

His father drew up. "You questionin me, boy?" He raised his hand again.

Screw this.

David dodged the blow and failure to connect sent his old man off-balance. Jackson fell against the dresser, and David shot out through the bedroom door as fast as he could.

"You come back here, boy!"

Fuck you!

He ran up the hallway and then heard his father in pursuit. David burst into the kitchen, the door bouncing off the cabinet, and ran around the center island where all the Tupperware was stored. His father was through the door, seconds behind him. The boy grabbed the handle to the back door and knew, once he got beyond the privacy fence's gate, he at least could run for a lot longer than his beer-bellied old man could.

"Boy!"

The word barked close behind him. David turned the knob and was out and into the backyard, his father almost on top of him. He angled left, meaning to run a wide pattern, hoping the old man would stumble over something on the back porch and give David the time he needed to get the latch on the back gate open. No such luck. He felt fat fingers wrap around the back of his shirt collar. The old man pulled him up straight like a fly caught in the web of a very nasty spider.

"Now boy, we're gonna teach you a little discipline." He shook the boy to punctuate his sentences. "You're gonna remember the next time I tell you to do something. You're gonna learn what it means to be responsible, follow instructions."

David was done. He was trapped. There was no escape. But he'd have his say.

"You only told me to check the caller ID," he said directly. Despite the footrace, the beating, the pain, his voice was very calm, hardly wavering at all.

Jackson raised his right hand again. "Why, you little—"

Out of the garage she came, barking savagely to herald her charge. Queenie leapt right for Jackson's upraised hand, and the vice of her jaws clamped down around his tendon-stretched wrist. The old man shrieked a high-pitched howl and dropped David to the concrete. Jackson fell backward onto the porch, spilling over and destroying a lounge chair, carrying the dog with him. She still held his wrist, as if she didn't know what to do now that she had him, but then he was beating on her, trying to drive her off him. David saw his father punching Queenie and shouted "Stop it! Stop it! Stop it!" but the dog released Jackson's arm, getting inside his defenses and nipping at his face. The old man's instincts kicked in then, and he slammed his arms over his face to protect it. Finally, he grabbed her under her legs and chest and heaved her off, sent her flying across the porch. She landed clumsily on all fours, working her legs like dynamos, preparing to charge him again. But David grabbed her collar and weighed her down as Jackson got his own feet under him again and shouted,

"Goddammit! God fucking *damn* it!" at the pain in his pockmarked face. The old man stumbled toward the back door. David held her down, not for his father's safety—the thought never entered his head—but because he didn't want the old man beating her again. Jackson stumbled into the house and slammed the door.

The boy could hear his father shouting obscenities as he walked through the kitchen and deeper into the house. Queenie stood there panting, growling, daring him to return. David held her tightly. He buried his burning cheek in her cool fur and burst into tears.

He didn't see his father for the rest of the day or night. David washed his face in the spare bathroom, testing its tenderness with his fingertips, then retired to his bedroom and watched reruns on television until he fell asleep. His father had never looked in on him once. He'd eaten a sandwich for dinner.

The next morning he was awakened at 7:30.

"Time for school, boy," the old man said. David thought there might be another chapter like yesterday. But nothing. No follow-up. The strangeness of that worried him. "Brush your teeth."

The boy rolled out of bed, his muscles aching from yesterday's chase. His cheek was a low, dull throbbing now. He'd tell the kids at school he fell on the sidewalk. They'd believe that.

He took a leak, brushed his teeth, and walked through the kitchen to the back door. He sleepily grabbed the bag of Ken-L Ration, walked outside and poured the food in Queenie's bowl. Usually she came padding along at the sound of the food. But not this morning.

He whistled for her. When that didn't bring her, he walked into the garage, where he kept her bed. It was there. Queenie wasn't. And her leash was gone.

He walked back into the house. The truth slowly began to melt into his brain. His father was sitting at the table, reading the paper and drinking a beer.

"Where is she?" the boy asked.

His father looked up. "Who?"

"You know who." David wasn't in the mood for games. He was very much awake now. His voice was defiant. Downright challenging. But his father didn't seem to care. Not this time.

"Oh. I went hunting this morning. She run off."

David blinked.

"I was gonna go fishing," said Jackson, as if rehearsed. "But then I decided to go hunting. Took the dog. She run off after somethin in the woods. I looked for her. Couldn't find her." He turned the page of the paper, flicked it straight.

David's heart emptied at that moment. It sank into his stomach where, deep down, he knew—he *knew*—what his father had done.

Chapter 14

"Hey man, final's in thirty minutes," his roommate said, shaking him. David Jackson rolled over and sat up, trying and failing to retrieve a line of drool. He sat there weaving back and forth in his bed. He'd been up till three A.M. studying for his macroeconomics final, then put himself to sleep by splitting a six-pack with his roommate. The same roommate that now seemed much more awake and ready for the final than David was.

"How the *fuck* can you be so chipper this morning?" David asked. His mouth tasted like ass.

Larry Brackett smiled. Standing with legs apart, he put his fists on his hips and looked off toward infinity. "It's in the genes, buddy! Supergenes!"

David worked his tongue in his mouth like it had just been installed. "Fuck you."

"No thanks, though I *did* notice you tried to get me drunk last night." He waved his right index finger. "Tough luck, roomie. I don't play for that team."

David fake-laughed really hard for about three seconds, then immediately regretted it as his head pulsed. "That's very funny. You should work Northgate as a comedian."

Larry smirked. "Living with you for a year now, I *should* be a comedian."

"Yeah-yeah. Ha-ha. What the fuck time is it?"

"8:32," Larry said. "Now you've got twenty-eight minutes till the final."

David's eyes sprang wide open. "Oh, *shit*." He launched himself off the bed and headed for the shower.

"No time, buddy!" called Larry after him. "Wheels up in ten minutes!"

"I'll be ready," shouted David back at him. "Promise!"

Larry rolled his eyes. "I'm not missing this test so you can smell pretty," he yelled back.

"I'll be ready, goddammit!"

Larry sat down on the couch in the apartment's small living room and looked around. There were lots of empty beer cans. *Hey, at least they're upright*, Larry thought. Two pizza boxes, one of which still had two slices slowly growing old in it, sat askew on the coffee table. He grabbed one of the pieces and thought about cleaning up things for a few minutes while David took his shower, shrugged off the idea without too much effort, and picked up the TV remote. He fired up their brand new 3-D TV's Web browser.

Nothing better to do. Might as well look at some porn for a few minutes.

He'd been surfing around looking for blondes and streaming the free video grabs (using that term for Web porn always made Larry laugh) for about a minute and a half when the phone rang. Larry smirked at it for interrupting his body surfing and let it ring twice more. Finally he got up to answer it. He was tempted to let it go to voicemail but then decided it might be someone calling to let them know the nine o'clock exam—the one that was now less than twenty minutes away—had been canceled. He didn't want to miss the news.

"Joe's Morgue, you kill 'em, we chill 'em."

There was silence on the other end, then, "Um, may I speak to David Jackson, please?"

"He's in the shower. Can I take a message?" Larry went into routine mode, turning his attention back to the busty blonde on the screen.

"Well—this is kind of important."

"Hey, no problem. You have my undivided attention." *Now those are breasts*, he was thinking as he said it.

"Well—it's about Mr. Jackson's father. I really should speak with him directly."

Larry stopped clicking. David's old man had been sick off and on for the last six months. David had joked to Larry that he couldn't wait for the old fucker to die, and the sooner the better. But Larry heard something else in his roommate's voice the few times the topic came up. What, he wasn't sure. But he knew enough to know that, whatever this call was about, it wouldn't be good news. He clicked off the TV.

"I'm listening," he said. "I'll make sure he gets the information."

Driving home from Texas A&M University, David was furious with his father. If he had to die, why the hell did it have to be *right* in the middle of finals? But that was just like him. Always thinking of himself.

The road thrummed under him, the sound of rubber gripping pavement. It was early May, and already the heat had forced the windows up and the A/C on. David held the wheel with both hands but released one to tune the radio to a new station. He was nearing Houston, about halfway home, and they always had better rock stations than he was used to. He found a retro station playing heavy metal and cranked it way up. He was tempted to roll down the window and let the wind blow through the car, but then decided it was just too warm for that.

When he'd called her back, the woman on the phone had said the old man was really bad off. He wouldn't leave the hospital again, she'd said. And if David wanted to see him before . . . Well, he'd better come on.

"Yeah, well," he said out loud as he drove. David could barely hear himself because of the radio pounding the rolled-up windows. "I wouldn't say *want*."

Ozzy Osbourne was singing about a crazy train. *He used to eat the heads off animals on stage*, David recalled the lore. *What a fucked-*

up bunch of people his *fans must've been*. The song was only thirty years old, but to him it might as well have been from the Civil War.

Progressive, degenerative liver failure. And because of his father's drinking, he wasn't a viable candidate for a transplant, though he was on the list. And even if a liver was available, the old man's pension from his company wouldn't cover it, not by a long shot. And there was no money saved.

"I'll be lucky to get anything out of the old man," David told Ozzy. "The house isn't worth the ground it's sitting on. He let that go, just like he let himself go. Wouldn't follow anyone's advice and would curse you for giving it to him."

He bit his lower lip and focused on the broken stripe in the middle of the road as it lapped by. He vaguely realized there were cows in the pastures beyond the barbed wire that bordered the highway. Bluebonnets were in full bloom along the roadside. But David focused on the road in front of him. "Driving's a full-time job, son," his father had said when he taught him. "Pay attention and try not to kill anyone."

"Well, you're one to talk. You dumb sonofabitch. Drink yourself to death and then fuck up my finals to boot!"

He didn't remember starting to sweat, but he must've, because the road was getting blurry and he *damned* sure knew he wouldn't shed any tears over the old man. Not *his* old man. How many times had David wished he would die—just *die*—when he was growing up? How many times had he *prayed* for it? And now, that moment you've all been waiting for—and here he was, sweating like a baby.

He wiped his eyes again, cranked up the radio and A/C a little more, and drove on.

"Room 302?"

The nurse at the floor desk glanced at him, decided he was worth helping, and pointed down and around the elevators. "Down the left corridor and it's on your left, about ten rooms down."

"Thanks."

Though he hadn't been in many, the smell of a hospital always made him uncomfortable. The sterility. The cleanliness. The likelihood to get you sicker than you were when you came in the door. He never understood that irony.

David walked down the length of the corridor past the other rooms, some with open doors, some closed, and some he wished had been closed. In one room he saw out of the corner of his eye an old woman lying cockeyed in bed, as if she'd fallen there after a long drinking binge and was just glad not to have hit the floor. She stared glassy-eyed at a television that sounded excited to be on. A bouquet of get-well flowers sat dying in her window. He passed back by the elevators he had come up, watching the one-foot-square speckled floor tiles coming toward him.

step – step – step

He superstitiously tried to place his feet in the open area of each square where he stepped

(step on a crack, break your father's back)

and felt stupid for doing it.

David hadn't seen his father much since leaving for college. *Escaping, more like*, he thought to himself. He didn't send cards on birthdays or holidays, but then neither did his old man. About every six months, David worked up the courage to go home, perhaps driven by the masochistic need to see the old man again, for what reason he couldn't fathom. But deep down David knew: It was mandated. You had to love your family no matter what, even when you hated them, when you told yourself you didn't need them or couldn't love them. None of that mattered. It was in The Rules. The price of admission to the wonderful world Louis Armstrong used to sing about.

step-step-step

He would usually drive down on a Friday evening after classes and pull into the driveway of the old house

(seems smaller now, doesn't it)

and ring the front doorbell. His father would greet him with a smile, which didn't seem as forced now that he was older, and they would shake hands, because that's what men did. They would retire to the kitchen table, where his father had a small television running constantly set to Fox News, as if he were afraid of too much silence. The old man would ask how school was and David would say fine, and David would ask how retirement was and his father would say fine. The uncomfortable non-conversation, with a subdued game show or comedy rerun usually droning in the background, would give way to discussions of whatever Houston sports team had its season at that time. When that topic dried up, the weather would come along, or something exciting would happen on the television to elicit a shared giggle from the two men. During commercials, his father would ask him if he wanted a beer. Sometimes David would say yes, sometimes no.

This was their ritual.

stepstepstep

The visit would last until David couldn't stand it anymore, which varied between Saturday afternoon and Sunday morning, and he would drive back to Texas A&M feeling for the hundredth time as if he'd just been paroled. And then it would occur all over again in another six months or so.

He reached his father's room and stood outside the door, not really wanting to go in but knowing he had to. David thought of the old woman lying sprawled in her bed like a drunk. Maybe he should have brought flowers or something. He had the devilish thought of running back and stealing hers, since she wouldn't notice

(you'll go to hell for that)

and then, smiling at his own deviousness, decided his father wouldn't want them anyway. Flowers weren't a man's gift.

He pushed the door open.

The television was on, of course. It was midday on Tuesday, and watching *Wheel of Fortune* was his father's favorite pastime these days. David opened the door quietly, not sure if the old man was asleep or not. It was a semi-private room, but the second bed, the one nearest the door, was empty for now. From the door he could see his father was snoozing, so he walked in quietly between the two beds and sat on the empty one. He was vaguely aware of hospital policy and that, specifically, this bed was to be kept neat and clean at all times in case a second patient needed it. So he made a mental note to smooth the covers back out before he left so they wouldn't give the old man a hard time about it.

David looked at his father's face. His thinning wisps of gray hair splayed out on the pillow under his head, uncombed. His head was cocked to the left, as if looking at David from behind closed lids. His mouth was open slightly, the way the body does when it's providing a contingency plan in case the sinuses fill up. His skin looked like it might crack open, a dry, clay reservoir after a week of constant, baking sunlight. His cheeks were sallow, his color pale. His hands grasped the thin, gritty sheets of the hospital bed and held them to the top of his chest, as if warding off Death with a cotton shield. The lumpy form beneath didn't move. If not for the chart at the foot of the bed, David wouldn't have recognized the old man. He was an emaciated form of the man David remembered his father having been. Older now, of course, but also withered. Time had bleached the life out of him.

David reached over and picked up the TV remote, noticing it controlled an old-fashioned cathode-ray set. Of course it did. Hospitals didn't have the money to invest in higher-end flat-screens, much less 3-D TVs like the one Larry's father had bought them. Hell, hospitals didn't even have the money to make beds in real time, when they were needed, right? They had to send the bed leprechauns around to do it in the wee-wee hours of the morning, laddybuck, for when those emergency patients—all those drunken old people who couldn't wait for the nurse to make the bed—needed a place to fall that was soft and non-liable.

He turned down the volume, and the lack of noise immediately woke his father.

"Who's there?" the old man asked. It was the weakest David had ever heard his voice. It sounded like an old steam engine that lacked the pressure to start. Instead of lungs driving the sound, it was like the voice was hitching a ride on a ragged breath that just happened to be passing through. David had heard of the "death rattle" before, and now he'd *actually* heard it, coming out of his father. *Where's your bluster and blow now, old man?* he thought and immediately regretted thinking it. It was disrespectful somehow. Not to his father. To the natural order of things. To God. To the way he knew he ought to feel about the old man but didn't.

"It's me, Dad."

"David?" The old man worked his eyes. You could see it. He was trying to focus.

"Yes."

"Hello, son," he wheezed.

"Howdy."

"It was good of you to come down. I know you're busy with school and all."

David felt guilty for lambasting his father for being sick during finals. And anger quickly followed that feeling. Anger at whom or what he wasn't sure.

"That's okay, Dad. How are you feeling?"

"Fine," his father said, his eyes going to the TV and only finding a commercial there.

"Where are you on the list?"

"List?"

"The *donor's* list, Dad." Though he'd just turned twenty-one, a bit of the know-it-all sixteen-year-old crept back into David's voice. *The* donor's *list, dumbass*, his tone said.

"Oh, that don't matter anymore," his father said.

"What do you mean?"

"They tell me I wouldn't get one anyway. Drunks don't get new livers. It's in The Rules."

David knew that was reality, but he'd made sure his father was on the list just the same.

"It's all right," the old man was saying. "I won't be around much longer anyhow. I don't need anything from those fuckers."

David heard the words and, perversely, almost burst out laughing. Even now, his father's disdain for the rest of the human race trumped his common sense. Then again, there wasn't much to be done, truth be told. What bothered David the most was how definitive the old man's voice sounded. Like they were in a meeting and it was on the agenda in black and white. Next action item: Death.

"No, Dad, that's not what we agreed on."

"We?" said his father. "Since when do *we* make decisions for *me*, boy?"

"I . . ." David decided not to take the bait for the argument. "I just think it's too soon to be talking about—"

"Nobody's talking about *nothing*." The old man's voice was weak again. He had used up his reserves staking out his position on the subject. He picked at the sheet, looking for a tighter grip. "This is just the way it is."

David's inner voice raged, *Let the old fucker die! The sooner the better! Let the old fucker poison his own blood the way he's done yours! Idiot!* But another part of him, the part that felt like it had a debt yet to pay for his two-way ticket into this world, wanted nothing more than to keep his father alive. At any cost. No matter what. He struggled with what to say, trying to climb over the years of walls he'd built. But the old man was asleep again, snoring softly and evenly above the muted celebration of the TV's studio audience.

Then his father's lips began moving. David could hear the tired mutterings of a conversation. The old man seemed to be speaking to David in his sleep, perhaps dreaming of a conversation the two of them had had once, or had never had. David moved closer to catch the words.

". . . anything else . . ."

Snatches only, partial sentences. And one line, whispered between breaths, came out very clear. "I lost everything—everything I ever loved—when you were born."

David recoiled, as if he'd just seen a snake in his father's bed. He bumped into the second bed, knocking it out of its perfect alignment. He stared at the pasty flesh of the near-corpse clasping the bedcovers to its chest. The open mouth

(so like Old Suzie's now, old and soured with hospital food)

spitting its venom at him, even from sleep.

There, see? Told you so, you bleeding-heart idiot!

David leaned backward on the bed and stared at the old man dying as the TV crowd clapped and cheered without a sound. The flesh might have been hardly recognizable, but the sheer delight the old man apparently took in torturing him—even now—was as telling as a fingerprint. *A heartprint*, David thought. *A black* heartprint.

He turned and fled the room, never looking back. His father died exactly one week later, alone in the hospital bed. *Wheel of Fortune* was on TV. It was a Tuesday. The empty bed next to the old man was perfectly made.

Standing at the graveside after the dozen or so locals had left, David stared down at the headstone. It had the standard name and life dates on it, then simply "Beloved Father."

"Well, it's half-right," David slurred. He'd slammed three beers just before the service, so he swayed a little. But this was one of those times when people forgave that kind of behavior. He was in mourning after all, so it was acceptable to be a little tipsy in public today.

An exception to The Rules.

His conscience attacked him then, the part of him that hadn't wanted to let his father go. *Be respectful to the dead*, it said. *Else they come back to haunt you.* That made David laugh out loud.

The minister, who hadn't known his father and who had to be reminded once of the deceased's first name during the actual service, stopped and looked back. He shrugged his shoulders and opened the door to his Cadillac.

But the voice of his conscience had been the old man's.

What do you mean "come back" to haunt me? David replied to the voice. *You think I can forget him anytime soon? Ever?*

His conscience seemed to mimic the minister's shrug. The other voice in his head merely rolled its eyes in disgust. *Idiot.* A burp tried to come up and brought up partially digested beer and stomach acid. The heartburn spread through David's chest. He grimaced, and it began to recede slowly back into his gut.

He looked in his paper bag. There were still three beers there. Shiner Bock, a local Texas favorite. Brown and rough and less sweet than Guinness. He pulled the first bottle out and twisted off the cap. He slammed it, nearly choking himself.

And then the second.

And then the third.

He was drunk all right, but he wasn't stupid. He looked around several times, almost making himself dizzy. No one was around now that the minister had driven off. *Fuck The Rules anyway*, he thought. Out loud, he chortled the old joke, "Y'know, you only ever really rent beer."

Slowly, deliberately, he unzipped his fly. His bladder was so full it took no time at all for the flow to come. He watched it splatter, yellow on the fresh mud—brown, white, and foamy as gravity did its work. It formed a little river, charting a course of primordial liquid, carving out a tiny yellow canal in the dark earth. By the time he'd finished, his urine had made a small pool of rented, processed beer near the tombstone.

"See, old man?" he sobbed. "You *can* take it with you."

PART 3

(15 YEARS FROM NOW)

You've got to be successful
Just to be all right.
Lest the old man's ghost come walkin'
In the middle of the night.
—James McMurtry
"Stancliff's Lament"

I'm not from here, but people tell me,
It's not like it used to be.
They say I should've been here,
Back about ten years,
Before it got ruined by folks like me.
—James McMurtry
"I'm Not from Here"

CHAPTER 15

"Hello?"

Elizabeth half-whispered the word.

It was the only breath she had. Her lungs were hitched. Her hands felt wet and cold. She readied herself to rise and run, placing her palms flat on the floor. They picked up the dusty decay like magnets.

"Mom won't like that," her 3V voice smirked at her dirty hands.

Shut up.

Elizabeth's mouth hung open. Her eyes sought the dog in the depths of the parlor, where the voice had come from.

"Hello." The word croaked into existence a second time. It was rough, the shade of a voice that hadn't spoken in years. As if air, breathing through the house, had created sound.

She was truly frightened now. Before the frog-voice had spoken again, Elizabeth had hoped that hearing it was her mind playing tricks on her; her 3V voice tickling her fears with a memory from her nightmare. Or maybe an echo from the past had slipped from the walls around her. An old ghost, scary but harmless. But then the voice had made its second hello, and Elizabeth knew she wasn't alone.

"D-dog?"

Pant-pant.

"She's here," said the man. The shadow had taken shape. A thick, tired form. "She brought you to me." He sounded happy about that.

I know! Elizabeth wanted to scream. *Bad, bad dog!*

"Don't be such a baby," her 3V voice said, mimicking Michael.

"Where are you?" she whispered. She had pushed herself up onto her knees now, not quite to her feet. Elizabeth wanted to look around for the roaches, but something inside countermanded the order.

179

Somehow, a roach crawling on her had become less fearsome than just a few moments ago.

"Here," answered the man.

She had one leg under her now. Her hands felt grimy. "That's not a very good answer," she said quietly. "I can't see you."

The house seemed to relax around her.

"Don't mean I'm not here." It was strange. If Elizabeth could have heard a smile through the darkness, she thought she might have just heard one.

Her eyes began to adjust to the room's low light. She saw the silhouette of an old man sitting in an old chair.

(Old Suzie's chair)

Watching her.

(watching her shows)

Elizabeth had both feet under her now and stood up. She felt a single drop of sweat trail down her left calf. She shuddered as the house breathed a chill across it.

He motioned toward her. She thought of the old wizards from her fantasy stories. Perhaps the old man was casting a spell on her. She had seen news reports. She knew what could happen to little girls. He would paralyze her and then . . .

The dog padded over to her slowly, tongue drooping, mouth pulled back in a dog-smile. She stopped in front of Elizabeth, her eyes gazing up, flounder-like, at her. Elizabeth took her eyes off the old man and looked down. *I don't like you anymore!* she projected.

The dog saw the anger in her eyes and closed her mouth. Elizabeth was afraid the animal would growl at her, but instead the dog just lowered her ears and inched forward a bit more to nuzzle Elizabeth's hand. *Oh no. No you don't.* But the dog wasn't looking at her anymore and didn't see the anger that remained. She moved her head around in Elizabeth's hand.

Elizabeth suddenly realized she hadn't been watching the old man. Maybe he'd moved.

Maybe he'd moved toward her.

Slowly, reaching inward again for Elsbyth's strength, she looked back at the chair. There he sat, motionless. Again, and strangely, she felt more than saw that he was smiling at her.

"I have to go home now," she said. "It's getting late."

The old man breathed out slowly. She'd decided to name him that—old man. The rattle of his deep voice, the wheezing of his breathing told her that's what he was. "There's still sunshine," he said. "Not much, I admit, but some."

The dog was panting again. Elizabeth was unconsciously scratching her furry head. "Mom taught me never to talk to strangers," she said.

"Well, she's right. My name's Rocky. Now we ain't strangers."

Elizabeth was silent. She didn't want to talk to this man. She didn't want to share anything with him at all, not even words. She realized she'd bent over to more easily scratch the dog's head and stood up again abruptly.

"Dog has a way of putting you off your guard, doesn't she?"

"Did your mother teach you manners as well?" asked the old man.

"Oh, sorry," said Elizabeth, an automatic response to an adult's correction. "I'm Elizabeth." She was immediately upset with herself for falling for such an old trick.

"Maybe he'll offer you candy next," her 3V voice poked at her. *Shut up.*

"Hello, Elizabeth," he said, prying his arms from the chair as he spread them wide around him. "Welcome to my house."

The girl cocked her head to one side. "This isn't *your* house. It's Old Suzie's. And she's dead."

She felt the smile coming again from him. "You're right on both counts. But dead people don't own nothin."

"And you don't own this place," she said matter-of-factly.

A head—more than an outline but less than a face—shook slowly from side to side. "No, I'm just stayin here awhile."

"Oh," Elizabeth said, awareness suddenly dawning. It seemed to take the edge off her fear. "You're homeless?"

The old man chuckled, a slow, churning sound, like an old lawnmower engine starting up after a long winter. "You could say that." Then he paused before asking, "Did you know your name means 'oath of God'?"

"No." What a strange thing to say. "I didn't know that."

"He's a weirdo," her 3V voice said.

But then the feeling came to her again that this man—this *stranger*—knew too much about her already. She was afraid of his knowing so much.

As Elizabeth's eyes adjusted to the waning light of early evening, she could make out more than a shadow now. He had a thin face. Grizzled. Unshaven. Dirty.

Like the floor of this house.

"Well," he said, exhaling heavily as if he wanted to discuss her name's significance but knew it would only bore her. "Why not stay awhile? This place gets lonely. 'specially at night."

There it was. The invitation. She felt the paralysis creeping over her again. The wizard was casting his spell. And what was worse— she was consciously letting herself be spellbound.

"I—"

"The dog would like you to stay."

Elizabeth managed to break her gaze from the chiseled gray eyes inside the lined face. She looked down at the dog staring up at her from beneath bushy brows. The orange eyes with coal centers reassured her for some reason. *He won't hurt you. Not while I'm here*, the eyes seemed to say.

And then, within a heartbeat, Elizabeth completely changed her mind.

"Okay, I'll stay. As long as you promise not to move from that chair."

She saw the old face crack. It took a moment for her to realize he was grinning, and she could actually see his expression this time. It was exactly what she'd pictured when she'd felt him smiling before. *Weird*, she thought.

"I don't think I could move from this chair too easily right now even if I wanted to," he said. "I'm very tired, you see."

He motioned for her to sit down on the floor opposite him. It must have been where Old Suzie's television had once sat, Elizabeth realized. But she sat there anyway. The dog walked over and curled up next to her with a slight creaking of joints and a contented moan as she laid down to rest.

The old man in the armchair smiled at her. Elizabeth smiled back, letting her imagination take over. Being homeless, he must've traveled to a thousand different places. She wanted to ask him about all of them. Then she noticed he was just staring at her—wouldn't take his eyes off her. It made her uncomfortable again.

"So you live here," he said, just when she was getting ready to stand up again and run out through the kitchen. "In town, I mean."

"Yes," Elizabeth said. She was grateful for the conversation beginning at last. At least she thought she was. But she'd rather talk about the thousand other places he'd visited instead of boring old Hampshire. "Just not very long."

"Oh? Where did you move from?" The old man's voice had a strange quality to it, almost scripted.

"Houston. My dad moved his practice from there. He's *from* here." She said the last with a sour voice.

"Practice? He's a doctor?"

"Lawyer."

"Ah."

Again, there was something in his voice.

"You don't like lawyers?" she asked.

"Shakespeare didn't," he said, with a grin that wasn't quite a smile.

"So?"

"Do you even know who Shakespeare was?"

"Sure. We've read some of his plays in school."

"Really?" The old man seemed genuinely surprised. "You get better schooling nowadays, I guess."

"You didn't read his plays in school?"

"They taught them."

He left it hanging, and Elizabeth didn't understand the difference. Then she did.

"Oh. *You* didn't read them."

"Lawyers aren't so bad, I guess," he said, changing the subject.

"They defend people," confirmed Elizabeth. For some reason she thought she needed to do the same for her father now.

"Jesus, what's wrong *with you?"* asked her 3V voice.

"Even when they don't deserve defending," continued the old man.

Elizabeth thought about that for a second. "Doesn't everyone deserve a chance to tell their side of the story?"

For the first time, she saw the old man shake his head. "Some people don't. Those that aren't sorry for what they've done."

She quietly considered what he'd said, reaching down to pet the dog pressed against her. The fur was soft, oddly cool. Not knowing really how to answer the old man, she asked, "So what are you doing here?"

"Just passing through. I found this old house and decided to stay here awhile. It gets a little chilly for old bones on the road this time of year."

"How do you eat?"

The question was a natural one, but it seemed to make the old man uncomfortable. *I'll bet he steals and doesn't like to but has to because he's homeless*, she thought.

Then he smiled again. "With my right hand."

Elizabeth rolled her eyes. "Oh, *brother*. You know what I mean!"

The smile faded. "I get by."

She decided not to press. "Do you know the story of this house?"

"No," he said, intrigued. "Do tell."

"Well, they say it's haunted," Elizabeth explained. Her voice took on a conspiratorial quality, like when she shared a secret with Michael.

"Really?"

"Yeah. The ghost of Old Suzie, the witch-woman who used to live here."

"*Witch*-woman? Which woman would that be?"

"Huh?" Then she saw the silver moonlight twinkle in his eye, and she got it. "Oh," she said, "that's pretty bad."

"The witch-woman?" he asked.

"No, your *joke*. Gawd. You're worse than Dad. Old Suzie was supposed to be a witch."

"Oh. I see now."

"She used to catch little kids and cook them for supper."

He was pensive for a moment. He had the look on his face a person gets when they're trying to dredge something up from the back row of a fallow mind. "Wasn't that what the witch in *Hansel and Gretel* did?"

Now it was her turn to skim the rows of knowledge filed away in her head. "Well, that's probably where she got the idea," Elizabeth surmised.

"Oh."

"*Anyway*," Elizabeth said in an exasperated voice, "she died sitting *right where you are now*." She emphasized the last five words the way camp leaders do when they're trying to scare children.

"My goodness!" he said, feigning concern. "Do you think she minds that I'm sitting here?"

"Dunno," said Elizabeth sheepishly. "Why don't you ask her?"

"Huh?"

"She's standing *right behind you*."

The old man started forward in the chair, twisting and looking over his shoulder. Elizabeth was laughing as loud as a girl her age could.

"Got you!" she said.

He slowly turned back around, settling in the chair. "Yes, you did. A word of advice," he said, wincing, "don't make old men move quickly. We don't snap back as easily as you do."

She slowly stopped laughing and her face became concerned. "Are you okay? I'm sorry—"

"No, it's okay," he said, holding up a hand. "Let's just not scare old Rocky again, okay?"

"Okay. Sorry."

He nodded, settling back in the chair. "So, tell me about Old Suzie."

"Like I said, she was a witch. She used to eat children. Then she died. Watching her shows."

"Who told you that?"

"Um. . ." She wasn't sure how to answer. She didn't want to get Michael in trouble. "A friend of mine."

"Not your dad?"

Elizabeth cocked her head to one side. *Another odd thing to say.* "No."

"Weird old coot."

"Mmmm," he said thoughtfully.

"Why did you think that?"

"Well, you said he was from here. Stories like that don't start up overnight. I'm guessing Old Suzie was the talk of this town for years before you were ever born. Stories are like that. They get started and take on a life of their own. A spirit, you might say. They hang around and haunt you when the person they're about is long dead."

Elizabeth hadn't even wondered where the story came from. It just . . . *was.* "I don't think I understand."

"That's okay," he replied, the smile returning. "Not many folks do. Else stories like that wouldn't ever get started. Least you'd hope that was true."

She shook her head. The old man was talking like an adult now. They were entering you'll-understand-when-you-get-older territory. "Well—what *was* she like?"

"Oh, I don't know," he said. "I'm not from here. I just live here."

Elizabeth rolled her eyes again. She could tell he was baiting her, but she bit anyway.

"Well, what do you *think* she was like?"

"Well now," he said, his eyes lighting up, "like I said, I don't rightly *know*. But if I had to guess . . ." He looked around. Despite the dusky haze of the early evening, some light still crept into the corners. "I'd guess she was a hardworking woman, looking at that big used-to-be garden out back. There's a rusted-out tractor in the garage, but you can tell by looking at the engine—when you open it up, that is—it was well taken care of for a long time. I didn't see no children's bones anywhere, so either she was a very *neat* witch, or those stories were maybe a little too tall for the truth."

"Her husband left her and she worked the place alone," supplied Elizabeth. It was a tidbit of Michael's story she hadn't really thought about till now.

"Really?"

"Yes."

"And she died watching television, sitting in this very chair?"

"Yes."

"So what, dear Watson, can we conclude from these facts?"

She looked quizzically at him. "My name's *Elizabeth*."

He looked quizzically at her. "You never heard of Sherlock Holmes?"

She shook her head.

"I take back the good stuff I said about your schooling," he muttered. "They've shortchanged you, girl."

"Whatever 'shortchanged' means," her 3V voice snarked.

"Okay, answer the question," he said. "Forget the Watson part. Put the facts together."

Elizabeth put her mind to it. It seemed like a game to her now. "Her husband left her. She kept up her own garden. Kept her equipment in good order. Loved watching her shows on television."

"That's the stuff on the left side of the equation. What about the right?"

It struck her then. "Maybe she was lonely. Maybe that's the stuff she did to keep from feeling alone all the time."

He didn't smile, which she thought he would've done if she'd gotten the right answer. Her monitor did that at webschool. "Positive reinforcement," he called it.

"Well, like I said," he said, "I didn't know her. But that sounds about right from what little I know *of* her."

Elizabeth turned her eyes down to watch her hand petting the dog. She'd been stroking her fur while they talked, but now she felt a particular need for something soft and pleasant.

"I wonder why people tell the other story about her, then. I mean, she wasn't like that—a witch, I mean—was she?"

"I'm guessing not," the old man said. "But folks believe what they want to. It's how they stay sane. Most everyone believes that black is black and white is white, only each person really defines the colors in their own way. And sometimes—like with Old Suzie, I'm guessing—sometimes they agree on what's true and what's not, and that becomes the reality of it."

She looked at him with that confused expression again. "I don't understand."

He sat back in his chair. "Well if you don't now, kiddo, you might one day."

"Okay, that's as bad as 'You'll understand when you're older.'"

"That's not fair. If you don't help me understand, you shouldn't make me feel bad for *not* understanding."

The old man muttered agreement. "That's a fair thing to say. All I meant was, most people decide what something means—or what someone is—without bothering to find out what's true and what's not. Without *thinking*, really. People tell stories about a person when they never even know that person." His voice turned flat, spitting out the words to get them out of his mouth. "They're like sheep. Baa-baa-baaing their way through life without saying anything meaningful. And whatever they *do* say is often hurtful to someone else. Cuz they usually speak from fear and ignorance, not a thoughtful place."

Now, that was something Elizabeth understood. Without asking, her father had simply assumed that the monitor's call yesterday had been bad news.

"Because it usually is," admonished her 3V voice.

Yeah, okay, she answered back, *but yesterday it* wasn't. And her father hadn't even bothered to find that out.

"To use your brain and figure out the truth always takes more effort," the old man was saying, as if reading her mind. "And people can be lazy by nature."

"I understand now." She felt her nose starting to run and realized then that her eyes were tearing up. *Why didn't Daddy just* ask *me? Why did he assume the worst?*

"Yes, I think you do," Rocky said. "Good for you."

She nodded, beginning to stand. "I think I better be getting home now. My parents are going to be pretty worried."

"It *is* getting dark out there," he said.

"Well," she said, hesitating as the dog looked up at her without raising her head from the floor. *She really does look like a hairy flounder*, Elizabeth thought. "Maybe I can come back tomorrow. If I'm not *grounded*, that is."

"That would be nice. It's nice to have people around, now and then."

The dog perked up and panted at Elizabeth. Her vote seemed to confirm the old man's.

"I'll see," she said, turning to walk back through the kitchen. Then she stopped and considered the front door. The moonlight streamed in through the half-rotten wood but lit her path well enough that she wasn't too afraid of going that way. And it *was* the shorter route for getting home.

"Oh yeah, let's rush that. Man, you're in so much trouble."

"Tell me something I don't know," she whispered.

"What was that?"

"Nothing," she answered him. "I'll try to come by tomorrow." She walked past the old man, through the parlor, and into the entryway.

"All right then," he said as she passed.

A hallway was to her left and a door on either side, just before she got to the foyer.

(just like in the dream)

"Weird."

She stepped onto the porch, but before pulling the door closed behind her, she said quietly, "Sorry, Suzie." Then she walked out into the grass, brainstorming about what her punishment might be.

So focused was Elizabeth on her parents' wrath she failed to notice that, unlike in her dream, the porch had been quiet beneath her feet.

Chapter 16

The moon was a solid disc reigning over the smaller stars in the sky. Elizabeth's skin tingled under the crisp air.

But it wasn't so much the cold as the fear that gave her goose bumps. Walking along the street toward home, Elizabeth pondered how bad it would be when she got there.

Her father would lay into her. He'd yell at her for, first, getting kicked out of school for the day and, second, leaving the house that morning without telling her mother. And then he'd ask her if she knew she'd done wrong, and after she'd admitted the sin, he'd give her penance and grant absolution.

The penance would probably involve revoking her 3V privileges for a week. Some kids didn't care about that. Some even reveled in the fact that they'd *earned* the punishment. Not Elizabeth. If she could avoid the confrontation, she would. If she could short circuit the yelling prior to the punishment being doled out, she would. And she would take the punishment and be grateful it wasn't worse. The routine of that cycle was what she was used to. It was almost comfortable. Because there was always worse.

The gravel crunched under her feet, and she kicked a loose rock into the drainage ditch. The loss of her 3V privileges—that was the cruelest punishment of all. Her parents thought it was fitting because they knew she enjoyed the 3V tank. They thought if they took the privilege away, she'd learn her lesson. *And they might be right,* Elizabeth thought. She mulled that over as she walked the plank toward home.

Adults seemed to think the way they handle children is some sort of super-secret recipe for creating a proper person, a formula that only adults *really* understand. They think all children know is they've been bad and that being bad is, well, bad. Wasn't it adults that performed the psychological studies and monitored behavior? Wasn't it adults who mapped the path to responsible adulthood through a process called parenting? But children know what's really going on.

We always know, thought Elizabeth.

Adults who grow up and *remember* what it was like to be a child realize this truth about the same time the generation behind them is moving on to college. For Elizabeth the understanding had come early, a way of keeping her sanity. It took on the stony shape of knowing exactly what was to come. Punishment fitting the crime. Loss of her 3V privileges.

For Elizabeth, losing those was like losing her own imagination, that safe place where she escaped the voices calling one another names in the other room. When she became Elsbyth, the Warrior-Queen of Rheanna, *no one* could stand against her. Her Horse Companions looked to her for leadership. They asked *her* what to do and *she* made the rules. There were no dueling parents. No disappointed monitor. Nothing but a fantasy world of wondrous creatures and endless adventures, where conflict was a simple matter of good versus evil.

"But not for another week," her 3V voice moped.

They would take away her 3V games. And her father would probably *enjoy* the thought that now she would spend her time studying as she should. And her imagination would die for a week, a slow, emaciating death of boredom and parental assault. Already she was looking forward to a week from now, when she would ride again with the wind in her hair.

"Where the hell could she be?"

David Jackson was furious. He paced the living room with only a floor lamp and the constantly changing video feed of the muted *Web Report* lighting his path. "She knew damned well her monitor would call about her dismissal. That's why she ran. So typical. Refusing to face the consequences. To take responsibility!"

Susan sat on the couch, focused on the arrangement of fake flowers on the coffee table. David had been ranting since she'd told him about the monitor's call. At first she hadn't said anything, hopeful that Elizabeth would appear and the two of them would discuss her absence from school without involving David. He'd turned on *Web Report* as usual to check the stocks but then, after night fell, Susan had gotten worried and told him everything. For all she knew, Elizabeth had been out all day. On the streets.

(what's in your basket, Red Riding Hood)

Wandering around.

(something sweet . . . to eat)

With God-knows-who ready to take advantage of her.

"When that girl gets home I'll—"

"You'll what?" demanded Susan. Her mother's protective impulse welled up inside her. David stopped in his tracks, staring at her. Now that she had his attention, Susan went on. "You'll spank her? Put her to bed without supper? Take away her games? *What*?"

His face became fierce, offended by the question. By the *questioning*. Why was he always the bad guy, goddammit?

"I'll make her understand what it is to leave this house without *telling* someone. She'll know what accountability is all about. She'll know what it means to—"

The back door opened to the kitchen, the hinges tattling on Elizabeth. David looked at Susan, who stared hard back at him. Their eyes parried and dodged. David knew Susan was angry with their daughter too—angry at Elizabeth for leaving without letting her know, angry at herself for not noticing for hours, angry at him for thinking of punishment when Susan just wanted to wrap her arms around Elizabeth and welcome her home, safe from the wolves in the forest. He listened to his daughter's footsteps trying to be quiet on the tile of the kitchen floor. He suddenly experienced a profound sense of déjà vu. Doubt overcame him. Should he do what he thought was right here? Ambivalence always plagued him when it came to disciplining Elizabeth. He was keenly aware of his own baggage but unsure how to handle it.

David knew Elizabeth would be off and down the hall to her room quickly if he didn't intercept her. And if he was going to confront her, he wanted to do it here, on *his* turf. And really, that was for her benefit. Unlike her space in the house, the living room was a place she could leave behind when she needed to. *Doesn't she realize I think of things like that?*

"Elizabeth!"

His voice was short and loud. He thought of it as his drill-sergeant voice. Not something she could pretend she hadn't heard.

Susan was still staring at him, daring him to be too hard on their daughter. *Don't dare me*, he thought. *That's dangerous*. And then he realized his anger was directed at Susan, not Elizabeth. He promised himself he wouldn't let it affect what he said to the girl.

Elizabeth mounted the steps to the living room slowly. "Yes, Daddy?" Her voice was light, lifted at the end with the question, trying to soothe the savage beast with the music of her twelve-year-old voice.

"Come here, Elizabeth," he said. David kept his voice as neutral as he could. He really didn't want to scare his daughter. He maintained an image of the overbearing father-ogre in his mind's eye to keep himself in check. When someone two-and-a-half times your size yells at you, it's hard not to be scared. So he tried to control his voice. "Why don't you sit on the couch there, beside your mother?" He killed two birds with one stone with that. David knew Elizabeth would feel safer next to Susan, and he knew the same would be true of his wife.

Then he realized that he'd had that thought.

God, safer? The idea made David's skin crawl. *Safer from* me?

"Your monitor called today," he said, putting aside his sudden feeling of self-loathing.

Elizabeth nodded, swallowing. "I know," she said quietly.

"He said you were dismissed from class today because you hadn't prepared properly."

She closed her eyes once, then opened them again. "Yes, sir."

He leaned forward in his chair and saw Elizabeth lean back on the couch. Five feet at least separated them. And she'd leaned back. Away from him. *God, safer from* me? he thought again.

He reclined and put the footrest of his armchair up. He hoped it would put them at ease.

"Why were you not prepared?" David formed his words carefully. He wondered to himself, *How would a how-to parenting book approach this*? He thought that trying to apply an objective standard to his approach to the conversation might keep him from getting upset.

"I . . ." Elizabeth broke off. She had tried the lie on the monitor and it hadn't worked. And Mr. Skinner had called, just like he'd promised. Nothing to do now but tell the truth. Take the punishment. Get it over with.

"Next week," her 3V voice said. *"And we ride in Rheanna again."*

"I'm waiting."

"I'd been on the Web." Her eyes began to well up.

"Good, that always helps."

But these weren't crocodile tears. They were for the words she knew were coming.

"Mmmm," her father said. "Mr. Skinner called. He said you lied to him about why you weren't prepared."

"Goddamn that fucking prick!"

Elizabeth was horrified at the words in her head, clenching her teeth to keep the obscenities in her mouth. But they were her words, even if they'd been spoken in her 3V voice. And despite their nastiness

(Michael would be proud)
she couldn't say they weren't.

"Skinner's always out to get us!"

Nothing for it now but the truth.

"Yes, sir."

David lowered the footrest of his chair, and she tensed immediately. Susan put an arm around her, stroking her shoulder, ready to step between them if need be.

"That's unacceptable, Elizabeth," he said.

"Yes, sir." She was crying now, her face crumpled in on itself and flushed red, the wrinkles of her emotion hinting at her face as an old woman.

"We paid for today's class, and we'll pay for the makeup session before the end of the year," David said. "You don't take school seriously enough. As a result, we'll pay twice as much for the same amount of teaching."

Elizabeth felt the mucous running thickly from her nose. She reached a hand up to wipe it off. "I'm sorry, Daddy," she said, but her mouth was contorted with her crying, and it came out as a long, baleful moan.

"Sorry's not good enough," he said, his voice rising.

Susan's eyes began to speak through her mouth. "David—"

"When I need your input, I'll ask for it," he said, darting his attention briefly to her. Her eyes flattened, and he immediately regretted having said it. Not because he was afraid of his wife, but because it would only fan the flames higher.

His own fire was burning now, his fuse shortened by the thought of Elizabeth failing in her education. Failing *herself* in the long run, something he never could get her to understand. It was so frustrating! Couldn't she see what was best for her? Couldn't she understand that what she did now would *mandate* the rest of her life?

"You must do better in school," he said, leaning forward in his chair. He tried to give his voice a helpful quality, like the adults in those children's educational shows he watched growing up. *This is the number three. Threeeeeeee.* "Elizabeth, it's not so much the money that bothers me"—and he'd hoped to leave it at that but couldn't help adding—"although that's something that your mother and I have to consider. But if you don't turn your performance around, the webschool will drop you. Don't you understand, without a good education early on, college is questionable, and then *everything* changes?"

Elizabeth formed the next line in her head a second before her father spoke it. *You know, Elizabeth,*

"if you don't apply yourself, you'll never"

amount to anything

"and you'll end up"

serving drinks somewhere

"in some cyberbar."

"Yes, sir," she said, crying less as she reached the cliché in the conversation. She knew the ending now. Not happy. But not *worse* either.

Her father sighed. "No Web privileges for a week. Use it for school research only. And I'll have the home computer send me daily reports of your online activity to make sure that's the case. Understood?"

"Yes, sir," she said, beginning to cry again as a week without Rheanna solidified into reality.

"I'll keep you occupied," her 3V voice promised. Teased, really.

"Go to your room," he said. "I want you in bed by . . ." He looked at the clock, which showed 8:30. "I want you in bed, lights out, by 9:30, understood?"

"Yes, sir."

"You're dismissed."

Getting up from the couch, her mother's hand slipping slowly down her back as she pulled away, Elizabeth was relieved and despondent at the same time. But at least it was over. She made her way down the stairs from the living room.

"Not too quickly, or he'll get you for that too."

When she got to her room she closed the door and got into bed, pulling the pillow over her head. Without her 3V world, the pillow and closed door were the only things that muffled the yelling.

"Well, that should take care of it for today," David said, unmuting *Web Report*. "Tomorrow on the other hand, I'm not so—"

"Oh, shut *up*," said Susan. Her voice rose quickly, thunder in front of an approaching storm. David stared at her, dumbstruck. "Don't you know *why* she left today, David? Don't you understand that you can't talk to your own daughter?"

He muted *Web Report* again and stood up, putting his hands on his hips. "Enlighten me, since you seem to know everything."

"You push her too *hard*." Susan's hands were out, her fingers working, as if she could somehow help him grasp what she was saying. "You're always threatening her with failure. Do you know what it's like at her age to be warned against being a failure day after day by the man you look up to more than any other in the world?"

"Do you *really* have to ask that question?"

Susan stood up too then, her hands now clenched fists at her side. "No, I suppose not. But that's why you of *all* people should understand her!"

"Then what do you want me to do?" He was shouting now. "Let her get away with disobeying me? Enable her failure in school? Set her up to fail for the rest of her life?"

Susan's head drooped. "There it is *again*! You measure everything in her so many different ways that none of it means a goddamned thing! So all you do is confuse her. You hold your love out to her on a stick, a reward for applying herself. Some parents spoil their kids with *stuff*. You promise you'll love her *if* she measures up to your definition of success!"

"That's not true!"

"Of course it is! Everything you do shows it, whether you know it or not! Jesus, David, you were more upset when I told you about the monitor's call than you were when I told you she was out after dark." Susan was close to tears now herself. She heard the words she was saying, and hearing them out loud showed her just how bad things had gotten.

They stood there, faces taut, each daring the other's eyes to give ground. David looked away and turned around to find his chair. He fell into it. Susan remained standing, her eyes never leaving him, pinning him to the mat of his recliner.

"That's not true either," he said. His voice was level. "I'm just as worried about her as you are."

Susan took a deep breath. "But that's not what I hear from you, David. That's not what you *say*. That's not what she *sees*."

"I don't give a good goddamned what you . . ." He grimaced. The hounds of his anger were dragging him forward into rage. He could feel their leashes straining. But he held on. "You should know me well enough by now to know that I worry as much as you," David said coolly. "For godsakes, we've been married long enough."

Susan sat back down on the couch. *He's relaxing, now you relax*, her mind advised her. "I used to think I knew you. Before we moved back here."

He flashed her a look. It warned her not to start *that* particular argument. *Let's at least finish the one we're having first, deal?*

After fifteen years of marriage, she knew what the look meant. "David, for once I'm not digging at you for coming back here. But it's this *town*. It's cursed or something. I can't imagine why—"

"Jesus, *please*—"

Susan threw up her hands to ward him off. "I'm sorry. It's just that—"

"It's a safer community, Sue!" David heard his own raised voice and flinched away from it. He lowered his tone. *Down, boy.* "We talked about this. It's simpler living here."

"*We* talked about it," murmured Susan, "then *you* made the decision to move back here."

"Here we go—"

"But I'm telling you, David," she said, cutting the other debate short, "it's this *town*. She has no real friends here. And kids need more than . . ." She motioned at the muted *Web Report* with its horizontally scrolling numbers and interactive stock-buying options. "She needs more than the Web." *And so do I,* she thought but didn't say for once.

"She's making friends. It takes time to get adjusted. I realize that."

Susan grabbed onto that. "Then *tell her that*. Don't come down on her so hard. *Help* her. Don't berate her."

David stared at the scrolling numbers on the screen. He forced himself not to focus on the MerChrysler numbers. "I'll talk to her again tomorrow, after school."

"Better yet, talk *with* her. David, she's a wonderful girl."

"I *know* that," he said defensively. *Don't you think I know my own daughter?*

"Almost a teenager."

He rolled his eyes. He remembered what he and Theron had looked for in teenaged girls. At that moment he recalled the ridiculous memory that he and Theron had pooled their money to buy X-ray glasses from the back of a comic book so they could see through girls' clothing. The X-ray specs hadn't worked, dammit. *Jesus, what am I thinking?*

"She's growing up," Susan pressed. "We have to help her with that."

"Don't remind me," was all he said, running his hand through his hair. He unmuted *Web Report*.

Susan, sensing maybe she had made some progress, let the conversation end there. She walked into the kitchen to putter around. Nothing really needed to be done. She'd spent her day worrying over Elizabeth's whereabouts and cleaning the house so much it almost shined.

David sat in the living room, hearing *Web Report* but not really listening to it, unable to think of anything else but the body language of the two people he loved most in the world as they'd sat on that couch.

They pulled away from me.

He played the scene over in his mind. He had leaned forward; they had leaned back.

They felt safer sitting away from me.

He rewound it again, replayed it. And again.

They felt the need *to feel safer.*

The thought broke his heart.

CHAPTER 17

Elizabeth pulled the pillow down tighter over her head. The Parent-Free Zone sign on her door implied they couldn't enter without her say-so, though sometimes, like now, she couldn't keep even their voices out. Still, it remained her sacred space, unspoiled by unwelcome visitors if nowhere else but in her mind.

She lay face down on her bed, tempted to cry more but ashamed for wanting to. Instead, she settled for clamping the pillow over her head. She thought about her fantasy world, imagining the landscape of Rheanna around her. The smell of the horses and the blooming sweetness of the green grass. The power of the horse beneath her and the feel of his muscles as she rode across the plain. Her Companions riding at her side to meet the evil Mallus on the field of battle.

But it just wasn't the same. She couldn't really smell Rheanna's grass. Caomos didn't jostle and jolt her in the saddle. No Companions pledged fealty to her, come what may. There was only the dull roar of her own blood pounding, amplified by her stopped-up ears. And it was already getting hot under the pillow.

She took it off her head and sat up, brushing her tangled hair from her eyes. Elizabeth could hear another dull roar now, the low, occasionally not-so-low argument between her parents. Her mother once called it a "disagreement" when Elizabeth had asked her about it a long time ago. As if using that word to describe the yelling and cursing could somehow make it better, maybe even soften the loud voices in her memory's ear.

But children always know.

And so she called it an argument in her head and never asked her mother again what it really was because Elizabeth already knew, and all the calling-it-something-else in the world couldn't convince her it was anything other than what it was.

"Let's get in the tank," her 3V voice said.

No.

"They're too busy arguing. We can ride in Rheanna—"

"I said no!" Elizabeth shouted it out loud, a ringing echo in her sanctuary that drowned out the mumbling, heated voices from the other room. She put her fists to her temples, hoping the pressure would drive out the demon voice tempting her to do what she knew she shouldn't. Seeing no other option, she was about to put the pillow over her head again when she heard the scraping at the window. It was a quiet, shy sound, and it spooked her. She turned slowly

(don't bother, monsters can still see you)

and stared at the glass. The glare of the streetlight sliced through the window. The automatic shading for the window was turned off, so only clear glass separated her from whatever had made the sound. The curtains hung to either side as if framing a stage, ready to show her— what?

The scraping came again, this time a little louder. There was a specter arm, elongated by the streetlight, reaching up to the window. It made its scratching noise again and was gone. Never taking her eyes off the window, Elizabeth curled up very slowly into a fetal position.

(he sees you when you're sleeping)

She bunched her fists under her chin and held her arms in close. Again the scrape came, louder than ever, and then a larger image—a head—moved behind the glass. She almost screamed when it noticed her. Did it smile?

(he knows when you're awake)

"If you can't go to Mallus, maybe Mallus has come to you," her 3V voice said.

Shut up.

"Or sent a Wolf Rider to do his bidding."

Shut up!

(he knows when you've been bad or good)

But this wasn't 3V.

This was real.

And there was no such thing as Mallus or Wolf Riders in the real world. There were no Companions, no enemy army. The thought reassured Elizabeth for a moment, then pained her with its truth. How often had she wished that Rheanna *could* be her real world and that she never had to come back to this one? How many times had she been willing to take on Mallus instead of her father? How much easier would that battle have been?

But perhaps it *was* possible, somehow. Perhaps Mallus—the Dark King, the First Enemy—had come for her. All the way from Rheanna to her sanctuary.

(so be good, for goodness sake)

But if that was true, then it was also true that if she were Elsbyth in the world of 3V, then she could be Elsbyth in this world too. And Elsbyth wasn't afraid of Mallus. He had killed Ulaemeth, her beloved. And she would cleave Mallus with her sword for stealing him away from her.

"Um, what sword?" asked her 3V voice.

Then I will use my hands, Elizabeth thought, no longer fearing the shadow at the window. She uncurled her body slowly, less prey and more cat, now. The sweat from her fear soaked into the comforter as she moved over the bed. Quickly, her hands were dry.

All the better to strangle you with, she thought.

Elizabeth positioned herself below the window. The next time the sound came, she would find its source. And strangle Mallus, the Murderer of Ulaemeth.

She reached up and unlocked the sliding-glass window, then coiled both hands close to her chest like whips. And she waited. Since there was no screen, the trap would be easy to spring.

When the rapping came again, Elizabeth jumped up, whipping the window open. She grabbed Mallus by his shirt and yanked him hard against the outside of the house. The Dark King's groan of pain was very satisfying. Still, he felt way lighter than she'd expected

(spirit bodies are not heavy)

as she pulled his face into the slanting light, eye-to-eye with her.

"AAAAAAAAAAAAAAAAAAAGH!" shrieked Mallus.

"EEEEEEEAAAAA!" screamed Elsbyth, Warrior-Queen of Rheanna.

"Elizabeth?"

Michael's voice was relieved, embarrassed, and excited, all at the same time.

"*You're* not Mallus," Elizabeth said.

"No," said Michael hesitantly, as if internally debating that perhaps he *could* be Mallus, if that's what Elizabeth wanted him to be.

"Well," she began, her voice indignant, "what the hell are you doing at my window at ten o'clock at night?"

"Um, well," he began hesitantly, and then it spilled out of him all at once: "I thought you might be feeling a little bad about what happened in school today, so I waited till my parents thought I was asleep and I climbed out my window and came over here and rapped on your window hoping to get a chance to see you and I thought I could maybe make you feel better."

Elizabeth was impressed that he got all that out considering she still had him pressed chest-first against the window sill. Her first impulse—on a day when everyone except perhaps the homeless man in Old Suzie's house had seemed out to get her—was to kiss Michael for riding to her rescue. But that idea scared her more than the thought of finding a real Mallus at her window ever had, so she released him instead and heard a satisfying crunch of leaves as the boy's weight settled.

"What'd you have in mind?" she asked innocently.

Michael ducked his head.

"I dunno. I just wanted to make you feel better."

Inwardly Elizabeth smiled, though she kept her face neutral, in case he could see her despite the night. "I know someplace we can go."

Michael brightened. "Really, where?"

She placed her knee on the low bookshelf below her window. "You'll see," she said, climbing over the windowsill to drop onto the cool grass.

Elizabeth led him along the side of her house to the street. She tried to stay out of the streetlight as much as she could, in case anyone happened to be looking out their window. A neighbor's dog barked at their passing, and the two of them froze. After a moment, Elizabeth motioned Michael to follow her, and they were off again and made their way calmly down the street. They walked in silence for a while. Elizabeth seemed to be somewhere else, and Michael hesitated to say anything for fear of saying The One Wrong Thing.

"Did you get in trouble?" Michael asked finally, unable to stand the silence.

"Course," she said.

"Monitor Skinner called after all, huh?"

"*Course.*"

Her tone seemed to wonder why he would even ask such a stupid question. Michael thought he shouldn't speak again. Everything had been going pretty well before he'd said anything. "You didn't miss much in class," he said anyway. "It was really boring there without you."

"Really?" She looked back at him and saw the moonlight reflecting on his teeth as he grinned to himself.

"Yes." He whispered the word. "Debbie Maselic got three questions wrong in a row and then didn't say anything for the rest of the day!"

"Really? Debbie? I thought she *never* got a question wrong!"

"Well, she did today," he said brightly, glad he'd hit upon something that pleased her. They walked along and he said, "Did your dad take away your 3V privileges again?"

Even in the pale night he could see her shoulders slump. *Stupid, stupid, stupid!* his thoughts pounded him.

"Yes," she said heavily, "for a whole week." Her voice had curdled in his ears again.

Stupid, stupid, stupid! He decided to try to make it better. "Only a week? That's not *too* long."

She exploded at him, "It's for*ever* in that house!"

Stupid, stupid...

Michael again decided to keep his mouth shut. Then, Elizabeth stopped. He thought she would turn on him and lay into him again. *Oh God, why can't you just keep your friggin mouth shut, Mike?*

"We're here," was all she said.

He blinked, not understanding her at first. "We're where?"

"*Here.*"

Michael turned and stared at Old Suzie's house. "You gotta be kiddin," he said.

"Nope."

"So now what're we supposed to do?"

Elizabeth said, as if explaining to an infant, "We're going *in*, of course!"

Michael was horrified at the thought. Then he noticed his muscles constricting and tried to relax, to keep the fear from his face. His father had always told him not to show his emotions, *especially* to girls. "Oh," was all he said.

"You're not afraid, are you?"

"No, I'm not afraid!" he said a little too quickly. Michael stuck his hands in his pockets and looked down at the ground, finding the gravel quite fascinating.

"Well, come on then," she said, leading the way.

He stared after her openmouthed, unable to believe this was the same girl who hadn't wanted to go near the house just two days before. Even though he was scared, he also thought it was pretty neat that she was marching right up to the porch.

"Okay, I'll come along," Michael called after her as he jogged to catch up. "You know, just to make sure you're okay."

And though she didn't really know what she was doing yet, Elizabeth fell into the familiar response that women give when they know men are playing a part because they have to or they wouldn't be men. "That would be nice." She said her own lines quite convincingly. And she halfway meant it when she continued, "I'd feel much safer if you did." She walked up to the porch and placed her arm on the rickety railing and waited for Michael to catch up.

"It sure looks spooky in there," he said. There was a small light flickering—a candle, no doubt—and Michael wondered if Old Suzie was in there getting her cauldron ready. *Boiling water, vegetables, seasoning . . . only one thing missing. Oh! Here are the children now!*

"Is that what you see when you look at this old house?" asked Elizabeth.

"Well . . . *yeah*. Whata *you* see?"

"I saw the same thing until earlier today. But now I don't think it's so bad."

Michael stared at her. "Uh-huh." Was she nuts?

She stepped up onto the porch and stopped at the door. She knocked three times.

Michael stared at her. "Why knock, unless—"

"Shhhh," Elizabeth said, index finger to her lips. Michael wondered why she did that. She *had* just knocked. But suddenly he was very worried. Maybe Old Suzie had enlisted Elizabeth in her ranks. Yeah, brainwashed her, maybe. And her assignment was to bring other kids to the house to put into the cauldron for dinner. It was Old Suzie's revenge for all those broken windows and dare-runs through the old place. All those times they had disturbed her shows. Old people liked to can things, put them up on the shelf for eating later. She probably put canned kids up on the shelves to tide her over in the winter.

The screen door began to creak on its hinges, and suddenly Michael's bladder was full to bursting. Then he saw it wasn't an old woman who answered the door at all but an old man.

"Well, hello again!" he said to Elizabeth.

"Hello, Rocky."

"Who's your friend?"

"His name's Michael."

"Well, hello, Michael. Glad to meet you. Y'all come on in."

The old man led them inside and into the parlor. Michael looked around in wonder at the old house, as if he were passing through a ghost.

Maybe he's one, the boy thought, looking at the old man. *Suzie's run-off husband cursed to come back and haunt the house.*

A dog lay on the floor in front of the old man's chair. She raised her eyelids, took note of who'd entered her domain, and slowly closed her eyes again, satisfied all was well.

"You are *so* brave," Michael whispered to Elizabeth. He couldn't help himself. They were in *Old Suzie's house*. Elizabeth only smiled as she sat down on the floor and the old man settled into his chair again. He'd lit a small fire in the fireplace. It was turning into a cool night.

"So what brings you back so soon?"

Elizabeth hesitated, though she felt she could trust him. At least he hadn't given her a reason *not* to trust him. "My dad got upset because I got kicked out of class today. He revoked my 3V privileges for a week."

"Oh," said the old man. "And you think that was unfair?"

"Of course . . ." began Michael, but he stopped when he saw Elizabeth shaking her head.

"Not really, I suppose. But a week without 3V is pretty harsh. He thinks he's punishing me for doing poorly in school. But . . . he doesn't understand."

The old man leaned forward and the firelight danced on his face. "Spoken like a million other children before you," he said, nodding. "Including your dad, I'll bet. So, what doesn't he understand?"

Elizabeth shrugged, looking at the floor.

"It's the place she goes when her parents fight," said Michael. With that simple statement, all was revealed. Elizabeth felt her cheeks burning as the truth was blurted out so clumsily. But the old man seemed not embarrassed at all.

"Ah, now I see," he said. "Have you talked this over with your parents?"

Elizabeth looked at him, astonished at the notion. "Are you kidding?"

"Hmm, I guess that *would* be out of the question, now wouldn't it?" His tone was playful.

"You don't know her dad," Michael said.

"You might be surprised what I know," said the old man, his voice heavy. Michael took it as a sign that he shouldn't respond. Rocky continued, "So you came here to get away from your folks?"

Elizabeth nodded, again self-conscious. When he spoke it like that, so directly, it seemed like such a trivial reason for disturbing the old man's evening.

"I didn't want to come," Michael said before he could stop himself.

"Oh? Why's that?"

The boy swallowed hard once, not daring a glance at Elizabeth. "I'm afraid of ghosts."

The old man laughed. "Is that what you think I am?" he asked seriously. "A ghost?"

"No," Michael said immediately, then paused and shrugged. "I dunno. Maybe."

"He's afraid of Old Suzie," stated Elizabeth.

"Am not," said Michael, but unconvincingly.

"Well then," said the old man, clapping his hands together lightly, "let's talk about Old Suzie. And ghosts."

Long after Susan had gone to bed, David sat in his recliner in the living room, the always-streaming *Web Report* on the screen. The commentators were animated as usual, but he wasn't really looking at the numbers or listening to them. He was thinking about what Susan had said and replaying for the thousandth time in his mind how he'd handled Elizabeth's dismissal from school. Maybe he *did* push her too hard. Maybe he expected too much out of her.

Or not enough from yourself.

"What the hell does that mean?" he asked out loud. But his brain didn't answer.

Why *had* he moved back here? And why did he get so upset when Susan asked him that question? Was it because of what she asked or the way she asked it, in that accusatory, it's-all-your-fault tone? But— why *had* he moved back here?

Web Report was interrupted by a bulletin. The prisoner who'd escaped from Huntsville still hadn't been found. A 3-D picture of Wayne Alan Kitts flashed on the screen, and the grizzled old face had a leer to it that fit with his child-molester record. David focused on that. *That* was why he'd moved them here.

Because it was a safer place. Huntsville was close to Houston, and Houston was not safe, well-to-do neighborhood or no. But maybe there was another reason. A need to come back here, plant the flag, reclaim the territory for himself.

Maybe Susan was right about that. He winced at granting his wife's point but couldn't set the acknowledgment aside. Maybe he'd merely been selfish by insisting they come back here. Maybe his concern for Elizabeth had just been an excuse.

No. He loved his daughter more than his own life. He truly believed it was safer here. Or that he could *make* it safer here for her. That he could come back here and slay the dragon that had slept idle and ever present, breathing sulfur in the back of his mind for so long. And then nothing could harm her. But somehow that quest, the one he'd never even known he was on, had gotten twisted back on itself. And now his wife and daughter were pulling away from him. *Leaning* away from him.

They felt safer sitting away from me. They felt the need *to feel safer*.

How had things become so warped?

David stood up and walked from the living room, through the hallway, and to Elizabeth's room. He paused at her door, not wanting to wake or disturb her, staring at the Parent-Free Zone sign. He remembered how it used to be for him, his room. A base where no one could tag you to be it. That's the way he'd always felt about it when he was a boy. But he wanted to look in on her, know she was safe in her bed. He cracked the door just a bit and, when he couldn't see very well, finally opened it all the way. And saw the gaping window, its curtains billowing softly.

He looked around the room again, sure he must've just missed her. "Light," he said, and the overhead bulb blazed on. The room was empty. Had she run away again? His anger boiled up from inside, all his previous thoughts drowning in it. But then he noticed the bed.

It was a disaster. The covers were a mess, as if . . . as if someone had taken her. She had struggled. They'd dragged her out the window.

They.

The anonymous monsters that every parent knows really exist. The ones that don't hide in closets. The ones that come through windows.

What had *Web Report* been going on about? The escaped prisoner, Kidd or whatever his name was. Some detail was picking at David's brain, something about . . . the fugitive's home town?

"Susan!" His panic overwhelmed his anger. "*Susan!*"

CHAPTER 18

Aiming for the river, Kitts yanked his legs away from the bull nettles and Mesquite bushes grabbing at him. He didn't need to look back. He could already hear the dogs behind him. They wouldn't stop, so he couldn't either. His hands slapped at branches. The Trinity River wasn't far.

His breath sounded like a blade cutting wood, lungs aching with the effort. His bones hurt with the tight grind of age. His side was splitting, so he reached down to press, relieving some of the pain. When he felt the wet, he stumbled to a halt, brought his hand up to his face.

"Oh, shit," he rasped. "Jesus fucking Christ."

The blood cooled on his fingertips. The demon in the back of his head tempted him to lick his fingers. He was very thirsty.

"Those sumbitches shot me!"

He stared at the blood in disbelief. Kitts had thought the pain in his side was just the stitch you got from being old and out of shape. Adrenaline had kept him from knowing any different before, but the high had worn off now, and he felt every step, every year. It was like he'd been holding a handful of top spades heading for that ace-high royal flush, and then drew a club—right color, wrong suit. *So close.* The stab to his psyche hurt almost as much as his side.

But for one card I coulda won this little poker game. But for one lucky bastard making one lucky shot, I coulda made it.

He turned around and looked behind him, wishing he could turn back the clock now that he knew how the game would end. Groundhog Day it, try again tomorrow, and maybe next time the bastard wouldn't be such a good shot.

(too late for that)

"Goddammit!"

The blood coursing through his head was loud, too loud. Then he realized the rushing sound he heard was the Trinity. Couldn't be more than fifty yards in front of him. Now that he looked, Kitts could see the bright light of the moon dancing off white caps in the river. It was high, flooding with the first good Central Texas rain since July. Maybe he could float his way downriver, pick up on the other bank and head out again to boost a car at some all-night stop-and-shop on I-45.

(or maybe you'll just bleed out)

Kitts took in a deep breath and his lungs stuck him again. It felt like every time he breathed, he tore the wound open further. He stuck his finger in the hole and gritted his way through the exploration. He couldn't find the bullet and that was bad. That meant it was deep. Maybe gotten to the vitals.

Vittles, his grandmother's voice said in his head. She had always called dinner "vittles" when he was a boy.

Maybe that was why his lungs ached so badly, why he was so out of breath.

It's probably just old age and your slovenly ways, his head said in granny's voice.

(you hope)

If I only had another chance, he thought. *I'd break out and they wouldn't even see me.*

He fought a step at a time now for the river. "It was Stu, that stupid fuck," he told the nettles, struggling through. "*Stu* is short for stupid fuck!"

He reached the river's edge. A voice told him the water's roar would keep him from hearing the dogs. But hounds didn't need to hear, and they could run a lot faster than he could. And a lot longer.

And they ain't been shot, the Cooler King in his head offered coldly.

He followed the current upriver with his eyes. About a quarter mile down he saw a house on the bank, bright light against the black country night. Kitts knew that house. The warden's house. Ten years ago he'd been a trusty and almost taken his chance then.

Why didn't you, at least you were younger and, oh yeah, not shot, said the King.

But the guards had watched him like a hawk, so he hadn't moved. That was when Deadeye Floyd Parker had been warden. Pretty soon Ramirez had stepped up to the plate and taken his place, and Kitts was back on Shit Patrol, never allowed to leave the walls.

That's Ramirez's house, it dawned on him. And he realized in that instant God was on his side after all. He hadn't lost the game. The rules had just changed. He would make it after all. And he'd get a little more in the kitty to boot.

He dragged through the shallow water along the Trinity's shore toward the house, keeping one ear cocked for the dogs he hoped he was confusing. He let himself savor the images inside his head. Images of Ramirez begging for his life, of Ramirez's head caving in— the wet, cracking sound of his skull as Kitts swung a crowbar or baseball bat or anything else he could get his hands on.

Thank you, God, he thought, shivering.

Kitts almost slipped as he came up the muddy bank but caught himself. He ignored the persistent pain in his side as he stood up. He never took his eyes off the house. He saw now that it was the kitchen light that shone on the river. A figure was moving inside, only a hazy form at this distance. Kitts picked up his speed, the wound and hounds all but forgotten, the adrenaline flowing again.

He sidled up next to the house and leaned against it for a moment, then sank down to his knees, catching a ragged breath. He could ignore the pain stabbing at him from his lungs, but not so easily the wave of nausea drifting up his gullet. Kitts braced himself and slid forward till he was under the kitchen window. He knew if he let himself sit there, it would be where they'd find him, stuck like a pig and bled out. After another heavy breath, he pushed himself up to a crouch, his knee joints popping in protest. The mud was hard and cold under his knees. He could still hear the hounds, but they didn't seem any closer. Patting himself on the back for the river trick, Kitts whispered, "Fuck you, bitches."

His eyes crept up over the window sill. He blinked, adjusting to the kitchen light, then ducked quickly as a figure moved into view not two feet on the other side of the window. He heard the clank of dinner dishes, scraps grinding down the disposal, plates slipping into neat rows in the sonic dishwasher. Kitts chanced another glance inside. He saw her then, the light shining around her.

Caroline.

Ho-ho-ho, Ramirez's wife now, not just some piece of the week. Well, well, well.

He'd only seen her that one time before, when Ramirez had humbled him thirty years ago. Kitts remembered her coming to visit her beau on duty like it was yesterday, that day he'd been scoping out the fence and Ramirez busted his balls. Her name had stayed in his brain like a brand.

Caroline.

Kitts wrapped his tongue around her name, caressed it. He licked it into existence.

"Caroline," he whispered.

She had been in her late twenties then, Kitts guessed, remembering what he'd seen. A brunette in jeans, cowboy boots, a sleeveless buttoned shirt, sunglasses.

A walking-talking reason to escape was what she'd been.

Full breasts and narrow hips, the slimmest hips he had ever seen on a woman, and he could tell just by looking at them they hadn't yet birthed any babies. She had given Ramirez a sweet smile of promise and affection, and Kitts had stopped his escape planning and recorded the moment as she'd leaned up to kiss the sergeant on his cocksucking mouth, her scarf blowing in the breeze. Kitts had imagined her soft closeness, the smell of a woman, the thing he thought he missed most about sex with them. As she'd smooched her beau, Kitts's own lips had pursed as if he were Ramirez. He'd kissed her name on the wind.

Caroline.

He'd masturbated in his bunk for weeks to the vision of her on that basketball court until her face had been lost among the thousands of women they smuggled in over the Web. Eventually, he'd forgotten her in a blonde, brunette, and redheaded montage of tits, cunts, and asses. That is to say, he'd forgotten her face. But never her name.

Caroline.

And now, here she was on the other side of the window. Anything but his vision, anything but his fantasy.

Wrinkled. Tired. Washing dishes.

Her skin resembled the dishrag slung over the lip of the sink—used up, wrung out one too many times.

Look what Ramirez has done to her.

Kitts couldn't believe his eyes. The vision of her reaching up, kissing her then-boyfriend. Sometimes he substituted himself in Ramirez's place when he remembered it. It all came rushing back to him—standing on that basketball court three decades ago, watching her lean up and kiss Ramirez.

It should've been you. Cheated again, he thought.

The old woman washing dishes inside the house seemed a surreal corruption of the vision he'd first met. Someone had abducted the body of that goddess and sucked the life out of it. Kitts cursed the fact that he could still recognize her, because that meant it was really her. Caroline. Not as he'd remembered her—until he'd forgotten her—but what she had become.

Old.

She glanced without seeing toward the window, and he ducked his head again. Moving on his hands and knees, Kitts made his way to the front of the house. There was no car in the front driveway, so Ramirez must be gone.

(prisoner escape)

Of course he's gone, dumbass. Jesus, worse than Stu.

"*Fuck off,*" he whispered.

Kitts staggered to his feet and slowly climbed the wooden steps of the porch. He turned the front doorknob slightly. The knob was a little squeaky but not locked. That surprised him. *Prisoner escape and Ramirez didn't even bother to lock his front door?* Maybe country habits die hard. *Or maybe Ramirez is just a dumbass. Either way, I win.*

He cracked open the door and heard the dishes still clinking in the kitchen.

Moving inside, he slowly closed the door behind him. Looking around, he allowed himself a moment to notice the normalcy of it all. The coat closet, the family portrait of someone's ancestors on the wall. *Prob'ly hers. They're white*, he thought. The hardwood floor. The light from the living room. Insignificant things, unless you haven't seen them in thirty years.

The dishes clanked. Kitts stepped quickly into the living room. It was a dull yellow in color, and he thought a piss-yellow living room fit Ramirez to a tee. A couch, two chairs, a coffee table, a 3V center, a fireplace—all the amenities of home. Ramirez's home, anyway.

But Ramirez wasn't home.

(prisoner escape)

Which meant that Caroline was likely alone. Ramirez had never had any children; it was common knowledge and a running joke around the prison. *No Deadeye Floyd Parker, this one. Ramirez cain't shoot straight, haw-haw.*

Kitts walked over to the mantel piece. Grinning to himself, he picked out a poker from the fireplace tools and leaned on it for a minute as his side flared up again. His belly felt bloated, though he hadn't eaten in hours. But strangely, after all his exertion to escape, he wasn't hungry. In fact, the thought of food made him more nauseous. But he ignored that, feeling the cold steel of the fireplace poker in his hand. *Lost one poker game earlier*, he thought, smiling at his own word-play. *Now I've got me a new play in hand.*

He heard the dishwasher begin to hum. She was finishing up in the kitchen. No, not *she*.

Caroline.

Kitts sat down in what he assumed was Ramirez's recliner and waited for her to emerge. *Can Caroline come out to play?* his thought giggled. But he didn't laugh out loud. His side hurt too much.

"Rudy?"

The chair faced the 3V center, away from the kitchen door. All Caroline could see was the top of a man's head in the chair. It was gray like her husband's but dirty. She thought it strange that she didn't really recognize the back of her own husband's head.

"Hello, Caroline."

Not quite her husband's voice. *Not even close.*

Against all common sense, she walked over to the chair. The man stood up and Caroline rared back. An abomination clotted with mud and blood stood in front of her. The now-battered cardboard armor that had protected Kitts as he climbed over the razor wire made him look like he'd donned a hellish version of a child's robot costume for Halloween. His left side was wet. Caroline looked down and had the fleeting thought that the blood stain where he'd sat in Rudy's chair would be hell to get out of the fabric.

"Wha-what do you want?"

The abomination smiled. "Thirty years ago, if you'd only asked me that question. Instead, you laughed at me."

Kitts raised the poker in his right hand.

Caroline's mind screamed at her to run, but her feet seemed deaf. She knitted her eyebrows, trying to see past the dirt and years. "I don't even know you."

"You don't . . ." The man gasped, the poker faltering. Caroline assumed it was the stitch in his side. She had been married to law enforcement long enough to know a gunshot wound when she saw one. "How can you say that to me?" the dirty old man asked.

Caroline's feet were waking up now. She began to back away from him. Kitts advanced on her, step for step.

"I'm telling you, we've never met," she said. "I have no idea who you are."

The man deflated in front of her, then seeing she saw it, bowed up again and raised his weapon. "You're not my Caroline. You stole her body and used it all up."

"What . . .?" But she stopped, realizing that everything she'd said so far had only made things worse. "What do you want?" she finally repeated.

Kitts stopped, considering her question. Then, pointing to the phone with the poker, he said, "I want you to call your husband. Tell him there's a fire. The cat died. There's a cockroach in the kitchen. I don't give a shit what you tell him. But you get him here. Without suspicion."

Caroline shook her head. "I'm not bringing him here for you. You're that escaped prisoner they called him in for, aren't you? You'll just kill him."

Kitts raised a finger and wagged it from side to side. "I promise to let you both live. But I want to see him first. Talk to him face-to-face. Do that and I let you both live. I'll even turn myself in. It'll be a big coup for *Rudy*. Don't do it, and I promise you he'll die soon after you do."

She made the call.

"He says he's coming, but he's not happy about it, I can tell."

"Poor Rudy. Now, turn around and face the wall."

"What? Why?"

"I'm going to tie you up. *Turn around and face the wall.*"

She did as she was told. When she heard his next words, she knew complying had been a mistake.

"You stole it and used it all up, you bitch. And now you've even tainted my memories."

She heard the thin whoosh before she felt it, and then she felt nothing. Kitts smiled as he murdered the usurper harpy, hacking the curved tooth of the poker into her skull.

Kitts caught her as she crumpled, wrinkling his nose at the brains leaking onto his arm. He slid her to the floor, straining his side. He stood up with a deep breath and raised the steel rod again. And again. He pounded her skull, obliterating her face until there was nothing left but a bloody ruin, a madman's pumpkin carving of jagged lines and dripping holes. The pale yellow of the living room wall was dotted with red now, the floor slashed with blood and brains. Kitts stood up and stared at his handiwork, glad that he'd taken revenge on Caroline's doppelgänger, knowing that somewhere her spirit was silently thanking him for trying his best to preserve her perfection in his mind's eye.

He returned to the recliner in the living room, sat down with a heave of exhaustion only the old can really understand. His belly felt full to bursting now. He sat and waited.

It took almost fifteen minutes for the warden to get back home, and he wasn't sure what to expect as he stepped out of his car and onto the porch. When Carrie had told him she needed him home, he'd gotten mad. His job was on the line, and of all the sumbitches to escape, it had to be Kitts! Just *had* to be. And then Carrie had mentioned her hip giving her fits and their still-missing cat and how worried she was. But they didn't have a cat.

So he'd rounded up six county officers and asked them to give him a five-minute head start so he could scope out the situation. And now, as he mounted the steps to his own home—certain in the knowledge Kitts had violated that sanctity and burning with anger at the thought—he wasn't sure what awaited him.

The front door was hard to open, had become wedged against something. Kitts must've moved a bureau in front of it. *Best to move quickly*, thought Ramirez, putting his shoulder against the door. It scraped open slowly as Ramirez forced his way into the room, expecting to see Kitts there, possibly armed, waiting to cap him. What he saw instead was the dead weight of Caroline's body, pressed hard between the door and the wall.

Ramirez stared in shock. Her face was an ugly mess. His heart stopped in his chest as he stood, transfixed, looking at the bloody monster that had once been his beautiful wife, the best part of his life. His hands began to sweat, his chest expanding with the cold certainty of being too late.

"*Caroline—*"

In the moment of Ramirez's awe, the murderer came at him from the living room with the poker. Gasping for breath against his burning side wound, Kitts leaned forward, hoping to add his body weight to the waning strength in his arm. The rod fell short, embedding itself high on Ramirez's collarbone and raking down across his chest. Shouting his horror, the warden pushed himself backward, away from the blow. Kitts fell to the floor on top of Caroline, crying out as the shock of the fall brought new pain from his side. He lifted himself off the dead husk that had once been his wet dream

(wet work dream now)

and grabbed for the weapon he'd let go. Kitts pushed himself up to stand, crooked and leaning to his left to avoid stretching the wound again. Ramirez was still on the floor fumbling for his pistol, and Kitts knew if he didn't move now, he'd be dead.

He lurched forward as Ramirez pulled the pistol out of its holster.

"You murdering *bastard*!" Ramirez screamed through the tears of his loss.

His eyes sharpened to clarity by pain, Kitts swung hard, knocking the gun from Ramirez's hand. The warden watched the blurry arc of the poker as Kitts raised it for a backswing. Ramirez used all his strength to push himself backward along the floor. The rod wooshed through the space he'd been a second before. The warden shook his eyes clear.

Kitts seemed to be enjoying the game. Raising the poker again, he said, "I told you I'd kill you, you motherfucker." But Ramirez moved forward, not away, in and under the arc of the swing as it came down. He took the old murderer's legs out from under him, and Kitts fell on top of him, his weapon clanging to the floor. Before Kitts could recover, Ramirez turned him over, pinning him to the ground with his weight, pummeling and screaming at him. Kitts reached out a hand and, remarkably, found the poker with one grab. He brought it up clumsily to bash the side of the warden's head. The blow wasn't piercing but still dazed Ramirez, who fell to one side. Kitts struggled up slowly, powered by the widower's moans and the memory of that day on the basketball court when a sergeant had humbled a defenseless inmate in front of a woman. In front of Caroline.

Kitts spat on Ramirez, who laid there, delirious from the blow.

"I told you I'd kill you, you motherfucker," he said again, raising his arm.

Sirens in the distance.

Kitts stopped and stared past the corpse of the fake Caroline into the black night beyond the front door. He knew he had a minute or two before the troopers got here. Ramirez was crawling away from him now, would get to his weapon before Kitts could get to him, and while the two of them continued their mano-a-mano, the troopers would be storming the porch.

To hell with this.

Kitts dropped the poker and lurched away like Quasimodo. He felt as much as heard the shot from Ramirez's pistol hit the door facing as he passed into the kitchen. His hand fumbled with the back door knob before he realized it was locked. He heard Ramirez lifting himself off the floor, bellowing his rage in great gasping breaths, and finally Kitts had the deadbolt released and the door opened. He was out of the house and tripping through the night for the Trinity River again as the warden appeared in the doorway behind him, an avenging shadow. Kitts heard the troopers' cars grind to a halt on the shale driveway around the front of the house, saw the eerie reflections of their red and blue lights in his peripheral vision. But he didn't allow himself the luxury of looking back.

Ramirez took aim at the black figure loping toward the river and fired two shots that missed. Troopers were coming through the house to the kitchen and around from the front with hounds.

"Sonofabitch murdered my wife! He's going for the river. I want him *dead*, you understand me? Let the dogs have him first. When they get tired, you can shoot him."

"But Warden, if he surrenders—" began one of the younger officers.

He was cut off as his sergeant stepped in front of him. "We understand, sir." Turning back to the rookie, the sergeant said, "This man won't give himself up, Bob. He ain't the kind to. Understand?"

Whether he understood or not, the rookie nodded. They fanned out, and Ramirez led them toward the river.

Reaching the riverbank, Kitts heard the pursuers coming. Mostly he heard the dogs baying, but that was soon drowned out by the rushing water. The pain in his side warned him against attempting to swim, but the hounds urged him to it. He waded into the river for a few feet, then dove in, letting the current take him. A few random gunshots splashed the water nearby, and then the sounds of his pursuers began to fall off behind him.

He began to swim, and each stroke was like a knife dragging through his wound. He'd beaten the posse, knew they wouldn't catch him now. The river was just too fast. But he also knew, as his strokes became heavier, his stomach like the blood sac of a tick on a dog, he'd misjudged the water's temperature.

Who'd've thought to worry about cold water at this time of year in Texas? he wondered uselessly.

His limbs were growing more numb. Whether from the cold water or the shock his body had finally registered from the bullet wound, he didn't know. He also knew it didn't matter.

"Goddammit!" he cursed at the stars shining down on him, river water gagging him. He trod water as best he could while the Trinity carried him on, casting his eyes around for the bank. But as he raised his head to look for a reflection of any kind to gauge the distance, the river took a dive. Kitts rolled down with the whitecaps and went under. His wind-whipped lungs begged for air. He panicked and fought his way to the surface. Kitts spat the cold water out and gasped air again. His side stabbed him with pain like a bitter punch line.

"No, goddammit!"

The Trinity carried him roughly along. Kitts remembered the cardboard armor still duct-taped to his arms and legs.

Why didn't you throw it away, you retard?

It was soaked and weighing down his tired limbs.

Jesus, worse than Stu, stupid fuck.

He struggled to stay afloat, trying to remove the soaked cardboard from his arms. When the deadwood hit his forehead

crack

he fell backward in the water, forcing the air from his lungs. Stunned by the blow, Kitts went under again. His old-man reflexes betrayed him. His lungs demanded air but only found the cold water of the Trinity. His limbs faltered next, weighing him down as real panic set in, but he thrashed toward the graying light of the surface. Struggling demanded energy and energy demanded air, and the river in his lungs made him cough and gag, drawing in more water.

For thirty seconds, maybe more, seizures hit him as Kitts *willed* his lungs to create oxygen from water. The pain in his side was nothing compared to the burning desire for air and the certain knowledge his brain would live as long as it could—God's final, sick joke—knowing his body was dying, aware of every moment slipping away from him. Kitts cursed God, Ramirez, Stu, Death itself. Convulsions for air rocked him again. He clawed at the prism of light flickering ever further away on the Trinity's surface. Slices of the moon taunted him like reflections off a blade.

Sinking, his fighting feeble now, he saw the faces of children shimmering in the water. Every child he'd ever touched in secret. Millicent from behind the convenience store. Four-eyed Brad, behind the stacks in the library. Jimmy Schulenberg under the Little League grandstand. Others whose names he didn't even remember. They watched him from above, each pair of empty eyes, as he slowly descended.

He expected them to laugh at him, to smile at least, finally seeing justice served, the natural order of things restored. But their pale faces, rippling in the river, simply stared—vacuous, silent witnesses. So Kitts cursed them too, railed at them for not reveling in his death as he'd reveled in their fear, for failing to appreciate the universe returning itself to balance through his death.

As his body burned the last of the sugar in his bloodstream, movement ceased. Kitts could no longer hear the roaring river. Instead, he listened to the dull, slowing throb of the blood in his ears. At least the pain in his side was gone. Kitts felt nothing now, nothing in his bones, not even the iron chill of the river. His brain measured his last moments by the lazy thump of his heart, slower, slower . . . slower. A dimming circle of darkness closed in from the sides of his vision. The children with their staring eyes were gone, replaced by

a catfish swimming close, brushing him with its whiskers

a grain of dirt hanging suspended in the water

a lone bubble of precious air escaping his blue lips

until they too washed out of existence, melding into the gray curtain of the Trinity. The river and the life it carried seemed to be moving away from him even as it bore him down.

He could hear nothing now. Feel nothing.

Silence.

Death.

Kitts stared down. The black circle at last enveloped his vision. Yet still his brain functioned, aware of its own solitude in the void. Of its own, absolute aloneness in death. God's final, sick joke.

He planned to spit river water in God's eye when he saw Him. But his last conscious thought took even that small consolation away.

Ya won't be seeing Him, Kitts, his brain said in Stu's Czech accent.

Then oblivion swallowed him whole.

CHAPTER 19

"What do you think ghosts are?" asked Elizabeth. When the old man had suggested they talk of Old Suzie and ghosts, Michael hadn't looked too enthusiastic. A long silence had followed as Elizabeth glanced at Michael and Michael glanced at Elizabeth and they both looked to Rocky, who stared back, waiting for one of them to begin. So Elizabeth had.

"Well," said the old man, "I don't rightly know. Some folks think they're the spirits of the departed hanging around because they either don't know they're dead or they don't want to admit it. Others say they're just recordings on the fabric of time."

"What does *that* mean?" Michael asked, perplexed.

"Well," the old man said, rubbing his chin, "you see, all living things create an electromagnetic field. Your brain runs on electricity. Thoughts fire off, travel around your brain. When you burn your finger, your skin sends an electrical impulse to your brain and you register pain, so you pull your finger away from what burned it."

"We learned about that in life science class," Elizabeth said. "Electro-something-mical reactions and all that stuff."

"But what does that have to do with ghosts?" asked Michael.

"I'm getting to that. You see, electricity is energy. Like fire, another form of energy. You ever see any pictures of Japan after the Hiroshima and Nagasaki bombs?"

"The *what* bombs?" the children asked in unison.

The old man just looked at them. "You mean to tell me they don't teach you about World War II anymore?"

Michael said, "Ohhhhhhhhhh. That's when the U.S. and those other countries fought the Germans."

"Right."

"To free the Jews."

"Um . . . well, that happened, yes. But not just to free—oh, never mind. But the Allies—that's what the U.S. and their friends were called, by the way—didn't just fight the Germans. They also fought the Japanese."

"Oh," said Michael, still a little confused. "Yeah, they make great anime."

Again Rocky stared for a moment, reflecting Michael's expression. "*Anyway*, to end the war, the U.S. dropped atomic bombs on Japan. Do you know what atomic bombs are?"

"No. I guess we haven't gotten to those in history yet," offered Elizabeth.

"Yes, well, the atomic bomb was the most terrible weapon devised for its time. When an A-bomb exploded, everything for miles around was leveled. And the people were vaporized."

"Vaporized?" Michael sounded like he was pronouncing the word for the first time. "Like with lasers?"

"Sort of. They disappeared. They left only one thing behind."

Michael and Elizabeth leaned forward, wrapping themselves around the old man's words.

"*Shadows*."

The children's eyes grew wider.

"You can still see them today in the cities. Shadows burned right into the concrete by the energy of the bombs. Prone, screaming, totally surprised, disbelieving of their own deaths. Impressions from their present on ours, like there was no time in between."

Elizabeth closed her eyes and pictured what he described, making a mental note to go back through her history files and search the Web for photos. She wondered how they'd compare to what she'd created in her head.

"And you think that's what ghosts are?" she asked after a moment. "Leftover images?"

"That's one way to describe them," he said, nodding. "Or maybe they really are just people that don't realize they're dead yet trying to go on with their normal lives. Waking up every morning, making their breakfast, doing their daily business, and going to bed every night. Or maybe they're just people who *know* they're dead and don't *want* to be. Maybe they don't want to go to the afterlife because they know what's waitin for 'em. Nobody really knows for sure or even if they really exist. What do *you* think?"

"I think they're evil," offered Michael, glancing at the hidden corners of the parlor.

"Evil?" Rocky asked. "Why?"

"Because they scare people," said Michael. "They wait till it's dark and everyone's asleep and then they wake up and walk around the house and *creak!* on the stairs and *scrip-scrape!* in the attic and scare you. If they weren't evil, they wouldn't try to scare you like that." His tone confirmed he'd just delivered an indisputable fact.

"Is that so?" asked the old man.

"Yep."

Rocky nodded a dubious acknowledgment. "What do you think, Elizabeth?"

She glanced at Michael from beneath her eyelashes, then looked away. She didn't want to disappoint him. "I dunno."

"Sure you do. You know what you think, anyway. What do you think of Old Suzie then?"

Oh, great. Michael will hate me for this. "I think she wasn't so bad. Just a lonely old woman trying to find something happy in life when there wasn't very much happy in it for her. I dunno."

"But she was a witch!" Michael exclaimed.

"How do you know that?" asked Rocky.

"Well—because—that's what everybody says."

"Uh-huh." The old man turned to Elizabeth, asking, "So what do you think Old Suzie's ghost is like? If there *is* one, you understand. Not that I've ever *seen* her ghost, let's just be clear on that."

Elizabeth shrugged.

"Come on, you can do better than that," prompted the old man.

She rolled her eyes the way kids do when they have to do something for an adult but they want the adult to know they don't *want* to do it. "I dunno. I guess she was a nice ghost."

"A nice ghost?" Michael was staring at her, trying to comprehend blasphemy.

"Yeah. I mean, if she was looking for happiness in life, maybe she's looking for happiness in death too."

Rocky seemed to consider that, the sides of his mouth curling up a bit.

Michael looked dumbfounded. "What're you talkin about?"

"I think she disagrees with you about what ghosts are really like," said the old man. Elizabeth was looking at the floor, the ceiling, anywhere but Michael's face. "I think she thinks ghosts can be good too, not just evil. Is that about right, Elizabeth?"

She shrugged again, sure she had disappointed Michael after all. "I guess," she muttered.

"So, if ghosts are good," said Michael, "how come everyone thinks they're evil?"

The old man rubbed the grizzle on his chin. "Well, that's a good question. Not *all* ghosts are good, mind you."

"A-*ha*! *There*, see?"

"But Michael, some *are*. Some are good, some are bad. Just like people. I mean, think about it. Ghosts are just used-to-be people, after all."

"But Suzie was good," said Elizabeth. "Basically, I mean. People just thought bad *of* her."

The old man smiled openly at that. "That's a great point. Kinda like when you first came into this house, you were scared. Then, after we talked for a while—after you got to know the house, you might say—you weren't afraid of it anymore, were you?"

Elizabeth looked around the parlor—over her shoulder to the kitchen with the cockroaches, at the stairs leading to the second floor's unexplored rooms and whatever hid in them. "No," she said timidly. "I guess not. Not really." But Elizabeth seemed not entirely convinced.

"Do all bad people become bad ghosts? Why don't all good people just automatically go to Heaven?"

The old man leaned back in his chair, stretching out. "Now *that's* a big load of questions in a little bit of words!" He brushed off the knees of his coveralls and the dust hung in the firelight. "No, to answer your first question, Michael, I doubt all bad people become bad ghosts. Some see the error of their ways, I imagine. Again, kinda like living people do in life. And some good people lose it when they die—just go off the deep end. Become bad ghosts. As to your other question, I can't answer that."

"I always thought of God as Gandalf," said Elizabeth out of nowhere.

Rocky raised an eyebrow. "Gandalf?"

"He's a crazy old wizard in an old 3V adventure," said Michael. "He wears long robes and has a long, white beard and gets mad at people too easily, but he also has a lot of patience with them in the end. All in all, he's pretty cool. He does magic."

The old man laughed and said, "Well, that's about as good a description of what most people think of God as any, I suppose."

"Gandalf *isn't* crazy," Elizabeth said.

"She likes to pretend she's a heroine in her own 3V game," Michael explained, "named Elsbyth."

"Michael!"

The boy retreated.

"Elsbyth?" wondered the old man.

Elizabeth flitted her eyes at Rocky, a little embarrassed at having to explain her fantasy. "She's who I'd most like to be," she said simply. "I feel like I can do anything when I'm her."

"Is Old Suzie's ghost here?" asked Michael, trying to change the subject.

"Not at the moment," the old man said, casting his eyes about for Michael's benefit. "Would you like me to call her?"

"No." The word was quick, precise, and entirely audible.

Rocky said, "Well, just let me know. Maybe I can dig her up for you."

Michael swallowed hard and Elizabeth elbowed him in the side to tell him it was all right, it was just a joke. Michael smiled sheepishly with a look on his face that said, *Yeah, I know, I was in on it all the time. I was just playing along, y'know, pretending to be scared.*

"I would've liked to have known her," said Elizabeth.

The words died on the walls, and then there was silence. A breeze, fresh from the north, passed from the front to the back of the house. It sounded like someone settling down to rest after a long, work-filled day.

"I think you *do* know her," said the old man.

Michael looked from one to the other, uncomprehending again. Elizabeth was playing with a leaf on the floor, crunching it between two fingers, folding it, then unfolding it and staring at the new leaf lines lit by the crackling glow of the fire. Rocky was sitting back in his armchair, face hidden again.

"If Suzie was such a good person," Michael finally asked, "then why didn't she go to Heaven?"

Elizabeth was silently grateful for the question. She'd been wondering it herself. Good ghosts didn't make any sense. Good spirits should go to Heaven automatically. Right?

"Oh yeah, your second question. Well now, that's a poser," said the old man. "Maybe to get into Heaven she had to find in death what she couldn't in life, like Elizabeth said. Still looking for that happiness before moving on. But we're not even sure Suzie's ghost is here. Are we?"

Elizabeth looked up. "I'm sure."

Rocky leaned forward so she could see his eyes. "Really? And what makes you think that?"

She shrugged. "I just know."

He shrugged in return and sat back again. "Sometimes that's all you've got."

"I wonder what it takes to get into Heaven," said Michael.

"Another poser!" said the old man. "Well, it's always been my philosophy—and I'm just speaking for myself now, you understand, 'cause you can't tell nobody nothin about religion *or* politics—that there's a great big book up there. God keeps track of how many times you made other people smile and how many times you made 'em sad, like a pros-and-cons list. And if the pros outweigh the cons, you're in."

Elizabeth turned her head to the side. "You really think it's that simple?"

He nodded. "Most things are simpler than people try to make 'em, once you strip away all the fooferall."

"So God judges you by how many people liked you when you died?"

"Not quite, Michael. For me, it's kinda like a tug of war, and your soul is tied in the middle of the rope. All those lives you touched in a positive way come together and pull one way, making a light that leads you to Heaven. And if you were just awful to more people than that, well, they pull you the other way. The light gets blotted out by the blackness you created in other people when you were alive. Kinda like an eclipse." He leaned forward again as he said the last few words and blinked his eyes at them, as if bringing himself out of a trance. "Sorry, kids. Didn't mean to preach." He chuckled at that. "No sir, not for a minute. That's just what I think."

"That's what I said, Sheriff. She ran away this morning, came back, and now she's gone *again*." David Jackson's voice was tired. *He* was tired.

Sheriff Larry Applewhite put another check next to the comment he'd written in his notebook and nodded. He saw this kind of thing all the time. A child, spouse, or relative runs away from home only to turn up a few hours later. Unless it was a child, he usually waited for twenty-four hours before beginning a search, and then only after an official report had been filed. As it was, Jackson had called him at home and asked him to come out because his daughter was missing. Since she was a child, he'd come right over. Preliminary questioning had determined that Elizabeth had been dismissed from school earlier in the day and taken a walking tour around town, probably to wear off her own anxiety over the school thing. After that had come to a head, she'd run away again.

"I understand you're worried, Mr. Jackson," he said in the most soothing voice he could muster after being pulled out of bed. "But statistics show she'll be back by morning. She came back this evening, didn't she? And she even knew she was in for it after being dismissed from school."

"Yes, but now she's gone again. *Again.*" David paced the living room as he talked to Applewhite. The sheriff appraised his nervousness and, had he been interrogating Jackson for, say, a bank robbery, his lawman's instincts would've told him that the man was guilty as hell. "And I saw on the news tonight," said David, "that a prisoner from Huntsville escaped. A child molester! I mean, the streets aren't safe anymore, no matter *where* you fucking live!"

Applewhite sat down on the couch in hopes that, by doing so, Jackson would calm down a bit. "That's under control, Mr. Jackson. It's nearly a hundred and fifty miles away. And Wayne Alan Kitts is damned near seventy years old. I doubt he's made it this far this quickly."

"Yes, but you don't *know* that, do you?" The question came from Susan, who was sitting on the far end of the couch. She'd been pretty quiet until now, but she'd obviously been crying. Her fear at the mention of the escaped prisoner was too much to keep bottled up inside.

"No, ma'am, I can't say that for sure, that's true."

"Can't you at least look for her?" asked David, sitting down. His face seemed to have aged several years in the past few minutes.

Applewhite sighed. So much for finishing out at least six hours' sleep before tomorrow's shift started. Sometimes he really hated being on call all the time. Then he pushed the thought aside. "I know y'all are worried." He sighed again. *Make a commitment*, he heard his wife's voice say. "I'll tour around the neighborhood, see what I can find."

"Thank you, Sheriff!" The relief from Susan was like water on a fire. Someone was handling it, everything would be fine now was what her voice said.

"Do you mind if I ride along?" asked David.

Applewhite paused. Technically, he should say no. But he put himself in Jackson's place for half a second and said, instead, "No, I suppose not. You can look out one window and I'll look out t'other."

"I'm coming too," announced Susan.

"No," said David, and the fire in her eyes pulled him up short for contradicting her, particularly in front of company. "She might come back here. You should be here in case she does."

Susan swallowed her argument and waved him out the front door.

The two men got into the front seat of the sheriff's car.

"You're not supposed to be sitting up here," Applewhite observed as he started the car.

"You want me to move to the back?"

The sheriff considered the question. "No, stay where you are. It's all right." He backed the car out of the driveway and turned east down Elm Street. "We'll make the block and slowly widen our search area to cover more streets. If we don't find her by morning, I'll call my deputies and we'll go by foot."

He kept the car below five miles an hour, occasionally swinging his spotlight around to find a cat or a bush catching the wind.

"Elizabeth!" David yelled out the passenger window. His eyes scoured the dark patches where bushes and grass disappeared around neighbors' houses. "Elizabeth!"

With his spotlight and eyes scanning, Applewhite said, "She's not a dog to come a'runnin when you call, y'know. You're more liable to scare her off than anything by doing that."

Though reluctant to take his eyes away from the search, David glanced at him and said, "How do you figure that?"

"If she ran away, Mr. Jackson, she's not likely to come to the sound of your voice."

"We don't *know* she ran away. Her window was open. Maybe somebody *took* her. Maybe that child molester took her! Ever think of that?"

Applewhite decided the conversation might detract from the search after all, so he pulled his car over to the side of the street and stopped. "Yes," he said quite rationally, "I thought of that. But you said yourself that she ran away earlier today. Then you disciplined her and—by all appearances—she's run away again. We're a long way from Huntsville, Mr. Jackson, and Kitts is an old man. Odds are he didn't make a beeline for your house or anyone else's in Hampshire. Odds are he's lying at the bottom of the Trinity River, hounded there by prison dogs." Applewhite realized his voice had gotten harsh. He didn't like people second-guessing his work, as if he were an uneducated hick who didn't know his own job. But then he put himself in the other man's shoes again and realized David was just a worried father. He said a bit more softly, "I don't think anyone took her."

"You don't *think*."

"Mr. Jackson, do you know when the last child abduction was in this county? Twelve years ago. Little Shelly Meyer over in Sweeny. Mother snatched her out of the community park, the one across from the cemetery. The parents were estranged and the mother wanted the daughter, simple as that. Things like that just don't happen around here. Much."

David turned his eyes to scan out the passenger window. "That's what I used to think, Sheriff. It's why I moved us here." He paused, and Applewhite recognized the sign of a man trying to stifle tears in front of another man. Jackson cleared his throat after a long pause. "I just want Elizabeth to be safe."

Out of respect for Jackson, Applewhite made a show of turning his spotlight on the trees outside his own window. He counted the leaves on a branch just across the road before saying, "I know, Mr. Jackson. But let me do my job my way. Odds are, we'll find her and she'll be fine. No promises, but I have a feeling about this one."

David looked at him, despite his misting eyes. "How do you know that?"

Applewhite turned to him, let him see the conviction in his eyes. "Half my job is following my gut," the sheriff said. "My gut's telling me she's fine."

It was a sixth sense all lawmen—the good ones, anyway—developed over time. They could form a likely theory, more often right than not, with limited evidence and a lifetime's experience with human nature. This situation told Applewhite that they'd find Jackson's daughter safe and sound, and then the *real* trouble would pick up again. And if it wasn't taken care of inside their family, in about two years or so, an estranged Susan Jackson might decide to pick up her daughter one afternoon from the community park without informing her ex-husband. And then it would be Applewhite's problem again.

"Now, if we're done talkin," he said, "let's find your daughter."

David relaxed a bit. "Yeah, okay. I'll shut up. And do whatever you need to do. I know you know your job."

Applewhite nodded, putting the car in gear again. "Good. Look out that window. Tell me if you see anything."

CHAPTER 20

It was a rare thing for anyone to be prowling the streets of Hampshire after midnight. This late, the town was covered in a quiet calm that had once convinced David Jackson of its safety. And despite what he'd said to the sheriff, despite his sense of dread for Elizabeth's well-being, somehow driving these empty streets now with Applewhite helped reassure him that the town itself hadn't let him down.

They made a perfect square around the block but found no sign of Elizabeth. Then Applewhite pulled his patrol car into an overgrown driveway and parked, stretching over David to look out the passenger window.

"What is it?" David asked, then saw what was attracting the sheriff's attention.

Old Suzie's house.

Something inside David wasn't surprised to find them here. Since yesterday, he'd been thinking off and on about that Halloween thirty years earlier, and Theron's dare and having to hide his smelly Batman costume.

Old Suzie's house made it hard *not* to remember. There was firelight burning inside the house, and that teased the old fears of childhood. They climbed up his spine on spindly legs to stroke the back of his neck. "I, uh, I thought no one lived there anymore," he said.

"No one does," deadpanned the sheriff.

"Well then—kids? Someone set a fire?"

The sheriff unfastened his safety belt. David wasn't so sure he was glad to be along for the ride after all. Then his fear for Elizabeth—his *need* to find her—took over, and the little boy so preoccupied with Old Suzie and her Halloween cauldron was pushed aside by the worried father he'd become.

"I don't think so," said Applewhite as he opened his car door and stepped out. "Why don't you stay here until I get back?"

A voice in the back of his head, a little boy's voice that had once chanted "Regina, Regina, she's such a va-jeena," thought maybe that wasn't such a bad idea.

"No, I'm coming with you. Elizabeth might be in there."

Applewhite nodded wearily. "Suit yourself." It was just too damned late to argue about it.

They walked up to the porch, and the sheriff motioned David to hold up a second. Applewhite looked the boards over, assessing the decayed state of the wood, and decided there was only one way to find out if they would hold his weight. He placed his hand on the rail and stepped up. At first he had the palpable sensation the house was falling over on him, crushing him beneath its dead weight. During that moment he wanted nothing to do with Old Suzie's house. He'd known her when she was alive, and he hadn't approved when folks began to turn their children away from her at the grocery store. So he didn't see as how the house might have it in for him. But for that brief moment filled with vertigo and fear, he thought they might just be right and the house was cursed, as Frank McFreod, the last-of-his-kind real estate agent in town, claimed. But then the moment passed and after a few steps he found himself standing at the front door.

Applewhite could hear voices inside. *Children*, he thought, and before he could stop it, the other voice in his head—the same one that berated him for being a pussy when he didn't go all-in playing poker—wondered if they weren't the ghosts of the children she'd cooked and eaten all those years ago. He shrugged it off like he'd shrugged off the gossip about Suzie when she was still alive and opened the front door.

creeeeeak

The sheriff winced.

"Why are we going so slow?" asked David.

"*Shhhh*," said Applewhite, waving his hand. He hadn't even heard Jackson come up behind him. *Too late and too old*, said his poker voice. *Fuck you*, he shot back. "Go my speed or go back to the car." His tone was simple, direct.

They walked through the entryway, passing a closet on either side, and stepped into the parlor proper.

"Hello, Sheriff."

The voice startled Applewhite, and he thought with a sudden bitterness that he didn't have his gun in his hand. Didn't even have the flap unsnapped from his holster.

I ain't sayin nuthin, the poker voice poked at him.

He moved his hand to unsnap the holster but stopped when he recognized the voice. It was coming from the other side of the armchair, its dusty upholstery flickering with the light from the fireplace. Then he noticed the two children sitting cross-legged on the floor, one of them a girl petting a dog lying beside her. Her face matched the picture he'd been given.

See? Told you it'd work out.

"Elizabeth!"

Applewhite noted the quality in her father's voice. He'd heard it many times before. At first, the near disbelief that she'd actually been found, unharmed. Then the relief in knowing that she was all right. Then the love that losing her had recalled. All spoken instantly when he'd said her name.

"Daddy?"

David ran to her and, though she shied away at first, he picked her up anyway. He hugged her close and, after a moment, she returned his embrace. *Reluctantly*, Applewhite noted.

"I'm so glad you're safe," he said into her hair. "We were *so* worried."

"I'm okay, Daddy," she said. His emotion made her want to cry. She'd never seen him like this. Had never imagined in her fertile imagination that he could *be* like this.

There, once again the old gut is right on target, thought Applewhite. "Well, Rocky, how you been?"

The old man shifted in his armchair to watch the sheriff as Applewhite walked into the parlor. "Pretty good, Sheriff. You?"

"Fair," Applewhite said, his breathy tone adding, *for being up at one A.M. and wondering if my foot's going to go through the next floorboard I step on.*

David put his daughter down with a smile and turned his eyes on the old man. He'd known what he was looking at when he'd walked in here but had been so anxious to ensure Elizabeth's safety, he'd ignored it till now. "Who the hell are you?" he asked, losing the smile.

"Nobody you know," replied the old man. Someone else might've gotten up, a defensive move against the challenge in the younger man's voice. But the old man was old and so he stayed in the chair.

David's eyes narrowed. "I know you."

The old man leaned forward into the firelight. "Somehow I doubt it."

David shook his finger loosely. "No, I've seen you before. I'm sure of it."

Rocky shrugged.

"You probably have," said Applewhite. "He works the roads for me. I struck a deal with him. I let him kick around town, he scrapes up the roadkill for the county."

"That's it!" said David through his epiphany. "You're the Walking Man."

The old man grinned through wasted teeth. "I *do* walk a lot."

With that curiosity satisfied, David advanced, asking, "What've you been doing with my little girl?" The old man drew away from him, pressing back into the armchair.

"Whoa, hoss," said Applewhite, putting a hand on David's chest as he moved between them. "Hold up a minute. We don't know that he's been doing *anything*."

"Daddy, he's been nice to me!" Elizabeth said, coming up behind David and placing her hand on his arm.

The dog lifted her head from the floor and watched the scene unfold in front of her. Her ears were up, her eyes focused. She seemed to sniff at David to scent his intent.

"Nice how?"

"Mr. Jackson—"

"Hey," said David, throwing his arms up and away, freeing himself from both Applewhite and Elizabeth, "I just asked a question. Nice *how*, Elizabeth?"

"He . . ." She knew by hesitating she made it look bad for Rocky, but she wasn't sure how to answer the question.

"Nice how?" prompted her 3V voice.

"He talked to me," she said finally. "That's all. He just talked to me."

"Uh-huh," said her father, "and what did he say?"

"Now son," said Rocky, "I'd never hurt your daughter."

"I wasn't asking *you*," said David. He had it all now, the whole picture. Just the details were missing. What had the old man been saying to her and the boy she was with? Had he been trying to make them do things? Together? So he could watch?

"Ghosts, Mr. Jackson," said Michael. "We talked about ghosts and stuff. You know, for Halloween." The boy sounded scared.

"Ghosts?" exploded David, incredulous. The boy might as well have suggested they'd been talking about *Web Report*.

"Am I gonna have to knock you upside the head?" asked Applewhite. David's gaze met the sheriff's, and though Applewhite's tone had been playful, his eyes weren't. "Now, we ain't seen any evidence of any harm to your daughter, or to this boy neither, if anyone's keepin score." He knelt next to Elizabeth and put his hand on her arm. You can tell things by touching people. Whether they like to be touched or whether they're afraid of it. Though Elizabeth shied at first, she seemed to sense the protection in his hand. In turn, Applewhite sensed her need for it. A family portrait of the Jackson clan formed in his mind, the sketch he'd drawn earlier now filled in with some color by the brush of his intuition. "Did he hurt you, Elizabeth?" asked the sheriff. "Rocky, I mean."

"*No*," she said. "He's been really nice to me. And Michael too. We've just been talking. I met him earlier today—"

"Earlier today?" Incredulity again.

"Mr. Jackson, I'm *really* good with my baton." Applewhite turned back to Elizabeth. "You sure, honey?"

"Yes, I'm *sure*," she replied in her 3V voice, out loud for a change.

The sheriff nodded, knowing it was so, and stood up, looking over to the other culprit. "Michael Miller, your momma know you're out?"

The boy, hands in his pockets, looked at the floor. "No, sir."

"Then I think it's best she knows you're all right, at least."

The boy frowned, knowing that translated into being grounded. "Yes, sir," was all he said.

Applewhite turned to the old man. "You really shouldn't have that fire burnin, Rocky. Ain't safe in an old house like this. Don't make me look up the ordinance."

The old man shrugged. "Forgot to pay my electric bill this month," he said, motioning at a shady corner. "And the boy seems a bit skittish of ghosts." He smiled at Michael.

"Hey!" exclaimed the boy. "I weren't no more scared than *she* was."

"Liar!" Elizabeth proclaimed.

"All *right*." David's tone was less than patient and more than tired. "That's enough from both of you. It's too late to be arguing. Elizabeth. You're coming home with me. As for you, Michael, Sheriff Applewhite will take you home, won't you, Sheriff?"

"Sure," said Applewhite as he thought about it. Part of him was convinced Jackson might have more in store for Elizabeth than a good talking to. He'd seen the way the girl had drawn away from him at first. But it was hard to distinguish what might be a telltale sign of one thing from a simple case of the I-got-caughts. *Sometimes I really hate this job*. He made a judgment call and felt more than anything like he'd just tossed a coin in the air. Not liking that feeling, Applewhite decided to sit the fence. "Y'know, I can drop y'all off too, on the way to Michael's."

"That's all right, Sheriff," David said. "It's just a walk up the street for us. Night air might do us some good."

The sheriff hesitated a moment, then nodded. "Why don't you take the kids out on the porch, Mr. Jackson? I want to talk to Rocky here for a minute."

David gave him a look that said, *Uh-huh, you take your club to that old pervert,* which Applewhite shrugged off. Elizabeth felt her father's hand on her shoulder and moved a little faster in front of him so she wouldn't have to. They made their way through the entryway and out the front door.

"What's on your mind, Sheriff?"

Applewhite turned back to him and leaned against the wall. He had the passing thought that he might go straight through the wood rot and into the kitchen, but the old wall held his ten-too-many-hotdogs frame.

"Once things cool down in their house," he began, sounding like a doctor who's seen all he needs to see in the test results, "word'll spread that you're livin here. That in itself ain't a bad thing, though Frank McFreod will come down and bend my ear the wrong way about it. This is private property, after all."

"But Sheriff, there ain't nobody livin here. Ain't been in years."

"Doesn't make any difference. The long-story-short of it is, you don't own the place. But like I said, that *ain't* the biggest part of it. Hell, McFreod knows he can't sell this place. Too many spook stories. And it's too dilapidated. Nobody in their right mind'd buy it. And there ain't too many folks—Jackson there is a notable exception—beatin down the doors of Hampshire lookin for a home anyway."

"So what's the big deal? I ain't hurtin nobody by stayin here."

The sheriff paused a moment and looked at the old man. Rocky had always struck him as someone who didn't like charity. Would've been offended if you'd offered it to him. That's why Applewhite had suggested the job of cleaning up the animals who got hit along the highway. Nobody else wanted to do it, and it gave the old man a little spending money. But he *earned* it, and that was all the difference to men like Rocky. Besides, the fuckers from the county were always a week behind the sideswipe schedule.

"I didn't think you wanted charity, Rocky," was all he said.

"Didn't say I *wanted* it."

The sheriff looked hard at the old man, and if Applewhite had been a woman, he might've gotten choked up at what he saw there.

Abject surrender.

Humiliation.

He saw in the drifter's eyes the gray certainty that Rocky had chosen this course for himself. And now it was just a matter of playing out the hand. Fate forced down his throat.

The old man turned away from the probing gaze.

"Well," said Applewhite, wiping his mouth and standing up straight, "it doesn't matter anyway. McFreod doesn't matter. What matters is Jackson thinks you had designs on his daughter—"

"I never touched her!" The old man's voice rose, a shield.

"I didn't say you did. Never thought it, even. But that doesn't matter either. All that matters is that he thinks you did. He's a protective man."

The old man knew what was coming now. "A good father," he said, his voice cracking.

But the sheriff clucked his tongue against the roof of his mouth. "Well, his daughter might have something to say about that. But what I was gettin at was, he'll tell the other parents that you're here and what he thinks you had on your mind. And then one of the local bluehairs will bake a rum cake, 'cause that's my favorite, and bring it to my office and, just as they start to shamble out the door, will say, 'Oh, by the way, can you run that nasty old pervert down at Old Suzie's house out of town? Thanks, Sheriff.' And then I'll be right back here tellin you what I'm tellin you now. Only it won't be your choice to leave then."

Rocky leaned forward and put his head in his hands. "I have a home here," he said simply. "Finally. It just ain't fair."

The old man looked up at him, hoping to find—*something*. Applewhite decided to let the cliché in his head die in his throat. *No use tellin him what he already knows.*

"Tomorrow, Rocky." The sheriff walked by him and stopped. The dog, chin flat on the floor, stared up, watching the sheriff. Applewhite cleared his throat. "I'm sorry, old-timer," he said, heading out the front door.

As he stepped onto the porch, Michael walked up to him. "Can we go home now, Sheriff? I'm sleepy."

"Sure," said Applewhite, placing a hand on the boy's head. "It's no wonder, either. Your momma'll make me a pecan pie for bringing you home."

"Really?" Michael's eyes lit up. "Can I have a piece?"

"Sure. If she's still letting you have sweets after she grounds you."

The light faded a bit. "Oh yeah."

"Well, I'll put in a good word for you," grumbled Applewhite. "But you only get a small piece."

Michael looked up at him, beaming. "Deal!"

The sheriff glanced over to Jackson and his daughter. He was kneeling down in front of her, talking low but hard. *It's late, bub*, thought the sheriff. *Let it go for tonight.* "Y'all sure you don't want me to give you a ride?"

David looked over, a little irked at being interrupted. "No, that's okay, Sheriff," he said in a fake phone voice. "We were just getting ready to walk on home."

Applewhite nodded. The thought came to him that the girl, Elizabeth, might've been safer with old Rocky than walking home alone with Jackson, but he dismissed it. Truth be told, it was almost as groundless as Jackson's suspicions of the old man had been. "All right then, come on, Michael." He led the boy to his squad car, muttering in answer to Michael's excited tittering, "*No*, I'm not going to run the siren. It's too damned late for that. And I've got a headache."

As the sheriff's car pulled out of the driveway, gravel popping like muted firecrackers, David and Elizabeth watched them go.

"Come on, honey," said David. "Let's go home. It's late. And your mother's worried. Damn near worried herself to death." He was so relieved to have her back safe. He turned an eye up to the stars and aimed a thought at the center star in Orion's belt: *Thank you, God*.

They began walking across the wide front yard, the grass stroking their shoes with midnight dew.

Chapter 21

"I'm sorry, Daddy," Elizabeth said for what seemed like the millionth time. She didn't really care about the punishment this time; she was just *tired*. It had been a long day, full of fear and fun and frustration. Now all she wanted to do was go home and crawl under the covers and dream of riding in Rheanna.

"I know you are," he began, not really knowing where he was headed, "but you can't just run off like that."

"I know, Daddy."

"It's about being accountable, Elizabeth. I mean, webschool is the same thing. You got kicked out because you played your game too late. And then instead of staying home and reflecting on that and maybe catching up on your studies, you ran out today without permission. And *then*, after your mother and I talked to you about it and we agreed no more webgames for a week, you go and run off *again*."

"I *know*, Daddy."

But he wasn't listening. His fear had given way to his need to lecture, to reestablish control. "I moved us here because I thought it would be safer for you. And then you go and run off. Again. Did you know there's a child molester escaped from prison up in Huntsville? Did you know that? What if he came down here and found you? Hell, how do you know that old man in that house wasn't him?"

"Daddy, Rocky's a nice man. He just kept me company."

"Elizabeth, you're too young to tell the nice men from the not-nice men. Your mother's right about some things, and one of them is that people will take advantage of you if you give them half a chance. And being irresponsible is like handing them a key to your room."

My room, she thought. *Wouldn't I like to be there now . . .*

"Being irresponsible is just plain—un*safe*."

"That's it!" shouted her 3V voice. *"No more. Enough!"*

"Is that all that matters, Daddy? Being safe?" She stopped and stared up at him, fearful but defiant, her heart thumping a million miles a minute. "I've been *safe* all my life. I want to have *fun*. I want to—"

"Stay alive till you're eighteen!" he said. David's face was on fire. He had uprooted them, brought them here, paid the tuition for the best webschool he could find, and come looking for her in the middle of the night for . . . what? *Fun?* "Then you can go to college. Having *fun* is half of what it's for."

"I'll be dead by then!" Elizabeth shouted. She felt like she wanted to cry and hit her father at the same time. Her stomach hardened around butterflies, her fists clenched. "I'll end up just like *you*!" Elizabeth pummeled him with her tone because her fists couldn't. "I never want to be like you!"

For the first time, David realized what it all meant . . . the running away, the *leaning* away from him when he was near her, the retreating to her room (now, he saw, simply to get *away* from him)—she hated his guts.

She couldn't stand being around him.

His own *daughter*.

David remembered those precise feelings. He also remembered never having the courage to voice them. Even that day when Queenie had . . . when Queenie disappeared. Or the day his old man lay delirious in the hospital bed. He started to shake as the realization sank in. His hands felt cold and slick. He felt detached, like on those cool nights when his mother would come visit him in his bedroom. Like he was standing outside himself, watching someone else use his body, speak with his voice. He wanted to tell Elizabeth to run away, that she was absolutely right to be furious with him, afraid of him even.

Children always know, he thought.

Despite thinking exactly the opposite, he spewed a line at her from the Adult Handbook: "You're too young to know what's right for you!" Adrenaline coursed in his arms as he gestured over her to make his point.

Elizabeth flitted her eyes back and forth, watching her father's arms. Without even realizing it, she guessed their distance from her, their power, and identified an escape route behind her. Her eyes returned to her father's.

He saw her gauging him, planning her escape from his physical threat. Again he saw himself in her. Again his heart ached, seeing God's ironic sense of humor. He wanted to lower his arms around her, *protect* her, but knowing she would run from him kept him from hugging her. If she ran from him—that really would send him over the edge. Instead, to fill up the space between them, he said, "Your mother and I have done everything we can for you. We moved here for you!"

Elizabeth glared up at him with brimming eyes. "That's a laugh, Daddy! We moved here for *you!*"

Watching from outside himself, from over his own shoulder, David wanted to say, "You're right," but the man who was his father's son stood over Elizabeth, fists working, enraged. Feeling like a spirit displaced from a reality it could no longer touch, he struggled to regain control of the burning anger possessing him.

Elizabeth tracked his fists, knew that she should take her escape route now, before it was too late. But a greater part of her, the one that dared face down Mallus in Rheanna, wanted to make her stand. "Go on, then! Show me who's right!"

(that's enough)

"You're gonna learn what it means to be responsible and follow The Rules," said David, his voice flatly reading lines of déjà vu, one fist arcing back.

Elizabeth's breath hitched as she prepared to run. Time slowed as she focused on his fist. David tensed for a blow he struggled to withhold. Then, a sharp, insistent growl came from beyond his peripheral vision.

David looked to his left. Rocky's dog stood there, steady as a statue. Her lips curled away from her fangs, the crinkle around her eyes framing fiery slits. The will drained from David. He stared at the dog, her rumbling snarl warning him. He had stepped through a looking-glass into an alternate universe where black was white, up was down. Good was evil. Sapped of their strength, David's arms fell to his side.

He felt himself reenter the sweating reality of his own body. He heard quick, crunching sounds and ripped his eyes away from the dog to watch Elizabeth running across the grass and up the street toward their home. "Elizabeth, wait! I'm . . ." But he didn't finish. It was an insult to her to even think of saying it. He looked back to the dog. She hadn't moved an inch. He saw himself reflected in her eyes and a voice spoke in his head.

If you ever move to hurt her, ever again, I'll come back for you. And make it right.

A man's voice speaking through the dog. That crazy thought scared the shit out of him because he knew it wasn't crazy. It had just happened. Hadn't it?

David looked past the dog, her ears still flat, and saw Rocky standing on the rotting porch, staring at him. Had it been the old man's voice he'd just heard? Had it been in his head or had Rocky actually spoken? Not that it mattered. Not really.

"No." The word breathed out of him. "Never again."

He slowly backed away from the dog. She watched him warily as he went but made no move to follow. Turning his back on Old Suzie's house, David walked home by way of a dozen streets he hadn't seen in thirty years.

Elizabeth could feel him in her doorway.

She couldn't see him because she had the covers over her head, but she could hear him there, breathing. She didn't move. Maybe if she was still, he'd pass her by.

David watched her listening to him. He wanted to go to her, put his arms around her, but he knew she would pull away.

And can you blame her? he asked himself. *You frighten her. You* terrify *her.*

His chest deflated with the thought. How could reality have become so inverted? How could he have become the thing he'd hated most? He'd guarded against it, dodging from wall to wall to avoid it as he'd walked the pathway of his life. And all that caution for what? The shadows had outmaneuvered him by hiding in the light.

Everything was reversed in this parallel universe. So familiar and so wrong at the same time.

Her words flew up at him inside his head.

(I never want to be like you)

Maybe she's right to think that way.

David wanted desperately to tell Elizabeth she was wrong. That he'd stepped back from the brink. But he couldn't bring himself to enter her room, her sanctuary. A holy place of ownership, a sacred circle into which no evil could step. And that's what he felt like at the moment—an evil thing.

(she's afraid of evil)

Twisted inside.

But he couldn't make himself leave the doorway either. He was afraid if he did, he might miss his only chance to tell her he loved her, to *make things right*, like the old drifter had said. To make her understand that it wasn't him that had almost . . . But that was a lie too. It *had* been him. And that's why he couldn't move now. Nothing he could do, nothing he could say could change that he'd almost struck his own daughter in anger.

Goddammit, I can't just stand here all night.

Hiding under the covers, Elizabeth felt him move into the room. She lay very still, unconsciously starting to plan her escape route again. When he sat down on the bed next to her, the bedsprings creaking under him, a great calm descended over her.

Elizabeth thought it through as the seconds passed. She was surprised she wasn't hyperventilating, shivering, *something*. But she wasn't. Animals can sense earthquakes, she knew. Cats and dogs, even insects start to act funny before the ground shifts. She'd found it true in humans too. You can sense—see, hear, smell, feel, taste, *know*—something's coming, and so you prepare for it in your mind. You pull in the patio furniture and tape the windows and duck and cover inside yourself because that's the safest thing to do when trouble comes.

If that were true, it made sense the reverse must also be true. When something's *not* coming, when the coast is clear, you must be able to sense that too.

So Elizabeth just lay there, letting him sit next to her. And David just sat on the bed, watching over her.

The next morning Elizabeth awoke before she even knew she'd fallen asleep. She made slow movements beneath the covers. When her brain began to think again, she realized she might very well touch her father by stretching, since the last thing she remembered was him sitting beside her. Still pretending to be asleep, she edged her head from under the covers, peeped beneath her eyelids, and looked around the room as best she could without giving herself away. But she didn't see her father.

He must've left while I was sleeping.

"Good," her 3V voice answered. *"And if he's gone from the house, maybe we can go pay Mallus a visit before he gets home. I feel the need to kick some ass."*

But Elizabeth ignored the voice, which pouted in response, and stretched in her bed. She enjoyed with sinful awareness the luxury of not having to run to the bathroom, get dressed, and be at her computer for webschool at eight A.M. sharp.

Saturdays rock! she thought, smiling to herself.

She remembered the night before, her conversation with the old man, and her father's behavior. She had been genuinely afraid of him then. She had known—not sensed, not hoped it wouldn't happen, but *known*— he was going to hit her in that moment. If the dog hadn't shown up when she had, this Saturday morning would feel very differently.

Elizabeth wondered about that. She had heard him speak, even as she ran away, a quiet, fear-struck phrase. It repeated in her head using her 3V voice in as serious a tone as it had ever used.

"Never again."

And then he had come and sat on her bed. Had he spoken at all last night, she would've screamed. Elizabeth was sure of that. Had he touched her, she would've retreated. But he hadn't spoken, hadn't touched her. He'd just sat beside her. And she hadn't—after all and perhaps most unbelievably—minded him sitting on the bed beside her. And then she must've fallen asleep.

Shrugging off the strangeness of it all, she decided it was a waste of a good Saturday to lie in bed. So she got up, went to the bathroom, got dressed, and went tentatively into the kitchen, where she found her mother viewing *Web Report*.

"How are you this morning, Elizabeth?" Susan asked.

Elizabeth could sense the hesitation in her mom as well, as if she weren't sure how to form the sentences she needed to address her daughter. Susan had been relieved beyond words when she'd come home, and that had segued quickly into anger and worry and a speech about how harsh the world was and wouldn't she *please* be more careful and let her mom know where she was going from now on? Elizabeth had responded at first defensively but then was genuinely sorry she'd caused so much worry. "I'm fine."

"Your father told me about that old bum you were hanging out with."

Elizabeth considered her response, wanting to jump to Rocky's defense, but then decided to avoid the conflict altogether. "'Hanging out'? Mom, you are *so* out of the language loop."

"*Elizabeth.*" Susan stopped, reining it in. "I don't want you doing that anymore. Your father thinks he might—might do you harm, and I agree with him."

"Now *there's* a first." The retort spat out of her, and she immediately regretted it.

"*Elizabeth.* Promise me."

Elizabeth made a show of it. Slumped body language. Slightly whining tone. Dejected, end-of-the-universe look on her face. "All *right*, Mom. I won't . . . *hang out* with him anymore."

Susan Jackson nodded her head like a judge's gavel signaling the case was over. "Breakfast? Sausage and eggs and toast?"

"Maybe. Where's Dad?" She asked the question nonchalantly.

Her mother cleared her throat. "He went into the office this morning. But he said he'd like us all to go out to a movie tonight, if you're up for it."

This time Elizabeth didn't have to fake astonishment. "Go out? *Dad*? Aren't outhouse movies expensive?"

For the first time in as long as Elizabeth could remember, her mom laughed out loud. "Well, they're certainly more expensive than inhouse ones. You know, when I was your age, kids used to love to go to the movies. Anything to get away from mom and dad."

It dawned on Elizabeth that her mother was making one of those laughable but lovable attempts to connect with her. Despite the seeming ludicrousness of the gesture, it genuinely warmed her heart to think her mom was at least trying. "But you just said you two were going. So much for getting away from you."

Her mother's face clouded. "So you *don't* want to go? Your father will be disappointed."

"Screw him! Let's ride in Rheanna!"

"I was *kidding*, Mom!" said Elizabeth, ignoring her 3V voice. "I'll think about it." She grabbed a piece of toast and wrapped a sausage and some eggs in it as she headed out the door.

"And *where* are you going?"

"Oh, sorry," Elizabeth said, turning around. "I'm supposed to meet Michael at his house. I want to see how bad he got it last night."

"*Elizabeth*, that's not nice. But I want you to stay away from that old man!" shouted Susan as the back door slammed.

Elizabeth cut across her backyard and then the neighbor's to make her way back to Old Suzie's house. She used this route, which wasn't as direct, in case her father happened to be driving home from the office already. Walking along, she kicked stones every few steps and wondered what she'd say to Rocky. Her father had really embarrassed her, and she had no idea what she *should* say. Her 3V self reveled in the thought she was making a beeline for Old Suzie's house in direct violation of her mom's rule.

"If we can't go to Rheanna, at least we can visit with Rocky. Better'n nuthin."

Elizabeth looked up and noted that the first day of November, with its blue sky and pillow clouds and cool breeze, promised to be a good day. She passed Michael's house and thought about stopping to see how he was doing, to maybe help explain to his mom about what had happened yesterday. But his house looked shut up, battened down, and she assumed they were doing Saturday family things and that her visit might just make things worse for him anyway. So she walked on.

She'd come up behind Old Suzie's house, the way she'd followed the dog, without even realizing it. So she made her way up the weed-grown driveway, past the unkempt gardens, and up to the back door, its screen still hanging limp. Carefully sliding her way through the back door, she called out for the old man. No response.

"Dog?"

She had never thought to name the dog or ask the old man what he'd named her, and she felt silly calling for her like that. But it didn't seem to matter anyway because there was no answer from the dog either. Not even a pant-pant.

Elizabeth moved through the kitchen. The house was shady inside despite the sky-blue sunlight shining through the broken windows. She heard the scurrying sound of dozens of tiny legs as the roaches retreated to their hiding places, making way for her giant, deadly feet. Doing her best to remember they feared her more than she feared them, she walked straight into the parlor.

Elizabeth called again for the old man to no avail. There was Rocky's chair and the fireplace, which had been dutifully doused. The dust and cobwebs in the chair looked undisturbed, which was weird. But there was no old man. There was no dog.

Now she began to worry. Had her father returned here and taken his wrath out on Rocky after all?

"If he hurt that dog . . ." warned her 3V voice.

But Elizabeth dismissed the idea. The man she'd run from last night wasn't her father of today. He wasn't even the man who'd sat beside her as she'd fallen asleep. At least, she was pretty sure he wasn't.

She found herself in the entryway, staring at the open front door.

"Rocky?"

Elizabeth stepped onto the porch.

creak

"Dog?"

With her hands on her hips, she crossed the front yard and walked all the way to the road. Calling and looking, looking and calling. She walked up Elm Street toward the two-lane highway and stopped at the intersection. Traffic was sparse, but then, it was still early for a Saturday.

Elizabeth looked left and saw a car coming. She looked right and saw the old man and the dog. He was using a tree branch for a walking stick, ambling slowly but surely up the highway toward the slight hill that led out of town.

Then what she'd seen a moment ago registered in her mind, and she looked left again. It was her father's car coming. It slowed down as it neared her, and she knew it was too late—he'd seen her. But she wasn't concerned about that now as she looked to the right again. Quite clearly, and strangely at this distance, she heard the old man beckon the dog to his side, away from the carcass she had gone to sniff.

"Come on, Elsbyth, this is the way we're headed," his voice said, carried on the wind.

He named her after me!

"But he's leaving!" her 3V voice responded, sounding for the first time in its life as if it might cry.

"Rocky!" she shouted, but the wind was blowing the wrong way. He didn't turn and wave or give any sign at all he'd heard. She considered running after him. Then the wheels of her father's car popped rocks as it pulled up next to her. She heard him get out, saying something about going to the movies later.

Elizabeth ignored him until he stopped speaking and followed her gaze, staring after the distant figures on their way out of town. She felt his hand come to rest lightly on her shoulder. Neither said anything to the other. Feeling the cool wind on their faces, they watched together as the old man and his dog crested the hill of the highway and faded from sight.

ACKNOWLEDGMENTS

Few creative works are actually produced by just one person. In the case of *Shadows*, I've had a number of first readers who gave me encouragement and feedback along the way: Michelle Benoit, Mary Cearley, Alison Cohn, Noel Garza, John Groppell, Michelle Hoelscher, Leslie Janac, Dorothy Pourteau, Courtney Prince, Ravenna Romack, Bridget Young, and Lauryn Zepeda-Groppell.

I'd particularly like to thank Valerie Yaklin-Brown for the photograph on the cover. I'd bet good money you felt a sense of foreboding or isolation when you first saw it. That's Valerie's skill at work. Fun fact: Valerie is old school and still prefers a Rolleiflex TLR camera to the digital kind. Check out her photography at http://www.valerieyaklin-brown.com/. If you're like me, you'll come away feeling like you've just toured a gallery on your desktop.

Also, a big thank-you goes to Kim Miller, an old friend and colleague from our work together at the Texas A&M Transportation Institute (TTI). Kim designed the wicked cover that fronts the novel. Kinda creepy, eh? (The cover, not Kim.) She's applied her considerable talents for the past few years as creative director for marketing and communications at Texas A&M University. I'm just glad she was available to lend me those skills for a while. Kim, I wouldn't have wanted anyone else putting the final touches on this. I owe you a drink at Veritas.

John Henry, art director at TTI, took Kim's design and made a terrific cover for the paperback edition. John and I trade recommendations for reading and viewing material on a regular basis. He turned me on to *Vikings*, and I introduced him to David Gemmell. Thanks for the awesome cover, John.

I had two excellent proofreaders—Marcus Trower and Dawn Herring—who helped me purge as many mistakes as humanly possible before I carefully placed my newborn in your hands. Sometimes I didn't take their advice, so any flaws, errors, or cases of "why the hell did he say it that way?!" are entirely my own.

Thanks also to the writers, classical and modern, who use their words to inspire my imagination. This list is representative, if not exhaustive, and I've learned something from every one of them: Suzanne Collins, Glen Cook, Bernard Cornwell, William Faulkner, David Gemmell, Ernest Hemingway, Washington Irving, Stephen King, Sir Thomas Mallory, George R.R. Martin, Toni Morrison, Edgar Allan Poe, Gene Roddenberry, John Scalzi, William Shakespeare, J.R.R. Tolkien, Mark Twain, and Chelsea Quinn Yarbro. And here are a few relatively new authors just starting out in independent publishing who've also inspired me through their excellent storytelling: Roberto Calas (the *Scourge* series), Nick Cole (the *Wasteland* books), Edward W. Robertson (the *Breakers* series), and Manel Loureiro (the *Apocalypse Z* series). I highly recommend you try their stuff.

The lyrics at the beginning of each of *Shadows'* three sections are by James McMurtry, a fellow Texan and singer-songwriter based in Austin. I've listened to his music since he released *Too Long in the Wasteland*, his first album, in 1989. McMurtry is one of the best wordsmiths on the planet, an opinion Stephen King seems to share: "The simple fact is that James McMurtry may be the truest, fiercest songwriter of his generation" (quoted from *Entertainment Weekly*). I urge you to give his music a listen—but only if you value superior storytelling. Thanks, James, for many years of incredible music.

And finally, to you, dear reader: *Thank you* for taking a chance on this novel and giving me the gift of your time. I hope you enjoyed it. I'd like to ask one last favor of you: unlike traditionally published authors, who have a publisher's marketing department advertising their work, independent authors like me rely on word-of-mouth and customer reviews to spread the word about our books. Would you mind taking a few minutes and telling others what you think of *Shadows* at the vendor site where you bought it (e.g., Amazon) as well as Goodreads? I would very much appreciate it.

Chris Pourteau
July 2014 (first print edition)

ABOUT THE AUTHOR

Chris Pourteau has been a technical writer and editor for over twenty years. He's published numerous technical articles and several literary essays and short stories. This novel is his first foray into the world of long fiction. He lives in Bryan, Texas.

If you'd like to let him know what you think about *Shadows Burned In* or just want to say howdy, feel free to email him at c.pourteau.author@gmail.com.

www.ingramcontent.com/pod-product-compliance
Lightning Source LLC
Chambersburg PA
CBHW020310200626
46814CB00006BA/2182